KNOPF
75
YEARS·OF·PUBLISHING

ALSO BY MICHAEL BRACEWELL

The Crypto-Amnesia Club

Missing Margate

DIVINE
CONCEPTS *of*
PHYSICAL
BEAUTY

DIVINE
CONCEPTS *of*
PHYSICAL
BEAUTY

a novel by

MICHAEL
BRACEWELL

ALFRED A. KNOPF   *New York*   1990

THIS IS A BORZOI BOOK
PUBLISHED BY ALFRED A. KNOPF, INC.

Library of Congress Cataloging-in-Publication Data

Bracewell, Michael.
Divine concepts of physical beauty : a novel / by Michael
Bracewell. — 1st ed.
p. cm.
ISBN 0-394-58383-3
I. Title.
PR6052.R234D5   1990
823'.914—DC20   89-43383
                                                    CIP

Manufactured in the United States of America
FIRST AMERICAN EDITION

'Suddenly Dinah burst out again. "Neil, however did it all come to happen? Life seems utterly different. It used to be so splendid and clean and jolly, and now — Could we have been rotters all the time, really, and not known it before?"'

Nancy Hayes, *The Castle School*

With thanks to Suzy Jenvey

CONTENTS

PART ONE
'IN EVERY FACE SEE JUDAS'

One: Them Were Rotten Days   3
Two: The Oil-Seed Rape in Flower   29
Three: Fanlight Gassy   57
Four: The Imperfections of Stella   85
Five: 'Joy Division'   112

PART TWO
'THE POWER OF LOVE'

One: 'I once returned from a party of which I was the life
and soul; wit poured from my lips, everyone laughed and
admired me – but I went away – and the dash should be as
long as the earth's orbit ————————————————————

———————————————————————————————

——————————————— and wanted to shoot myself.' 141
Two: The Best Thing   168
Three: Death In Telford   193
Four: 'Please tell me at what time I must be carried
      on board . . .'   219
Five: 'Love Divine, All Loves Excelling'   248

PART ONE

'In Every Face See Judas'

ONE

Them Were Rotten Days

It was Lucinda Fortune (to her friend Katie) who had first made the statement 'I hate art students.' She had neither prefixed nor suffixed this comment, nor even localised the zone of her loathing to any one art student in particular. She had simply said it (whilst watching a wreath of cigarette smoke slowly strangle a demure spray of eidelweiss), and then changed the subject.

Kelly O'Kelly (female) would have been – had they ever been formally introduced – the epitome of Lucinda's hatred. Kelly O'Kelly had been placed on this earth by some divine collaboration between the individual and the universal law to be an art student. At six years old she was capable (untutored) of not speaking to her mother for days on end when lovingly questioned about the subject of her infant aquarelles. By early puberty she had more or less given up talking all together, but filled her silent hours in the rambling family home near Twyford (Berks.) with feats of amateur dissection. Mice, sparrows, and, on one particularly disgusting occasion, a pregnant bat, had all been brought to the attention of Kelly's elderly scalpel. The family encouraged her eccentricity, even going so far as to annex off a portion of the potting sheds for her in which to pursue her ghoulish activities.

At school her teachers could find little to say about her. 'A fair start' and 'Could contribute more if she tried' were typical of the bet-hedging epithets listed upon her half-term reports. Playground unpleasantness resulting from the discovery of feline remains in Kelly's duffel-bag was written off as the morbid curiosity of youth, and it was only upon the appointment of a vigorously modern art mistress that Kelly finally found a friend and ally. The school was relieved, the family were pleased, and Kelly O'Kelly discovered art on a similar scale to that on which Columbus discovered America. This was in the early nineteen seventies, when Kelly was twelve.

The new art mistress was called Frances Wadham (R A), and was herself a misunderstood surrealist. Forced into teaching by the critical hostility with which her spectacular – if lurid – anatomical landscapes were received, Miss Wadham had said 'Cheerio!' to her bedsit in Bayswater, presented her folio of signed Balla prints to a close friend, and headed with the speed and determination of a lady-shot-out-of-a-cannon in the direction of St Mary's School for Girls (nr Reading). She knew that one day British surrealism would become fashionable and its practitioners rewarded as they justly deserved and, of course, she was right.

In the meantime she established at St Mary's an 'Arts Laboratory', and the school quickly divided into those who thought it was a jolly-good-thing and those who did not. The Headmistress (happily for Miss Wadham) fell into the former camp. Introducing the new teacher on the first day of the Michaelmas term, the Headmistress predicted a 'Renaissance at St Mary's', and outlined the artistic future of the school in glowing terms. Surveying the faces of all the girls in the assembly hall, the dim, the bright, and the partially eclipsed, she addressed them as follows:

'For too long' (she said) 'we have thought of the arts as something to do on a wet games day. Under the professional artistic guidance of Miss Wadham' (and here she pointed at the newcomer) 'St Mary's will replace the visual arts to its proper position of importance in the correct curriculum for any modern schoolgirl. I am sure that we will all – not just the Arts Sixth – benefit from, and enjoy, the presence of our new art mistress . . .'

It should be pointed out that the Headmistress had no prior knowledge of Miss Wadham's own work. The enlightened Friend of the Royal Academy who sat on the Board of Governors at St Mary's was a landscapes man himself, and being too embarrassed to admit ignorance when questioned about Miss Wadham's work he feigned admiration and thus the appointment was approved. Sweeping briskly back to her study after assembly, the Headmistress recalled the motto of her old school: 'Knowledge is no more a fountain sealed' and wished that the Founders of St Mary's could have come up with something better than 'Obedience Above All!', which she found rather common.

For Kelly O'Kelly the world was transformed by Miss Wadham. As the Christmas term drew on into its thrillingly fog-bound hours of evening school, the amount of time that she spent in the third-floor 'Arts Lab' beneath the turrets of the East Wing increased into the maximum allowed. Recognising a genuine interest, and seeking for some talent therein, Miss Wadham was generous with both time and materials. Having enjoyed their first shy conversation about the putrefaction process in small animals, Miss Wadham obtained (via discussion with the science mistress) a pair of frog's legs and set Kelly the task of drawing them – a difficult assignment but carefully chosen. Some days passed, during which the frog's legs went rather brown and Kelly's fair-haired head (reminiscent, thought Miss Wadham, of a Bonnard sketch or a winter's morning in Brighton) was bent conscientiously over her task. Having completed her drawing she timidly took it up to Miss Wadham.

'Why Kelly – this is really very good. You've captured the break in that bone quite beautifully. I must show you this book etc., etc.'

It was only later that the surrealist in Miss Wadham spoke out. 'Of course Kelly, the short cut, with those frog's legs, would have been simply to glue them onto the paper . . .'

The simplicity of this solution provoked a proto-sexual sense of excitement in Kelly. The freedom of it! The daring! To not care if people were cross!

Amidst many varied and colourful projects, Kelly began to study for her Art O-level and struggle her way into adolescence.

For as long as she could remember Kelly had had 'a thing' about restriction and confinement. She loved the sensation of not being able to move, and many of her favourite childhood games had been those in which she attempted to tie herself up. Skipping ropes, a length of garden hose, a discarded bicycle chain of her brother's found one gloriously still August afternoon – all of these accessories had been worked into a complicated series of ritualistic pastimes that Kelly placed second only to the joy of cutting things up.

There were various gradations of excitement to be derived from these activities. As Kelly grew older her ability to create narratives in her head which included the necessity for her being tied up increased to a strength that was a credit to her imagination. Soon the stories were limiting themselves to simply more and more complicated prisoner scenarios. Sometimes, on the spur of the moment, Kelly would decide that she had to take off her skirt in order to play out the scene to her satisfaction. On these occasions it was the sense of secrecy and privacy which excited her as much as the physical sensation of straining with all her might to tighten the cords she had tied about her legs. She would watch her skin turning white and red as she pulled herself around on the floor. She would bore of the game quite suddenly, and then she would undo whatever it was she had tied around herself and go off in search of a new pastime. These games were played best when played spontaneously.

Kelly O'Kelly had never sought after friends, and as a consequence few of her classmates had made much of an effort to seek after her. The classroom cliques formed and reformed; spite, passion, gossip and sulks followed their usual course. Kelly began experimenting with charcoal, and Miss Wadham lent her two large books on Leonardo and compound fractures. In her private world of prisoners and victims Kelly's interest in bondage began to take on a new dimension.

*

Kelly first became aware of St Valentine's Day just before her mock O-levels. Much classroom and bus stop boasting, exaggerated nervousness and feigned indifference had provided the terrifying overture to this important festival. Kelly could think of absolutely no one to whom she would consider sending a Valentine, but having recently completed a life-like picture in line and watercolour of a lamb's heart she rather wished that there was some special boy to whom this image could be sent.

Of boys she had very little knowledge. Infrequent local discos under parental supervision had revealed only a group of very young-looking schoolboys, full of bravado and furtive sexual interest. These boys would usually stand around in the garden of whatever large detached residence the disco or party was taking place in and conspicuously share two cans of beer whilst maintaining an air of immense importance about the depths of their indulgence and its Caligula-like proportions. It is fair to say that many of these boys never changed with age.

Kelly would sit on the windowsill in the cleared living room or echoing Parish Hall in which the Saturday night disco was taking place, and wonder at how unsympathetic the early evening daylight was to either decadence or romance. Miss Wadham had told her that the behaviour of the local boys at these functions was largely a matter of class. Had Kelly been born in the Old Kent Road, or in a large industrial city she would find the attitudes far more advanced. Advanced in what sense Miss Wadham refused to say, thus rendering her suggestion all the more impressive. Kelly could not help but wish from time to time as she lolloped around half-heartedly to a record which she didn't particularly like, that Providence had deposited her in one of the tougher social ghettos. Twyford, in the mid nineteen seventies, was not known for its teenage glamour.

Most of all it was an impression of gardens and twilight that Kelly retained from her early social experiences. Beyond the noisy boys pretending to be drunk there was always a vivid stretch of carefully kept lawn. An ornamental rockery containing one or two dwarf conifers and a specially 'aged' statuette generally marked the halfway point. Beyond that the light faded into khaki and then spruce; increasing densities of green which terminated in a wall of darkness beneath the inevitable trees at the bottom of the garden. At the wilder of these functions, the King Boy would manage to annoy and outrage some girl to the point that she would chase him out into the garden shouting. He would shriek and laugh, possibly run around the rockery a few times, and then the whole event would be analysed and discussed the following week with an attention to detail which bordered on the pathological. Kelly wondered whether she simply ran with a particularly innocent set. She appeared to be alone in being unimpressed by this clumsy budding of early sexuality.

She had no one to discuss the matter with, and suddenly, never having thought much about it before, she realised that she was very lonely: lonely and angry at everyone. This was Kelly's first depression.

The depression coincided with a sequence of painful periods and the conspiratorial anxiety surrounding the school craze about Valentine's Day. There was talk of little else – who 'fancied' whom, who was 'going out with' whom, and who had 'got off' with whom. Kelly listened to all this with amazement and dread. An entire romantic and erotic play appeared to have been performed around her without her having the slightest idea that casting had even begun. By the end of the first week of February it seemed to Kelly that every girl in the school was in the middle of, at the end of, or anticipating, a glorious and rewarding passion. She suspected that she was surrounded by liars. She asked Miss Wadham.

'Oh it's one long anguished scream,' said the art mistress; but Kelly didn't believe her.

Kelly rediscovered her fantasy games of restraint and victimisation with a physical violence that both shocked and mocked her. She walked around the misty crescents and avenues looking at the wet drives and dripping trees. She knew that happiness must turn into disaster but she didn't know what followed after – this was her pessimistic guess, and she longed for summer, and a bunch of flowers to paint.

Neither her French mother nor her Irish father seemed in the least bit approachable to discuss this vague but piercing sense of isolation. Her mother looked upon her as a chocolate-box prodigy and her father only spoke of the O'Kelly family pride. Meanwhile the dreaded Valentine's Day crept closer. Kelly looked long and sentimentally at her painstakingly painted heart. She knew that it was the wrong kind of heart – neither satin, nor witty, nor suggestive, but it was her heart, she had spent hours on it, and it spoke for her.

February 13th brought with it an unexpected interview with the popular girl of the Fourth, Christine Smart. It happened as the form were changing for PE.

'Kelly did you know that Brian Hutton really fancies you? He told Jason Carnes, who told Sally Emmerdale . . .' And then (impressively): 'Sally's going out with Andy Henshaw, you know, Susan Henshaw's brother . . .'

The effect of this information was curious. Bending to do up her plimsoll she felt as though she had lost her previous personality without being given a replacement. She broke her lace. Rather late, and hobbling in a tight pair of borrowed gym shoes, Kelly shuffled into the gymnasium, where girls better-looking than she (she thought) were lining up to vault the horse.

Brian Hutton – he was the rather short, moon-faced boy with glasses whom Kelly had seen loitering uneasily by the bus stop on the other side of the road to the school gates. Physically there was little to be said for him it was true, but given the advertised hierarchy of local male talent (headed by the adorable David Essex lookalike Andy Henshaw) he was by no means the worst catch.

All day Kelly thought about this name – Brian Hutton – which had suddenly endorsed her passport to the state of romance.

February 14th dawned as a sudden spring day in the gloomy last month of winter. On waking, Kelly could see a crack of blue sky between her curtains the way that she usually saw it in June. She had woken early; the postman would not call for at least an hour. She dressed quietly and went into the sunny kitchen to make herself a cup of tea and have some cereal. The garden looked warm and inviting; a carpet of sparkling lawn, and here and there some timid shoots were pushing up in the flower beds. Her mother came downstairs and smiled at her. 'Oh, Valentine's Day – you must be very excited to be up so early!' Kelly smiled despite herself. She couldn't care less about Brian himself, and wild horses would not drag her to go out with him – and then the post arrived. Hardly believing her eyes, Kelly saw on the hall carpet, peeping out between a bill and a catalogue, a neat yellow envelope, addressed to her in felt-tip capitals. The moment was too good to waste quickly. Gulping the remains of her tea, Kelly set off for school with the unopened envelope in the inside pocket of her blazer. She would open it away from everyone, in the Arts Lab, where she could enjoy the whole process.

It was not until lunchtime that she finally tore open the envelope. Inside was an 'Artist's Reproduction' card. It depicted a sleek femme fatale poised cooly by the side of a limousine. Kelly was thrilled by the rather daring sentiment that the airbrush slickness of the image implied. Brian Hutton had never really struck Kelly as being sophisticated or urbane, but for the rest of the day the boundaries between the real and the imagined were a blur. She forgot what the real Brian Hutton was like and floated on a swimming pool of imaginary romance as she went into the dining hall to eat her mince. It was a personal awareness that the card had triggered.

Leaving school, Kelly saw Brian at the bus stop. Looking anxiously down the road for his late bus, Brian was wearing a creased school suit and had a football bag at his feet. Kelly sauntered across the road towards him.

She smiled; she even simpered a little. She said that Christine Smart had 'told'. Brian, for whom Kelly had never figured as even a remote candidate for his nocturnal harem, began to look genuinely confused. Kelly accused him directly of having sent her the Valentine. By the manner in which Brian fled gratefully onto his bus there could be no doubting his innocence. Confused, embarrassed, but excited, Kelly walked slowly home. Who could her admirer possibly be?

The mystery endured for nearly three weeks until a tragic afternoon when Kelly and her brother had a violent and spiteful quarrel. Afraid of his sister's physical strength and unpredictable rage, Mark O'Kelly had finally spat out the truth about her precious Valentine. The family had sent it to cheer her up. Mark had ridden on his bicycle to the neighbouring village in order to post it 'anonymously'. She was a turd he said, nearly in tears. He wished they hadn't bothered, 'spastic misery guts'. Kelly swallowed and left the room.

★

The Valentine's Day humiliation was to remain close to the surface of Kelly's mind for the next three years. A slightly older person would maybe have wondered whether he or she needed a lover, a priest, or a psychoanalyst.

Kelly made no close friends, and she had no boyfriend.

As she grew older, around her sixteenth birthday, Kelly began to look at herself for the first time. Previously she had had little interest in her appearance. Now she found that she could only describe what she saw of herself in the mirror with contempt.

'I'm short,' she said; she was five-feet-four.

'I'm fat'; she was just under eight stone.

'I'm covered in spots' – she had two small red marks just beneath her hairline. And finally, 'I'm gross'; her dislike of eating had kept her figure.

Then she tugged at her hair: 'Lanky and disgusting.' Her hair was blonde, badly cut, but healthy. There was nothing cute or childish about Kelly's damning appraisal of her looks.

Liz Green, a girl in Kelly's Art History group, who was well-known throughout the school for being the height of fashion and 'pretty', unexpectedly invited Kelly out for a Saturday afternoon shopping trip; an extra-curricular activity at St Mary's which carried with it much status. Wary at first that this was some kind of practical joke, Kelly was uncertain whether or not to accept the invitation. On the Friday evening before the big outing was planned to take place, Kelly went for a walk around the reservoirs which backed onto the end of her road.

These oblongs of black water had always seemed to Kelly to be the size of small seas. As a child she had assumed that they were part of the ocean and had often wondered what would happen if there was a storm and a boat was shipwrecked upon one of the concrete embankments. It depressed her to see the packs of children cycling around them at sunset. The vigour of their amusement seemed to lack respect. A few wind-bent birch trees stood thin and black near the water's edge of the largest reservoir. The undisturbed surface of the water reflected the sky as clearly as a mirror. In the evening, after a fine day, the reservoirs were three flat pink windows set in ebony frames. Moved to frequent reverie by the solemnity of the place, Kelly had tried to photograph the reservoirs from time to time; but her prints always made them look completely unremarkable. The atmosphere of the water and sky could not be captured easily.

As Kelly walked along the cement rim of one of the reservoirs that Friday evening, she found herself looking at her shoes. They were scuffed black plimsolls. Then she thought about her baggy beige trousers, pullover and short jacket. The jacket belonged to her brother and the rest were things that her mother had bought for their 'practicality'. Her hair was tied up at the back in a black ribbon. Around her wrist she wore an old watch, two thin silver bracelets she had won at a fair and a piece of knotted bootlace. Her only scent was a trace of sandalwood oil.

As Kelly walked a little further on towards the view of the patchwork countryside with its distant line of motorway lights, she wondered which she hated the most: her current appearance as an acknowledged frump, or the pending incorporation of herself into the schoolgirl pastime of clothes and make-up. The former status maintained her autonomy – but she had been made fatally aware of the value of that independence; and the latter implied an acceptance of the corporate identity – a hydra-headed monster of silly by-laws and emotional compromise. Looking into the water Kelly could see herself face-down beneath the surface, bloated in her practical clothes. She wondered whether her hatred of the Shopping Is Fun And So Are Boys way of life was derived from jealousy. Attempting to regroup her shaken pride with the contemplation of her recently won

Art Prize and likely acceptance into a distant and famous art college on Foundation, Kelly inwardly sneered at her contemporaries. It didn't work. She would go shopping with Liz Green.

Heading home, the early foliage on the trees gave off a powerful scent that settled like dew on the roads and gardens. In the big surburban houses, pre-war family mansions on a strange architectural scale halfway between pomposity and thrift, Kelly could see pink and blue shampoo bottles on the windowsills of lighted bathrooms. Here and there white garden furniture stood out against the gathering dusk, and through open windows and patio doors the murmur of television and music spread out into the still air.

Kelly thought about the teenage children of these homes. It seemed to her, as she traced her finger through the film of pollen which had collected on a car bonnet, that they were all building up to a massive carnival of optimism in which every activity was granted new meaning by its relation to an as-yet-unspecified but nonetheless assured romantic happiness. Telephones, hair-driers, shopping trips and borrowed cars were all uniting to assist the youth of Twyford in their creation of a magical celebration of Saturday. The preparation for the event was the event; no date or party or disco could ever be as good as this most subtle anticipation of it.

This insight did nothing to decrease Kelly's sense of loneliness. She longed for a date or a party or a disco to look forward to, and for some boy whose movements she could monitor in earnest whispers with her friends. Shopping on Saturday (a phrase which reminded her of 'Games on Thursday') would maybe include her in the carnival, but she felt in her heart that two things would occur: firstly she would look a mess and be laughed at behind her back, and secondly, as regards the boy, that he would somehow be an idiot and she would have no real interest in him.

★

On Saturday the shopping centre in the middle of town was hot and crowded.

Ice-cream-soaked infants screamed beside their push-chairs whilst harassed parents bent down with barely controlled rage to snatch away the offending cones. Bored husbands stood smoking in the wide doorways of thronging shops. Tired women emerged from supermarkets with heavy bags of groceries. A constant stream of people kept making their way down the narrow concrete path which led between two buildings to the multi-storey carpark. This alley was cut directly down its middle by the sun, thus casting the outgoing crowds into shadow as the new arrivals emerged into the blinding glare. A man with some suitcases of shirts to sell had positioned himself on the beer-stained steps of the old cinema. On the four public benches around the concrete tubs of trees in the middle of the precinct a group of youths were sitting, the girls looking bored and watching the shoppers whilst the boys flicked cigarette butts into the crowd or got up to show off kung-fu kicks. A man dressed as a robot was selling tinfoil balloons just to one side of them.

As Kelly O'Kelly and Liz made their way towards the shops, Kelly looked at the scene before her through eyes which had felt peculiar since she had wedged her bus ticket into the back of the seat in front half an hour earlier. Her mind would not work properly, but she was absorbed by what she looked upon. A man was standing alone beside a traffic cone counting to himself out loud on the fingers of one hand. A boy walked by with a triangle of silver paper pinned to the back of his jacket. The words 'Hoo-Ha!' were written on the paper in poor Gothic script. He was with his mother.

Liz met many people whom she knew, and at each encounter she would dispose of Kelly in the opening sentence, by saying: 'This is a friend of mine from school.'

A parade of Boy Scouts was brought to a sudden halt by

a minor traffic accident. Oil dripped onto the road beneath a smashed brake-light and glinted in the sun.

The hours passed by in the regenerated centre of the county town. Kelly bought a pair of pleated yellow trousers largely out of embarrassment at Liz's repeated assurances that 'they looked all right really' when she came out of the changing rooms to 'do her twirl'. The changing rooms had been a ghastly experience, sophisticated in procedure and jungle-like in behaviour. Having had nearly all her clothes bought for her by her mother, Kelly was completely astounded by the complex ritual of changing-room tags and 'number of garments permitted' laws. Wanting to get her own clothes off and on again as quickly as possible, Kelly had taken too many articles into her little cubicle and been terrified by the sudden tearing back of the booth curtain by an irritated assistant demanding the immediate return of one skirt and blouse. Standing with her jeans half on Kelly furiously shoved the offending clothes at the mechanically repeating 'three-at-a-time' sales girl. Kelly's legs and thighs had several bruises and fading twine burns on them.

Overhead a speaker blared chart music. There was a humid and airless quality to the atmosphere of sticky cosmetic scents that drifted between the posters of dreaming white Juliets and pouting, deep-tanned disco princesses. The olive-green carpet was covered in pins. Someone had left a half finished hamburger on a chair.

In 'Metro' Kelly bought a little black shirt. Her friend disapproved.

'It isn't very bright,' she said.

Finally, it was knickers, bras, jewellery and make-up. After that Kelly would be free to go home. Underwear was always on the Lingerie Bar at the back of the shop, and here a waterfall of lace, nylon-lace, gauze-effect satin and wrinkled suspender belts came tumbling down to a foam of their fallen brethren on the floor. Squads of girls perused the racks, and here and there an established couple would be choosing 'nightwear' together. Kelly found herself absorbed in the complexity and range of items in front of her. She had never considered, as she fingered a string of white elastic with a minute triangle of see-through white lace attached to it, that she should give much thought to her underwear. She bought the string of white elastic and its matching bra. She wanted to see how capable she was of flattering her body. Liz had already selected and bought exactly what she was looking for.

With her remaining few pounds Kelly bought a pale red lipstick ('Ice Flame'), and a soft gold lip gloss to put over it ('Harmony Mist'). Then she bought an eyeliner pencil. The assistant put her purchases in a special white bag with Face Shapes written on it in pink.

In a last-minute decision Kelly also bought a pair of clip-on earrings without looking at them too closely. They were silver and dangled.

As they left the shop Liz met two more boys of her acquaintance. 'This is Pete,' she said, 'And Simon . . .'

★

Kelly O'Kelly, ludicrous and angry; Simon Haynes, her unwanted and devoted suitor – this was Kelly's first experience of the non-relationship relationship, a damp feeling in her heart which hinted at first truths about love/hatred within the couple.

The impression that Simon made upon Kelly as they stood facing one another on the precinct for the first time was slender. Kelly had been reading *Wuthering Heights*. She looked at Simon who was squinting at her as she stood with her back to the brilliant evening sun. With Simon – even as an academic candidate – she knew that she would never 'escape from the wash-house to take a ramble at liberty'. He was (Liz made a special point of telling her in the hushed reverential whisper which Kelly thought better suited to matters of greater importance) seventeen-and-a-half. He was re-sitting his O-levels at the local Sixth-Form College, and had so far only distinguished himself by one day swallowing half-a-lungful of soup in the canteen, which, as the dinner lady had remarked, 'Had nearly done for him.' Despite this dramatic event Simon was largely unknown on the St Mary's romantic circuit, except, perhaps, as Pete's friend, and 'the boy who choked on his soup'. With this, and only this, behind him, Simon Haynes took his first real look at Kelly O'Kelly and believed himself in love.

It is difficult to assess what kind of quiet, pastel, domestic incubator had hatched Simon Haynes. He had moved through a peaceful suburban childhood without displaying the slightest fragment of curiosity in anything. As a child he ate, played and slept in more or less the right order, and at the onset of adolescence this routine was hardly altered. Much given to wandering around the house in the gaps between television programmes (he would watch anything), the only activity Simon seemed capable of performing on his own initiative was that of making mugs of instant coffee. Sometimes he would take these up to his heavily postered bedroom to drink. Other times he would lean against the draining board quietly sipping in a way which his sister (Debbie Haynes) found sinister and irritating.

The truth of the matter was that Simon was perfectly content. His silence was not a mask for either anxiety or anger. Laziness had claimed him young, aided no doubt in its task by the ready availability of suburban family comforts and the fact that Simon had neither tastes nor standards. He was content, for seventeen-and-a-half years, to pursue his animal stupor; fed, clothed, watered, housed and partially educated. In recent years he had come alive for odd ten-minute periods when some particularly blatant set of sexual signifiers managed to trigger his junior erotic appetite. The pleasure he derived from masturbation was classical in its simplicity. 'Nude woman,' he thought, and ejaculated.

Such was the yellowish loam which constituted the fair-haired, blue-veined, chicken-white and adequately built English youth that was Simon Haynes.

★

Miss Wadham had wondered long and hard over the extra-ordinary talent of Kelly O'Kelly. Her considerations were possibly tinted with just a dash of jealousy. At first she had been inclined to write off Kelly's premature interest in the use of mixed media and performance as mere precosity resultant from an over-artistic background in the bosom of some family of Home Counties aesthetes. Having made a few enquiries she discovered that Kelly O'Kelly was the daughter of a quiet Twyford family whose normality and serenity could best be described as screamingly dull. There was no chance that Kelly had been coached in the latest visual outrage by some influential parent.

Then she began to look harder at Kelly's much admired portfolio. Her drawing from life was excellent. The 'Entrails and Blood' period of her earlier work had now been succeeded by a series of quasi-sexual self-portraits, partially watercoloured and deliberately left unfinished to emphasise the effect of where the paint had dripped and run. They could not be called 'beautiful' – at least not in front of Mrs O'Kelly – and they most certainly could not be exhibited on Open Day alongside the horses, fruit-and-decanters, and geometric abstracts of her classmates.

In one of the pictures Kelly had depicted herself as seen in the mirror, kneeling undressed and holding a lizard in her outstretched hand. In another she stared without expression at a blue-and-white soup plate upon which there was some white underwear and a piece of burned string. The Art College had offered Kelly an immediate place on the Honours Degree course to start as soon as she was seventeen.

Thus it was that Kelly began the last summer holidays before she left for college by meeting Simon Haynes. No sooner had she returned from her shopping trip to lie full-length on her bed in the twilight than the telephone rang. It was Christine Smart. Feeling bored and tired Kelly sat on the stairs with the telephone to listen to the latest gossip – her shopping trip entitled her to this service. The news concluded with an invitation.

'You've got to come to Susan Henshaw's party next week. Her parents are away and everyone's going . . .' The latter piece of information struck Kelly as being an excellent reason why not to attend, but no sooner had she put the phone down when it rang again.

'Er. Hello, may I speak to Kelly please?'

'Speaking.'

'Oh. Ha ha, I didn't recognize you – it's Simon . . .'

'Have you got the right number? This is 850 . . .'

'We bumped into you down in the town this afternoon, Pete and I . . .'

Then Kelly realised that it was Simon Haynes and felt suddenly dreary and embarrassed. She had nothing to say to him about anything.

'Ha ha,' said Simon again, as though this was some kind of conversational open-sesame. 'Ha ha . . . Hello?'

'Hello,' said Kelly.

'Sorry, I thought you'd gone. I was wondering if you'd come to Susan Henshaw's party next Saturday with me? Loads of people are going and we could meet there if you like or I could pick you up when I get a lift . . .?' Then (confidently), 'Sally Haversham's going . . .' Sally Haversham was obviously the trump card.

'Who's Sally Haversham?'

'Oh. I thought she was in your form. Someone told me she was a friend of yours . . .'

'I haven't got any friends. I'm a fat ugly failu . . .' By this time Kelly O'Kelly was speaking without thinking and

Simon was very embarrassed. He could hear his sister coming in to use the phone and she'd know he was trying to ring a girl. He had anticipated a refusal, a mocking refusal even, but this madness was unexpected. Pete had never said that this would happen.

'In fact,' continued Kelly, 'I'll be dead by next Saturday, at least, by the time Susan Henshaw's party starts I will be . . .'

'Oh well maybe see you there then, sorry,' said Simon.

'Bye,' said Kelly. And they hung up.

Kelly put the phone down very gently as though it was ill or she had just been cruel to it and was feeling remorseful. She sat on the stairs and looked at the light on the wall. It was staying light until quite late, and deep amber patches were lengthening down the white cracked-ice wallpaper. After a few minutes Kelly got out the phone book and looked up Simon's number. Without pausing for thought she dialled.

'86443,' said a brisk, soldierly voice.

'May I speak to Simon, please?'

'Who's calling?' snapped the voice.

'Kelly,' cooed Kelly.

'Who?' came the suspicious reply.

'Kelly O'Kelly,' said Kelly.

'Wait a moment please.' The voice suddenly moved from the phone and bellowed, 'SIMON! Telephone for you. KELLY O'KELLY.' There followed a noise of Simon frantically running down the stairs and then having to wait until the owner of the voice had stopped watching him before saying:

'Hello?'

'Hello Simon, it's Kelly. Look I hope I didn't confuse you just then, you must think I'm really mad. My brother was mucking around and I couldn't talk properly. I was just ringing to say that I'll meet you at Susan's party if you want. Why don't I see you there about nine?'

'Oh great . . . are you sure?'

'Yes. I'll go with Christine Smart or someone and see you there.'

'It ought to be great,' enthused Simon, without much conviction in Kelly's agreeing with him.

'See you then.'

'Yeah. Ha ha; see you.'

Returning to her room Kelly looked at the rhythmic arch of water from the lawn sprinkler, silver against the damp grass. The treetops were blackening against the pale blue summer sky, chestnuts and sycamore. Then she remembered her shopping. The gardens, the shopping and the telephone; the equipment with which people grew up so publicly. In September she would be leaving for the Art College, miles away, in Brighton. It seemed to have nothing to do with her, that plan, and yet her parents and Miss Wadham were so pleased. Flattered into submission by such an immediate and enthusiastic offer they had quickly forgotten their reservations about the distance. When her father took her for the interview Kelly had not really noticed the town and its white promenade. She had spent the time watching the students, and trying to picture herself as one. She had an aunt who lived in Hove.

It was now quite dark. Her father had turned off the lawn sprinkler and shut the garden-shed door. All of Kelly's side of the house was quiet, and downstairs in the drawing room the television was engrossing the rest of the family. Kelly hated television.

Picking up the smallest of her boutique bags, Kelly went silently into her own small bathroom. It was pale green and smelt of fern-scented soap, fresh air and water. Without turning on the light she slipped off her clothes and began to struggle with the price tags on her new underwear. In a minute or two she was looking at herself in the big mirror beside the bath. The knickers seemed outrageously small, like there was nothing there, and the bra felt tight and uncomfortable. She let down her hair and shook it, immediately feeling ridiculous. She struck one or two seductive attitudes and then twisted round to try and see her back in the mirror. What she saw was what she supposed Simon Haynes would like to see. She was quite certain that he wouldn't, but she felt as though she was supposed to do something. She would do nothing remotely intimate with Simon Haynes. The idea was vile.

Wrapping herself in a towel, the lingerie back in its bag, Kelly ran a bath. It was nearly dark in the bathroom. Without turning on the lights Kelly twisted a damp flannel around her left wrist until it burned her, and lay back in the moisturising bath foam, watching the darkness around her.

The following day she put three white streaks in her hair.

★

Susan Henshaw was the privileged only daughter of a wealthy family who lived in one of the largest houses in Kelly's neighbourhood. The evening on which the willowy and waspish Susan was to open the doors of her parents' enormous house to approximately two hundred teenage guests was sure to be rare in its loveliness. The party had been preceded by several days of fine weather, and by late afternoon of the big Saturday the Henshaw's extensive, if over-landscaped, garden was a lake of golden light upon which were floating orderly rafts of rose beds, wafted beneath the azure by a warm, grass-cuttings-scented breeze.

Susan's parents were not particularly understated in their hope that this party – Susan's seventeenth birthday – would be the last of its kind. They were yearning for more formality, a 'wider spectrum' of guests, and, above all, a marquee. Knowing that as Mr Henshaw's fortunes as an electronic components baron increased, so too did the inevitability of the marquee, Susan had compensated her parents for the rowdiness of this, her last fling, by inviting her young cousins James and Stella Walker-Jones. To the elder Henshaws the hyphen meant a lot, and when James (sadly the popular Stella was already otherwise engaged) arrived with a young Etonian friend of his to stay for the party weekend, they delayed their departure for Madeira to greet him. James was the same age as Susan, but his manners were a credit to youth, and his clothes, though casual, sighed decency. As he was standing rather ill-at-ease in the panelled hall of 'Glyndale' (the Henshaw's nearly Arts & Crafts movement house), Mrs Henshaw was friendly to the point of hyper-ventilation.

'And this is . . .?' She arched her head with a widening smile to indicate her anticipation of pleasure.

'Miles Harrier,' said James, 'he's staying with us this holidays.'

'How do you do!' cried Mrs Henshaw with scalding warmth, 'I'm so glad you could come.'

'It's good of you to have us,' murmured the two boys in unison.

'I think that Susan's in her room doing something with her hair; but Andrew's about. Why don't you come through and have a drink outside with us in the garden; it's been so hot today hasn't it etc., etc.'

So joined by the rugged, if slightly affected (thought Harrier) Andrew, the little party made its way into the garden to talk about schools ('Oh Eton! How is it?'), the family ('Do you stay with James every holiday?'), and the forthcoming party ('How many people are coming, Andrew?'), and to wait for Mr Henshaw, whose position on the Board (Mrs Henshaw explained to Harrier) made him increasingly late home from town.

★

Miles Harrier was nearly eighteen when he stayed for the weekend with the Henshaws. He could not have known, as he sat politely asking Andrew about his recently acquired careers literature from the Army, that at the same moment, two miles away, Kelly O'Kelly was smoking an illicit cigarette beside one of the reservoirs and was due to fall hopelessly in love with him that evening. Unfortunately, this was to be precisely the same evening that Simon Haynes, through the pink light and shadows of a suburban teenage party, was to realise that Love, although exciting enough when first encountered, is not afraid of offering itself in one invisible and lethal dose.

Inexperienced in romance and uncertain in his desires, Harrier found that he spent much of Susan's party talking to Kelly about nothing in particular as they sat in varnished bamboo chairs in the candle-lit extension which was called 'the conservatory'. Simon, his heart pounding, extracted Kelly's body (her mind was elsewhere) for one confused dance at about ten o'clock. He said nothing (for fear of lessening his chances through offence) for the first two minutes, and then (for fear of lessening his chances through reticence) garbled three further invitations to forthcoming 'do's' that were thinly disguised as statements of fact:

'Pete's having a barbecue.'

and

'I'm going down to London for a concert – I haven't got the tickets yet.'

and

'My parents are away next week.'

We will never know how deeply Simon felt Kelly's lack of interest. It is probably just as well that Simon never discovered that it was Miles Harrier's better-looking, more muscular and richer arms that Kelly wound up in at midnight, as the syrupy slow music was played in the darkened drawing room. Harrier was unaware of the immediacy and extent of his conquest. He was also unaware of Simon, and would probably not have pursued the romance either then or later had he known about him. But to Kelly this was love, overpowering and complete. Her yellow peg-topped trousers and little black shirt clothed a being in Heaven, and the subsequent dates which she had with Harrier – many over the course of that summer – numbered as the happiest times of her life.

They would meet in one or other of the pretty villages which lay between Kelly and the Walker-Jones, or they would go for long walks together in the country. One day they went to London in weather of Mediterranean splendour and stopped for lunch in the new Habitat restaurant on the King's Road.

The affair was largely innocent, although Kelly would have given herself in an instant if asked, but tragically it was also rather one-sided. Harrier was very fond of Kelly; he found her pretty and she made him laugh, but somehow contact was never really made. He was very much taken up with his friendship with Stella and James, and whilst his family lived so much abroad there was a bond between the children which was precious to him.

Harrier never told Kelly much about his family ('They live abroad most of the time'), and she never told him about her love. She didn't think it could ever end. She forgot about going away to college. She just thought about Harrier and waited for the next time they were due to meet.

Strange fireflies buzz around the happy mind. They distract, for a moment, or frighten, but they are never grasped and studied. Kelly O'Kelly woke up one September morning to three facts: firstly, it was raining; secondly, her mother was annoyed with her because she hadn't made any preparations for her departure to Brighton three days hence; and lastly there was a letter, short and unemotional, from Harrier. Postmarked Paris, it told Kelly that he had had to visit his family and would be returning from them straight to school. Kelly knew, not from the contents of the letter but from its tone, that she had recently become a thing in Harrier's past. It hurt more deeply, the vagueness of it, than any direct rejection. There was nothing to work on – no declared feelings to restate, and no acknowledged relationship to defend. She was floundering in thin air, falling . . .

★

The evening before she left for Brighton, Kelly sat for half an hour in her parents' drawing room with a tearful Simon. The family had tactfully absented themselves, except for Mark who made a point of coming in to look for a suddenly needed book.

As Simon spoke of his feelings – for the first time – and of his total and immediate forgiveness (this was a lie) for any 'infidelity' that Kelly might have been guilty of towards his just and Platonic cause, Kelly did not look at him once. She would have cried had she done so and not been able to tell him that he was saying things that she wanted to say to Harrier. So she simply sat on the sofa, with Simon leaning forward earnestly on a chair that was directly opposite but a hundred miles away, and began to finger an old Christmas decoration that the cat was apt to play with. Finding a loose end of the pink nylon thread which was bound around the little plastic ball to cover it, she began to tie two fingers of her left hand together, rhythmically circling them with thread and then pausing to pull them tight. By the time that Simon left she could hardly move her fingers at all, encased as they were in a cutting sheath of pink nylon.

As Simon was leaving, still hoping that Kelly would say something to either salvage the remnants of his feelings or forgive him for being so submissive to them, she just stood leaning against the side of the open front door and nodding from time to time. Having failed his O-levels again, Simon Haynes was now being hung with the old school tie of his sentimental education. Uncomforted, he disappeared down the drive.

The following day Kelly O'Kelly left for Brighton. Within a month she had made it clear that she intended to forsake Fine Art for Performance and Environmental Media.

Separated by darkness, and an inability to speak a common language, the young people all began to grow up.

TWO

The Oil-Seed Rape in Flower

The builder, suntanned, stripped to the waist and wearing dark glasses, had breasts. Lucinda Fortune, with all the indulgence of a young person who believes herself to be in love, studied his reflection in a shop window on New Oxford Street and wondered at how brown he was against the blue of the road. Heat waves were rising off a strip of freshly laid tarmac and the traffic seemed to tremble as it passed. Turning to squint up at Centre Point and study its effect of falling, Lucinda could just make out a few blurred bars of yellow against the late afternoon sky. It was July, and the heat made her momentary dizziness pleasant.

In front of her, Bloomsbury was cut with deep shadows, and a shabby pink-and-white awning sagged over a second-floor window. No breeze disturbed the hang of its grey fringe. At Holborn the crowds thinned, and beyond Holborn, along the Gray's Inn Road, it seemed as though there were no people at all. Lucinda had just an hour to get home, change, and return to the West End in order to meet the man she thought she loved.

From time to time a wave of traffic sped past, catching a sudden glint of sun. Lucinda was in love with everything that she saw because it all seemed to connect her to Harrier, the man she was hurrying home to change for. As she felt the sunshine warm her arms, Lucinda perceived the whole of London to be arranged to unite her with Harrier at dusk. This union was yet to be approved by Harrier for, with the exception of the thirty-second street-corner conversation that they had had the previous week to arrange this evening's meeting, Harrier and Lucinda had not met properly for some years. Lucinda's feeling of love was therefore unofficial.

The gap between a word and its precise meaning has been the subject of much debate. To those possessed of a more vulgar ambition than the urge which drives a theorist to understand the ambiguities of interpretation there is something perilous about the testing of words against reality. This peril lies at the heart of the confusion which distinguishes the lover's discourse from the discourse of others. When Lucinda had first confronted herself with the exclamation 'I love Miles Harrier' she had therefore been unconvinced. Trying the emotion out, as it were, over a period of thirty-six hours, she had now come to believe in it as certainly as if Harrier had first made the statement to her and then proceeded to prove it. Harrier had not, to date, said anything to Lucinda Fortune about love.

She recalled a conversation that she had once had with a drunk commuter in Victoria Station buffet. With words slurred by both emotion and drink this unhappy man had told Lucinda about the depth of his dislike for his wife.

'But I do not understand,' Lucinda had asked (at that time still apt to confuse a veteran bore with the person whom we insist in retrospect on calling 'interesting'), 'I do not understand why you say that you hate your wife so much. What can you possibly mean?'

'It's because I love the little woman and would not harm a single hair on her beautiful little head,' had come the truthful, if confusing, reply. Love, Lucinda had later decided, was most definitely a capricious and volatile condition. All this mature analysis had of course evaporated once the emotion in question had taken the name of Miles Harrier and rented the mansion of Lucinda's heart. Renamed Miles Harrier this capricious and volatile condition had been welcomed with open arms. Having yet to see whether Harrier would return the emotion, Lucinda saw only love, not a Trojan Horse.

Reaching her apartment in the Gray's Inn Road, Lucinda smiled at the seedy lingerie shop next door to the street entrance. Harrier would laugh pleasantly when he saw it. She paused in the high-ceilinged hallway to brush some dust off the communal sideboard where the mail was laid out for the tenants of the block. Harrier must not witness a dusty sideboard. Tomorrow perhaps she would buy some flowers to brighten the entrance to her home. She ran up the black-and-white tiled steps which led to the mezzanine lift. One day, hopefully soon, Harrier would stand in the lift beside her. The elderly railings and varnished panelling would house them close together beneath the dim twenty-four-hour bulb. The yellow light in the lift gave one's complexion a flattering tan.

Lucinda knew that on summer evenings the big sash window on the second-floor landing let in a sudden blaze of sunshine. After the darkness of the lift it was quite dazzling to step out into its glare. This evening the window was a tall oblong of brilliant white, the light falling like a solid shaft onto the grey carpet which led to Lucinda's front door. As the lift clanked shut behind her and descended back down to the hall, Lucinda walked up to the window and looked out over the rooftops towards the taller buildings in the middle distance. She knew that a mile away the city was following the curve of the river, and a pale gold mist seemed to hang between her and the skyscrapers. Towards the City even bigger buildings flickered a rich peach light like fire off their windows. The blue of the sky was darkening slightly, and a width of pale vermilion stretched across the horizon. It seemed as though London was drowning for the night beneath the surface of a sunlit ocean. To Lucinda (in love) it seemed that the sunset she was seeing was simply a glimpse of an infinitely more impressive one which Harrier alone could show her. Harrier's sunset would be the real sunset, just as Harrier's London would be the real London. The earthly beauties that Lucinda might study alone were simply an impression of just how beautiful the earth could be when seen standing next to Harrier. Content to speculate on the glories of the anticipated, Lucinda allowed London to carry on drowning and let herself into the flat in order to shower and change as quickly as possible. Her flatmate, Stella Walker-Jones, was not at home.

★

To the cynic who lacks charm – that is, to the person who looks on life with the grumpy knowingness which is the mental attitude of 'the old lag' – there is little to recommend the life of a twenty-eight-year-old man as a subject for prolonged study. The old lag will simply see and sneer upon a handful of facts and a ragbag of associated images: a job, an illness or two, some sunlight remembered on a street somewhere, love affairs, marriage perhaps . . . In short he will see only a tiny collection of standard experiences, the titles of which could easily suppress further interest by dint of their unoriginality.

But beneath this bland surface there must exist something more, a place not unlike a storeroom or a basement, where the banal translates, if not into poetry, then prose gone mad, and the standard takes on a unique meaning. In order to take soundings from these depths, or rather, wanting to believe at least in solids, one must turn archaeologist. To excavate into the life of a twenty-eight-year-old man, and try to read from the powder and the treasures and the rubble how exactly he has lived to make him what he has become, is a task that demands patience with the banal. Once sifted and sorted the monotonous uniformity of the evidence begins to assume new values, and patterns, and a story, begin to emerge. One could start almost anywhere; a drink, a scrap of shirt material, a telephone conversation . . .

Whilst Lucinda Fortune was standing on one foot in the square of evening sunshine which flooded her kitchen and trying to decide between a black canvas mini-skirt and a longer, cream woollen pleated one, Miles Harrier was making his way more leisurely towards their rendezvous.

For Miles Harrier, in his twenty-eighth year (the summer of his twenty-eighth year), it seemed that Youth, the epiphany of Hope, had passed him by without, as it were, delivering the goods. A sense of unfulfilled ambition and vague anticipation seemed to hallmark his days, and as a consequence he was prone to both vivid speculation about his future and sentimental nostalgia for his past.

These moods began with no warning, and a sight as workaday as that of a troubleshooting software engineer, delving with a micro-thin blade into the innards of a computer, could prompt hours of colourful rumination. There was no order to these thoughts, or underlying structure to their rise to the surface of Harrier's mind. Their pattern was that of a freak outburst of chaos on a minor scale, and it was neither usual nor unusual, this controlled appearance of the out-of-control. Anything could happen.

He would think of his childhood friends growing up; of Lucinda Fortune for instance, so recently rediscovered, whose grandparents had been cabinet carvers in Europe with a cottage garden backing into Czechoslovakia. Or he would think of James Walker-Jones, Stella's brother, an obscure figure now residing in Whitehall Court Mansions, spilling drinks into air-conditioning units and buying awful photographs of sailors with girls on their knees. Years ago it was James who made the claim that Lucinda was psychic. He believed that she 'saw things', so he told her so, and she didn't sleep properly for years. At twenty-eight Miles Harrier thought of many different ways in which his past might have turned into a different future but all that he had so far concluded was that there were no short cuts to happiness.

He did know however of a short cut down an alley off the Tottenham Court Road opposite Great Russell Street which came out some two hundred metres down Oxford

Street northside. This short cut was slippery with the juice from burst rubbish bags during the day, and unlit and dangerous at night. Like many short cuts it seemed to finally qualify for the title by virtue of the element of risk involved. This sense of risk was also central to the sense of romance which can attach itself to a small alley in the heart of a city.

The little Spanish bar which stood halfway down the alley was not particularly romantic, but glimpsed at dusk from the hurrying torrent of the main street there was possibly something mysterious about it to the passer-by who happened to see a few coloured lights gleaming in its steamed-up windows. On closer examination these will-o'-the-wisps turned out to be plastic flowers on stems of twisted green wire, the electric blossom of a former Christmas tree; and for every one that twinkled prettily in yellow or red there were a further two that were cold and dead, their colour an indeterminate plastic neutral now that their bulbs had gone. The prettiness of the few survivors increased the dereliction of the scene they attempted to decorate. It was maybe for this reason, or maybe due to the dinginess of the alley in general, that the bar was not a popular one and its advertised basement dive a rarely used annex. A few Spanish Londoners watched the television on the bar, and the rest of the drinkers were either those whose curiosity would be satisfied over one drink or anonymous regulars who sat by themselves and said nothing.

Miles Harrier – a man who was rendered just slightly exotic by being the Honourable Miles Harrier – would sometimes use this little bar as a place for meeting friends in the early evening. Thus it was that just after seven on a warm July night Miles Harrier came to be waiting for his childhood friend Lucinda Fortune in the little Spanish bar up the alley. That was the length and the breadth of it.

He was early, and leaning back on the torn plastic seat to regard his surroundings he was filled with a pleasant sense akin to a doze. The bar was dark, and cramped, its atmosphere uncertain between that of a side-chapel and a scullery. The yellow walls were covered with a collage of holiday posters, the faded landscape thus created being one of surf-slapped sands, palm-fronted hotels, sombre matadors and a solitary straw-hatted donkey. The overlapping corners of these images were peeling away in some places, taking with them a crooked bar of brittle sellotape and a vital slice of visual meaning. In the twilit alcoves around the room there were pin-ups of beach girls which had bulged with the damp, thus introducing an unflattering sag to the suntanned breasts and behinds which were saucily exposed from strips of minuscule bikini. In the alcove beside the payphone, 'Rosa', a brunette wearing only a G-string whom the photographer had ordered to smile coyly over a volley ball, had had her tanned thigh encoded with telephone numbers, half an address, and the inexplicable legend 'ici Londres'. Neatly gummed about her head, orbital to her winning smile and like panels in an altar screen, were a dozen white labels advertising personal services in careful primary-coloured handwriting. 'Big Blonde', 'Busty New Model', 'Tie Me Up and Spank Me', and so forth. The flagship of this little campaign was a slightly larger sticker which depicted in the image of a mis-registered smudge a suspender-belted and topless *femme fatale* whose right knee was resting on a chair. Beneath this portrait was the information: 'Carol', 'Weekdays after six', and a telephone number. Carol was dangling a whip. Her face was obscured by an orange card: 'Kresta Cabs. 24 Hours. Any time, any place, anywhere.'

One or two wine bottles wrapped in goatskin hung from the smoke-browned ceiling, and above the bar itself a dusty row of raffish flamenco dolls stood along the length of a little shelf. The green light in the bar created an underwater effect, and the bent and broken spears of plastic fern which pushed up from a window box in front of the netting over the windows combined with arbitrary flares of fairy light to give the impression of sitting at the bottom of a cheap aquarium.

A jukebox murmured Spanish love songs. From Harrier's scant knowledge of Spanish the lyrics appeared to be made up entirely from the words 'love', 'darling', and 'forever'. The jukebox itself was a masterpiece of greasy leather-effect plastic and chrome-style finish which had chipped to reveal a bone-like substance. The noise of its mechanism was slightly louder than the volume at which it played the records.

As one of the barmen chewed placidly on a small, extinguished cheroot, his partner stood quietly beside him picking the back off a beermat. The counter which they were standing behind as they did these things was rather too small for them both to be bored in comfort.

With his hands in his pockets and his legs stretched out lazily in front of him, Harrier studied his reflection in a long mirror opposite his table. Vanity snatched him from the maw of indifference to what he saw. He was well-built, with broad, powerful shoulders and a strong figure which effortlessly filled out his clothes without unsightly surplus. His neck was maybe rather too thick and he was in danger of getting a double chin by middle age, but for the present his athletically developed trunk seemed to extend into a highly presentable head. His handsome features included an extremely aristocratic nose, a wide, schoolboyish mouth, and a pair of gentlemanly blue eyes that registered his mood beneath black, streamlined eyebrows. A high forehead ran smoothly into a slick head of glossy black hair which was cut into the closest to a modern style that his father's London barber could manage. The sides were slicked back with scented oil whilst the back was cut short and the top left in a fashionably greasy mass of loose curls. The result of this uneasy marriage between tradition and modernity was, if anything, avant-garde.

His shirt was a standard blue and white City stripe; and

his tie either Old Etonian or a dark crimson 'boardroom'. His suits were always pin-stripe, usually double-breasted, and came in either navy-blue, charcoal, or black. Shoes were a sensible Churchill town brogue (black). In short there was little to distinguish Harrier from hundreds of other young men professionally employed in London except for the fact that Harrier managed to somehow escape looking like an advert. Harrier had no interest in clothes or fashion. As he studied himself in the dark mirror across the little bar it never occurred to him that the two barmen saw nothing more than arrogance in his well-proportioned and expensively dressed figure. The barmen however, having inwardly commented upon this arrogance, simply carried on chewing, and picking, and looking without expression towards the open double doors of their bar.

Harrier looked at his watch. Lucinda had arranged to meet him at seven-thirty and it was now twenty-past. He looked around the bar again, peering slightly into the watery half-light. He felt that soon he would see a large fish swim before his eyes prior to taking an exploratory turn around the derelict rotisserie which stood against the wall behind the bar. Perhaps the whole bar, not just its rotisserie, flamenco dolls and jukebox, had been thrown over a railway siding one eerily still dusk, there to roll down a steep slope of pinkish slag and disappear beneath the surface of a sombre and midge-carpeted pool of immense depth known as London. This piece of illegal dumping, mused Harrier, could maybe have been observed by a painter in oils on Highgate Hill, someone who, mixing his colours out-of-doors one fine evening beneath the residential blossom, would be forced by the spectacle of this drowning to reconsider the serenity of the View Towards St Pancras which he was labouring to create. How could one incorporate the drowning of an entire wine bar into some potentially Whistleresque nocturne? Harrier frowned and searched his mind for a memory of either an underwater experience or a disturbed vista. There was the aquarium that Stella used to have when she was a little girl, and the three cement-rimmed reservoirs near to where Kelly O'Kelly used to live ... Neither of these was likely. Harrier sipped his gin-and-tonic, which tasted of condensation.

Low stools clustered around the small metal-topped table, this clutter creating the impression that there were more customers in the bar than there really were. The shabby double doors were open onto the alley, damp and quiet after a brief evening shower which had passed freakishly through the sunset as warning of later storms. The pavement was strewn with bits of broken glass, and a humid breeze flapped the tops of some rubbish bags which were lying on a pile of empty boxes. Litter and light seemed to wash around the building like water to the pillars of a bridge. As the sun went slowly down the noise of London began to break with less force against the doorstep of the bar. High above the city a few strands of cloud the colour of cigarette ash were trailing west towards Hammersmith. As seven-twenty-nine winked onto the digital clock above the bar, Harrier had no thoughts about Lucinda. He could not even picture her in his mind except for an unfocused collage of pavement and the cinema across the street from where they had met. Added to this was the errant image of the face of Stella Walker-Jones, their mutual old friend. Somewhere in Texas there was an observatory which discovered new stars with such frequency that the public were invited to pay a small fee to have one named after a friend or relative as an 'original gift'. Harrier could give Stella a star for Christmas, if they ever met again. 'Stella Star'; a name to describe stars without the fear of not being clear ... And then Lucinda walked in.

Lucinda; simultaneously tall, myopic, pretty, reserved, clumsy, straight-backed, emotional, unable to cook or sew, and clever. She couldn't run in her work shoes and always walked around in her stockinged feet at the office. As a young girl of fourteen she had had no time at all for the printed word, and the thing which she had liked most about herself was her friendship with Stella and James Walker-Jones.

Harrier had been very young when he first came to stay with the Walker-Jones during his school holidays. With James and Stella and Stella's younger friend Lucinda he had founded a secret society which occupied them a great deal during their earliest teens. It had been called the Black Hand Gang, and at the time the complex ritual with which they decorated their games and adventures had seemed both mysterious and exciting. Exploiting the countryside around the Walker-Jones's home, the four children became absorbed in their use of it, and even as they grew up to acknowledge more commonplace priorities there remained between them a memory of their gang which they found hard to laugh at. Now Lucinda was twenty-five, and in love (she thought) with Harrier; and Harrier was twenty-eight (and certain only of just how many pretty girls there were in London). James and Stella would be twenty-seven and twenty-six respectively.

Now that the children were adults, and now that they knew about things like property and wages, and now that good things were harder to look forward to and less pleasurable when reached, it seemed to Harrier that the vision they had shared as children could only have narrowed. Thus localised, the details of the Black Hand Gang had begun to play tricks on his mind. He wanted to find out what it was that used to interest him, and this was – partly – behind his agreement to meet Lucinda for the evening.

For until this particular summer evening Harrier had not seen Lucinda properly for some years. Stella, the ultra-feminine, model-in-the-making Stella, used to say that Lucinda looked like a boy in a skirt to her, but Harrier had always privately felt that this was untrue. Looking at Lucinda now, as she came into the bar, he thought how striking she had become. Pale, with bobbed auburn hair and grey eyes, Lucinda had retained a freshness which adolescence can frequently dull. She was tall, and moved very lightly, her smile seeming always to be three steps ahead of her. Looking at her clothes, Harrier felt sure he could recognise elements of her outfit from their childhood holidays. She was wearing a cream wool skirt which stopped just below the knee, a fuchsia-coloured silk blouse open at the neck, and an ankle-length pale grey raincoat. On her feet was a pair of battered tennis shoes. It was difficult to know from this whether or not she was, as James had suggested, psychic. Studying her looking around the bar for him, Harrier thought that Lucinda looked as though she had just run in from the garden. Lucinda had been dodging the traffic in New Oxford Street; her hair still damp and her heart racing as she rushed to test a word, or a feeling, against reality.

Nervousness creates a private world which is simultaneously open to the public. The secret hopes refuse to articulate themselves and the heart deputises an untrustworthy and secondary sense to be its ambassador. Seeing Harrier smile up at her from his position of enviable nonchalance in the Spanish bar, Lucinda became aware of how far away he was from her plans for their life together. Her one concern was for her desires to remain concealed. Unexplored, Harrier was inviting her into a dangerous country.

'You look tired,' she said, breezily, 'which is a shame because I wanted to exhaust you with my brilliant conversation.'

Before he could answer she turned away to buy herself a drink. The barman winked at her as she paid for her glass of lager. Lucinda, feeling reckless, winked back. Then she went to sit down across the table from the man she thought she loved.

'Hello Lucinda,' said Harrier, 'looking good Lucinda, looking good . . .' She offered a smile that turned into a simper. She hated herself. 'How's the aspidistra business or whatever it is that you do?' he continued, already sensing that there was something not quite natural about the way in which Lucinda was glancing around the room and lighting a cigarette too quickly. She turned to him with a smile. 'Harrier, you could at least have remembered that your youngest, and, need I add, prettiest, acquaintance, is currently in gainful employment with Roebuck StJohn Maitland, a leading publicity company in an extremely competitive field . . .' Whilst Lucinda was speaking the volume of the jukebox began to increase. She continued in a semi-shout: 'I suppose that your facetious comment about houseplants was based on a . . .' The noise was deafening by this time and obviously out of control. Behind the bar a small group of Spaniards were gesticulating with feeling towards the back of an elderly amplifier. '. . . recollection of my earlier job as a hat-check girl and flower arranger at Sotheby's . . .' The noise suddenly subsided and the word 'Sotheby's' sounded loudly in the bar. Harrier sipped his gin and nodded.

'He's bored,' thought Lucinda.

'Well, maybe I was confused,' said Harrier, 'but I don't suppose that there's really that much difference between flower arranging and publicity. Seem linked to me. Appearance counting and all that. Window dressing. Fine career.' Lucinda looked at the floor. Why did she want him so much? He was, she thought, beautiful.

She slipped off her coat and crossed her legs, pointing her toes down to tap the floor. Harrier said something else about her job, but she wasn't listening.

'It's lovely to see you again after so long,' she said, 'I've been longing to get in touch and find out what you're up to . . .'

As she spoke Lucinda wondered whether Harrier had a girlfriend. She couldn't see a wedding ring. A wedding – Harrier married; the idea was absurd. It was even more absurd, she thought, to be thinking of such things. She saw herself as a ridiculous, ugly, stupid girl, fluttering her eyelashes in his indifferent face and embarrassing him with her interest. Cruel that her mind then immediately diverted to the thought of them in bed together, in her room, or in a hotel with an empty bottle of wine standing in an ice-bucket full of water at dawn, or in some vague place with high walls that she imagined to be Harrier's room. Dark wood, streetlight through venetian blinds, his jacket on the floor, the curve of his back and the cold pillows that smelt of musk.

'Business publishing, Lucinda, is what they call it . . .' Harrier's voice ran a blade through her veil of sighs. 'Text books for the European salesforce to swot up their techniques, and guides to the U K corporate empires. Most of it's on software now to anticipate reps on-line in their cars, but we still produce expensive leatherbound directories for lunch-dulled chairmen to keep on their shelves in order to find out whether old Harry's still at Debenhams and so forth. It's rather dull.' Lucinda smiled. The only way forward was to smile and ask intelligent questions whilst she studied his profile and the way that he sipped his drink. 'I buy and sell a bit of property as well. Conversions. London and Manhattan, but most of that's family stuff – I can't afford the architects . . .' Lucinda remembered that Harrier was quiet about his wealth.

Had Lucinda been psychic – a possibility which still troubled her from time to time – it is difficult to know what kind of premonition would occur to her concerning her future with Harrier. Would she suddenly see that he had a bottle of Hawkes Bay Sauvignon (1985) waiting for nothing in particular in his fridge at home? Or would she see a glimpse of their future happiness which killed her desire to achieve it simply by hinting at predictable walks on Sundays through predictable parks in a monotonous autumn haze; a yearned-for domestic idyll translating un-

expectedly into a stifling compound of unsuited lives? She
could have seen anything. A terrible accident perhaps, with
a death on the streets or in a shop. Or would she see a
wedding in the country, with all their old friends smiling?
Maybe the supernatural would simply tease, and she would
suddenly make out a spectral beer bottle which hadn't been
there a minute ago . . . Lucinda, driven mad by an awareness
of her strange new powers, would maybe lose her reason in
her twenty-fifth year, and thus be incapable of changing a
light bulb on her own without sitting on a kitchen stool in
the dark for hours, crying. Being in love, Lucinda felt
especially vulnerable to the powers of premonition. But the
only image that did come to mind as she smiled at Harrier
and tried to gauge his feelings from minute to minute was
the image of Stella's face.

Whilst they were talking, or circling one another, or
pretending to do either of these things, Lucinda and Harrier
had not noticed the arrival in the bar of two men, one
middle-aged and his companion barely twenty. The older
man was feeling weak, and emotional, and had spent the
afternoon lying on a sofa trying to read *The Memoirs of
Hadrian* and remove a bad headache brought on by a noisy
alcoholic lunch and a quantity of cocaine the previous
night. In his book he had drifted between the sentences
where Hadrian had just been visited by his physician. Attempting to reconcile old age, Hadrian commented that
although his body was now decaying, and unable to support
desire and ambition, he felt no malice towards it. His body
had done all right in the end, and the soul that it housed, an
Emperor's soul, was rich with the experience of an active
life. Douglas Stanshaw, the aforementioned reader, could
not say the same for his own body, which was simply
decaying. His boyfriend, Chris Patterson, with whom he
had entered the Spanish bar, was beginning to prove a
difficult companion to keep, a difficulty that was surpassed
only by that of trying to lose him. Chris had arrived in

London three years ago, and having found in Douglas a source of income and rent-free accommodation was not going to be removed without a fight. Their relationship was a mess. There had been two holidays to Spain, and one to America, there was the flat in Earl's Court and the pocket money. The fact that Chris was beginning to find Douglas physically repulsive, and sex with him a near impossibility, had not so far outweighed the material advantages of remaining with him. Chris found plenty of time to see his lover, David, when Douglas was working at the recording studio, and David, although poor, was good fun. But despite all these difficulties Chris Patterson and Douglas Stanshaw did love one another, and this was at the root of their problems.

The evenings out together which were so important to Douglas as a part of a 'relationship' were a much-resented necessity to Chris. As a consequence he acted as belligerently as possible on these occasions until he had got Douglas too drunk to care and pushed him home in a cab. Safely despatched to sleep alone and fully-clothed across the bed, Douglas could then be forgotten about until lunchtime the following day. In the meantime Chris went to the clubs with David. This was usually easy enough, but tonight, for some reason, Douglas was determined to drink only tomato juice and insisted on conversation, a pastime that bored Chris.

Already bad-tempered, Chris made a special point of knocking Harrier's briefcase onto the floor as he passed by him. When Harrier, presuming this to be an accident, had said 'I'm sorry – was it in your way?' Chris seized gleefully upon his accent and began to mimic it loudly to the two barmen. Having failed to find support for his performance Chris then went smirking back towards Douglas who was sitting alone and embarrassed in the corner.

Lucinda was telling Harrier about her holiday in Turkey the previous summer. She had gone with her then-boyfriend Andy. It was a theory of Harrier's that every boyfriend in the world was called 'Andy', and he could see the Andys of the world uniting into a vast legion. With carefree indifference to their stupidity, casual clothes and training shoes, each Andy was born with a quantity of manly sump beneath his fingernails. The earring came later, just after beer and slightly before sex. It depressed Harrier to discover that Lucinda had had an Andy, and this twinge of depression – or jealousy – rather shocked him. He began to study Lucinda more closely (which she immediately noticed), and found in her features a heart-quickening amount of sex-appeal to which he had not previously been sensitive. Her legs, for instance, were long, and slender, and tanned – as were her arms – and Harrier had to battle with himself not to start thinking about her chest beneath the loose fabric of her shirt. He blamed this curiosity on the cheap gin and asked a responsible question about exchange rates. He also determined that however late they might stay out he would refuse to get into any sentimental or intimate conversations with her. He knew that he determined this last condition because it lent a sense of thrill to the hope that intimacy would occur. 'There was one brilliant place that we visited,' Lucinda was saying, 'on the side of an amazingly hot mountain. There were these three semi-circular pools of natural mineral water, like Perrier or something, and they were all one below the other down the hillside. It was absolutely deserted and we swam in one for hours . . .' Harrier felt the twinge again, this time more deeply, a baby ulcer of desire. Up until the point that Lucinda had started talking about Andy, Harrier hadn't really cared how he came across, and now that he did care, and his self-confidence was suffering, he felt angry with himself. He glanced over to where Chris and Douglas were sitting. Chris was leaning forward to spit something inaudible into Douglas's down-turned face. It looked unpleasant.

'. . . fucking bastard . . .' drifted in a whisper from Chris and Douglas's end of the bar. Lucinda giggled.

In the back of his mind Harrier could see the mountainside that Lucinda had described, with the sparkling ocean beyond it, and high up among the hot rocks and olive trees the first swimming pool of Perrier. The sun was blazing over the perfect holiday.

'In one of the pools there were ruins,' continued Lucinda. 'It was a flooded house or temple or something and you could swim down between some pillars and see where people had scratched their initials in the stone. The light was incredible under the water; green with shafts of sunlight reflecting down – it was brilliant.' Remembering the drowned bar at the foot of the slag heap, Harrier thought about a non-religious building with Lucinda and himself in it. Broken fairy lights fusing with a hiss in the water. Years ago he had stood on a footbridge over a motorway one afternoon and watched the traffic flash by beneath him; brilliant fish in the dust heading somewhere or other between massive yellow fields.

'I can't swim,' he said to Lucinda.

'Well then, you'd drown . . . I'd rescue you anyway.' Harrier saw himself disappearing beneath the surface. 'I don't care,' he imagined himself saying, 'I'd rather drown than call to Andy for help.' Lucinda in a one-piece swimsuit, diving . . .

It would have been obvious to any casual observer that Harrier and Lucinda had passed an important stage in their relationship since seven-thirty. They were both becoming eager to allow one another to shine in their autobiographical anecdotes. They were beginning to talk in agreements. This generosity was derived from their mutual knowledge that they were establishing a physical sympathy which at present could only be registered in the spoken, and, worse, the ideological. Nods were common currency, and weak jokes drew excessive laughter. It is possible that they both hated themselves for this. Lucinda was beginning to fill in the details of Harrier's room in her mind.

At the table in the other corner the ritual of an evening out was not going so well for Chris and Douglas. As Douglas talked endlessly about the decline of the music industry and how bad the pop charts had become, Chris looked at his face with increasingly ill-concealed loathing. Every time Douglas passed comment about the un-professional flashy young kids whose records he had to produce, he gave a bitter, self-conscious smile. It was this smile, not the baggy denims, the drop-framed sunglasses and the leather wristband (to match the lighter on a thong) that really annoyed Chris. It was the smile that made him hate, made him want to murder: the smile that seemed to both hold him prisoner and tell him how rotten the affair had become. The smile, in the end, became the manifestation of everything Chris detested and wanted to destroy. The fake tan so obviously smeared about Douglas's neck he could stand; the disgusting pinewood aftershave that gusted in hot draughts across the table he could at least counter with cigarette smoke . . . but the smile. Douglas, he knew, was unaware of this hatred. Whilst Douglas was talking about the new groups his voice became monotone and fixated, a style that was caused by his finding the young drummers so sexy and the girlfriends that they brought to the studio to show off with so loathsome. Douglas and Chris had long since ceased to have a 'satisfying physical relationship' as doctors and concerned friends call it. Douglas took out his frustration on the youths he mixed and produced. He felt like a eunuch in a harem. He knew how they talked about his cowboy boots. He knew how quickly the word got around that the producer was an old tart. It hurt him. Desire, on the other hand, would not become subordinate to his behaviour.

Chris looked at Douglas and saw a dry, perfumed wash-leather. It seemed to him that the furrows on Douglas's forehead were filled with black grease. He was exhausted with feeling hatred for Douglas whilst still needing him –

and his money. Douglas had vaseline on his eyelashes and his mouth sagged at the corners. He had a metal briefcase. Douglas was the older beaten man, and it was hard to believe that old age would bring him a soul enriched with experience. It seemed that all old age would bring Douglas was pain and ugliness as the total reward for a lifetime spent looking for love.

Fifteen years ago, Douglas and two of his friends (one now dead, the other running a chain of high-street boutiques) had driven across North Africa in a Land-Rover, getting drunk and lying in the sun. They had tried the male brothels but been far more cautious in their experimenting than they later pretended to one another over back-slapping, rib-poking 'do-you-remember-when' conversations in the Chelsea Drugstore. In 1973 Douglas had believed for a few months that he had found the eternal carnival beside the sea, the good time; and the more that he realised he hadn't the more he convinced himself that he had. He acted now as though he was simply choosing not to stay at the party, and that even as he plodded through middle age there were thirty or so young and beautiful people on the beach who were calling him back to join them. 'C'mon Douglas – it won't be any fun without you!' With a paternal smile he had left them, and they, disappointed, would always miss him. There were of course no young people, and there was not now nor had there ever been a party at which his presence was really required. Thus he believed in the wild old days.

The bickering had been constant now for nearly two hours. Douglas had had enough. He wanted a break from the strain of it.

'Well young man . . . I suppose that I had better be on my way . . .' Harrier could not help overhearing the tired and false manner in which this had been said. Chris, on the other hand, was beginning to panic. If Douglas broke off their relationship completely he would be faced with an income problem that could easily end up back in Plymouth on the dole. Therefore, 'You leave and I'll burn the fucking flat down,' had come his spirited response.

'And anyway, I thought we were going to Stringfellows?' Despite the underlying menace in his voice, Chris came across as peevish and shrill. Douglas sighed uneasily. 'No – not tonight. And I think that what with one thing and another I've put quite enough money into Mr Branson's pocket . . .'

'What's Mr Branson' (the name was sneered) 'got to do with it?'

'He owns Stringfellows – Richard Branson owns String-fellows . . .'

'Crap.'

The older man shrugged, playing with a large bunch of keys on a swatch of creased leather that was studded with gold. Chris began to seethe. Feeling trapped by his dependence on his lover he began to despise him. He decided to divert some of his anger towards Harrier and Lucinda, who looked rich enough and self-satisfied enough to deserve it.

'What the fuck are you staring at ponce?' he said to Harrier, jutting his chin out with each syllable. Harrier, who had been staring at Lucinda's neck, did not at first respond. Chris threw an ice cube over at their table. Harrier looked at it and then spun round, 'What do you think you're . . .'

'You – fuckface. I thought you were taking that dog for a walk so what are you staring at . . .?' And then Chris, Douglas, Harrier and Lucinda all reacted differently to the situation. Lucinda tried to gaze with pitying contempt at Chris, Harrier half stood up, Chris shrank slightly at seeing how tall Harrier was and Douglas, having first rubbed his forehead wearily, put his hand on Chris's arm and turned with a weak smile to Harrier.

'I'm sorry about this. He's not himself tonight. Drink or something. Ignore him. We're leaving.'

Harrier frowned. 'Well can't you keep him under control?'

Chris tried to look like something impossible to keep under control. He could have been an A W O L soldier in his thin grey suit and open-necked shirt. Short, and heavily built, with cropped black hair, it was only the prettiness of his eyes which interrupted the coarseness of his looks. He wore a thick gold chain of linked squares around his hairy wrist which pinched him, and his big feet were poorly shod in paper-thin grey shoes and white nylon socks that scarcely reached his ankles. Douglas, in a satin tour-jacket and expensive jeans that didn't fit him properly, looked like an old and effeminate cowboy. His clinging scent seemed to conjure up the interior of a sports car somewhere and a neurotically tidy flat in West Kensington. Chris was standing uncomfortably between Douglas and Harrier. He looked very young. Harrier and Lucinda, turning once more to face one another and shut out the arguing couple behind them, were aware that their evening, which had been going so well for both of them, had been clipped by the wing of sordid and amateur violence. It was galling to be touched by the unpleasantness of other people's messes. They would have to struggle to recapture their earlier mood of partial intimacy. Chris and Douglas went out. The bar was more or less empty again and the light seemed even dimmer, making distance hard to judge. The alcoves were dark; somewhere in the distance a telephone rang.

Outside in the alley Chris and Douglas were staring at one another. 'What are you behaving like this for? I don't want a half-hour hysterical conversation with you again — I'm too tired . . .'

'Richard Branson might own a lot of fucking things but he doesn't fucking own Stringfellows . . .' Chris felt that the Stringfellows debate was the match point in a bout of significant argument and he was determined that it would not be his blood that dripped off the ropes. Stringfellows was linking with the smile as totem of what he was hating in Douglas. His face sucked into a pinched mask and his eyes shone.

'Come on then,' said Douglas, 'we'll go and get some dinner . . .'

To Chris, who wanted a fight with Douglas, the offer of dinner could be taken as victory. He lit a cigarette and inhaled sharply, looking down his nose at Douglas. They started walking towards Douglas's car.

Back in the bar Harrier and Lucinda had decided to go over to Kettner's. They were discussing the dangers of drink in a mature and analytical manner, constantly using Chris and Douglas as representatives of victims of the curse.

Fifty metres down the alley tempers were beginning to flare. Having agreed to walk over to Soho for an Italian meal, Douglas then decided that he wanted Japanese food and they should therefore walk up to Goodge Street where he knew of a cheap sushi bar. Chris, hungry, could not stomach Japanese food. A meal would never be enough to save the evening. Douglas had been living on bowls of anaemic pasta and anti-acid pills for weeks. He frequently felt feverish and dizzy, and his morning headaches now took most of the day to clear. The studio that he worked in on Wardour Street seemed to exist at the end of a metal corridor, the sight and sound of which, particularly during the chaos of mid-morning, dug sharply into his wet eyes and split a crude passage of noise behind his forehead. Standing in the alley he found it impossible to look into the demanding eyes that watched him. Chris threw his cigarette away and ran his tongue around his teeth.

'You sure it's not too late for you?' he sneered.

Douglas could feel a pain between his ribs on the right-hand side, and knew that this was a prelude to the quickening of his breath. He wished there was a cool breeze so that he could feel himself inhale. He looked at the streetlight at the end of the alley, the red and green signs in the shop windows on Oxford Street. If they could just get through the meal, and then Chris could be paid off to go down to Leicester Square and one of the clubs. The remains of Douglas's libido was so jealous of the young and good-looking friends Chris saw. They wore black jeans and white T-shirts, and some of them looked like models.

'You look all worn out,' continued Chris, 'I think I'll have to go out on my own and catch as catch can . . . I feel lucky tonight anyway . . .' And here he sniffed the air proprietorially. As he stepped back, Douglas felt a sudden wave of desire. 'Come back to the flat with me . . . we'll watch a video or something . . .'

Chris laughed scornfully. 'That really would be fun wouldn't it – fuck that . . .' There was a deep pit of pain in Douglas's stomach. He lost his temper, turning on one foot with his hands in the air and looking ridiculous.

'I've had enough of this, and of you. You can go straight to hell you lousy little tart because I'm sick of funding you and your flashy little git-faced tart friends.'

Chris had not been expecting anger. Confused, he began to babble. 'I wish you were dead you cunt – fuck you!' And having wrecked his chances of using Douglas for further immediate gain he decided to go the whole way, luxuriating in extravagant anger.

'I met a bloke the other night – and he's a friend of mine – who knows how to get someone killed just-like-that' (a snap of the fingers) 'for just three hundred quid . . .' Opening the car door Douglas shook his head pityingly as he fiddled with the lock. Then he looked at Chris and took out his wallet.

'Here's five hundred – now piss off.'

'You're grotesque – you'd better just look out. Three hundred quid . . .'

'Piss off you shitty little rent – go and hire your assassin or something. Prat.' And then he slammed the car door and reversed noisily back down the alley, his bumper clipping a stack of boxes.

At this point Harrier and Lucinda walked by. Chris didn't seem to notice them, but stood against the wall looking at the wad of notes Douglas had thrown at him. All of his life he felt that people had been laughing at him, and all of his life he'd wanted respect. Violence was the way to earn it; and he thought about Mafia films, and terrace killings. He wouldn't drink or waste the cash – he'd use it on Douglas.

Lucinda gripped Harrier's arm as they walked down the alley. 'What a horrible boy,' she said.

★

With nightfall, London reabsorbed the four dots of the two couples who had met in the Spanish bar down the little alley. Harrier and Lucinda made their way to Kettner's, displaying an unnatural degree of politeness towards one another. Douglas sat in his car waiting for the lights to change and thought about Chris. Seeing a poster of a girl in blue jeans hugging a giant lipstick he began to think of going away for a while, to America perhaps, but this brought back sad memories.

Chris rolled down the Charing Cross Road with his hands in his pockets. The railinged windows of bookshops, brilliantly lit hallways of a chemist, and the crimson interiors of restaurants seemed to pass by him on the far side of a moat of darkness. The traffic was heavy, and on the corner of Leicester Square, outside the Hippodrome, crowds of young people were pushing their way into the club's black mouth. In one glance Chris saw the Star Bar, green dresses with under-arm sweat stains, thin ties, gelled hair that had set too hard and too dry, streaked fringes brittle with peroxide and perms, creased suits worn straight from the office, lipstick on teeth and the absorbed flicking of eyes in search of late friends. Shouts and shrieked laughter filled the air. Chris never went to the Hippodrome.

Looking into the crowd he saw a girl and boy french-kissing greedily. As the boy's tongue sought the deeper recesses of his girlfriend's throat, his eyes were closed and his free hand that was not around her waist held a can of lager. Once disengaged the boy looked away and took a deep drink. The girl nestled her head into his shoulder and the boy, continuing to drink, stared at nothing across the street. The girl had red, bare legs. On an evening-paper newsstand beside them the headline poster blared 'Return to the School of Horror'. Rubbing his girlfriend's back for a moment the boy returned to dive for pearls in her mouth. In the next doorway down, beside a row of spitted scarlet ducks which were rotating behind a Chinese chef, a solitary girl, short, fat, with a new perm of over-tight curls and a pair of blue-framed glasses was touching a cold sore on the corner of her mouth with the tip of her tongue. She was hugging a bulging handbag to her stomach and looking around nervously. Across the street a mock fight was breaking out against the window of a bookshop.

'Go screw an A-rab!' the chief participant was chanting, 'Go screw an A-rab . . .' Behind the window some copies of a new book were displayed against a poster announcing its title: *The History of Psychoanalysis* (in 2 volumes). The small photograph of the psychoanalyst who had edited the book had mysteriously fallen over backwards on its little stand, thus directing a serene smile of knowledge into the lighting fixtures on the ceiling.

On the edge of Great Newport Street wine-bar conversation was in progress:

'This is John – John's in advertising.'

'Oh! A high-flyer!'

and

'I used to be religious until I met Tony, then I changed . . .'

and

'No mate, no – these are mine . . .'

Such was the city through which Chris was pitching.

Lucinda and Harrier were picking their way along the strip of pavement which binds the railings of Soho Square. They had rediscovered their interest in one another. Lucinda was beginning to feel breathlessly happy, her hopes rising. They passed a Suzuki jeep, which had bows of pale yellow satin tied in extravagant formations about its bumper, bonnet and roller bars. Lucinda jokingly tore one from its fitting and tried to rest it on Harrier's head – the birth of a new intimacy.

As they walked, Lucinda talked about the people she worked with and why she didn't think she'd stay in her present job for very long. 'I don't think that publicity is really a job,' she said. 'It's basically just making lots of phonecalls and trying to get the media interested in our clients. I know that sounds glamorous, talking to journalists and so on, but . . .' It didn't sound very glamorous to Harrier, but he didn't say this.

'I think that most jobs are the same,' he volunteered, simultaneously aware that this was not a generalisation to make in the company of a ticket collector and an astronaut. He wondered what Stella did for a living but didn't ask. Lucinda was already way ahead of him.

'Before I started working,' she said, running to catch up with him and slipping a significant arm through his, 'I wasn't in the least particular about where I slept. I could sleep in cars, on floors, on public transport – anything. Now I have to be in a bed; I just get tired and need to be . . .' A taxi blared its horn at them and they jumped back onto the curb.

'He didn't indicate,' said Harrier, and they headed off down Frith Street, an unspoken chain of thought to do with beds swinging cheekily between them.

Lucinda thought that the metallic clicking which Harrier's shoes made on the pavement was terribly sexy. As they handed their coats to the hat-check girl at Kettner's she found herself thinking about short cuts to happiness.

Kettner's had the air of a house party as Harrier and Lucinda began to chew their way through pizzas and the street outside began to smell of burnt sugar. An ice-cream van had caught fire in Cambridge Circus it later transpired. Lucinda, with feigned nonchalance, mentioned that the following month brought with it her birthday, and there was to be a party to celebrate the occasion. The party would be shared with that for the opening of her friend Kuzumi's new shop, and as the publicity for that was being done by Roebuck StJohn Maitland, and should Harrier be free . . . Harrier began to regard Lucinda with increasing pleasure, and leaning back in his chair explained that he would be delighted to come to Lucinda's party. Lucinda, thrilled to bits, squeezed Harrier's hand.

'I'm so glad,' she said.

Two streets away Chris was sitting in a pub re-running his scene with Douglas. Having taken a pill in the toilet his mind was now racing through scenarios of revenge. He would also, later, have to find somewhere to sleep, but first he must see Ray about what he had begun to call 'the contract'.

He glanced at an old man sitting next to him. 'If you do that again I'll fucking kill you,' he snarled.

The old man stopped rattling his newspaper.

THREE

Fanlight Gassy

It is now necessary to return to the career of Kelly O'Kelly, a girl who had decided to be sufficient unto herself, but who, despite all impressions to the contrary, was still to play a major role in the life of Miles Harrier.

Including the remarkable debut of her Foundation year, Kelly O'Kelly spent four years at the art college in Brighton. Walking along the broad promenade in summer she would follow the parade of tall, sea-facing buildings to their abrupt finish in the heat haze which obscured the suburbia of Hove. She saw the town as marshmallow-coloured, hiding, on sunny days, mysterious chasms and squares of deep shadow, particularly around the tiring incline of streets which led to the railway station.

On arrival Kelly had immediately preferred these quieter reaches of the town to their more impressive counterparts beside the pier and the Royal Pavilion. She grew possessive of the stillness of her favourite streets, and as one by one their bubbles were burst with the opening of a new shop or wine bar she felt her freedom to wander foreshortened.

Unhappily for Kelly it was to these same shops and wine bars that most of her contemporaries turned for both casual employment and a social focus. The hierarchical zoning of friendships and affairs which Kelly had grown wary of in Twyford was swiftly ventriloquised within her new situation. Having more time for places than for people, Kelly felt herself betrayed on all sides, and few evenings passed when she did not see the pavement beneath her or the grey-veined enamelling of the washbasin opposite her as an arrangement of memories, bitterness and speculation, with Miles Harrier at their centre.

The worst of these reveries were those which turned her repressed desires against her. As if at the mercy of a Karate master or a black magician, Kelly found that she was un-balanced most by this reflecting back onto herself of her own powers. Her capacity for love (and this was extensive) converted into hate, her ability to look forward to things turned into a superior talent for regret, and the not-in-considerable strength of her delicate lusts found new muscles to tone when indulged in the ultimately self-degrading release of a solitary orgy.

This deepened internalising of Kelly O'Kelly's emotions coincided with a widespread flourishing of flamboyancy and energy amongst many of the art students towards the end of the 1970s. Hair was worn short, and brightly coloured, trouser legs narrowed, and rips, zips, pins and chains took over from the ephemera of child-cult and mystical emblems which had provided the basis for student orna-ment during the previous decade. Throughout this public flowering of fashionable anger Kelly O'Kelly remained staunchly suspicious of any attitude which subscribed to a corporate identity. It was only when alone in her room at night, and she heard the second-year textiles student beneath her playing the unintelligible folk dirges to which she relent-lessly embroidered, that Kelly O'Kelly found herself scream-ing for the noisy and the irreverent.

★

Tertiary education formally accepted Kelly O'Kelly into the four-year Expressive Arts course on an exhilarating morning towards the end of September, just five days after she had received the fatal letter from Harrier. Despite the brilliant sunshine a strong wind was blowing off the sea, and as Kelly made her way back to her hall of residence at the end of the first morning, she was struck by the sweeping cloud formations which stretched high above the waves.

Her group had had an informal talk from their course tutor, Mike Reeves. One or two of the more socially advanced students had already begun to call him 'Mike' in the coffee interval, as opposed to 'sir' or 'Dr Reeves'. Calling Mike Reeves 'sir' or 'Dr Reeves' had drawn a mixture of concern and amusement from the bearer of that title. 'Now remember what we've been saying,' he had said, as the initial ripple of nervous laughter had died down from his shocked response to such titular formality. 'I want you to forget all about your schools . . .' (and here he paused impressively, his hands on his hips). 'We are here to do two things. Firstly, to try and understand why we have all decided to become 'artists', and secondly, to try and discover what is the best possible way that we can all, individually, express that decision in relation to ourselves . . .' A respectful silence followed this announcement.

The meeting had taken place in the performance studio. This room was like a small hangar at the end of a damp concrete path away from the main faculty buildings. Its skylights were still blacked over with wooden shutters from the end of the previous year's degree shows. On the dark green floor there were chalked crosses and a scattering of white paint traces. Mike Reeves was illuminated by a single spotlight which he had arranged in hushed whispers with a bored and contemptuous-looking technical assistant. The new students were not yet considered knowledgeable enough to be introduced to the technical assistant.

Whilst the twenty or so newcomers were being addressed, two people put their heads around the studio door and then shut it again quickly saying 'Sorry' as they left. Their sudden interruption had afforded Kelly a glimpse of wet grass and an overhanging branch of yellowing leaves. A brief gust of damp, autumn-scented air remained in the darkness for a few seconds. Kelly wondered whether they were allowed to smoke. She put up her hand.

'Kelly?' (The tutor looked pleased.)

'May we smoke?'

'Wait until the interval please.'

And then he turned away from her as if to strengthen his theme despite the distraction of an obvious *faux pas*.

Much was said about 'marks on paper', and 'making the correct mark'. Examples were given from the history of art of cases of famous artists whose greatest works had begun during their years of tuition. Valerie Arnus, the complementary studies tutor, would be running them all through that during her compulsory lecture course. And then the contemporary was referred to, its demands and its industry; and so the seekers after knowledge were told to look upon packaging, and design, with new respect.

During the coffee interval Kelly studied those with whom she would be joining down the difficult but rewarding path to self-expression. So far she had only heard various voices coming out of the darkness behind her, curiously disembodied. Sometimes these voices had been answered by name. 'Audrey', 'Chico' and 'Melanie' had stood out most from the group of seventeen- to nineteen-year-olds who were ranged upon or around the two rows of battered stack chairs which had been put out for their comfort. There were obviously some members of the group who were extremely self-confident. These were the ones who had made a slightly sulky entrance (inferring rebellion), and had then proceeded to sit on the floor, or lie at full length, despite the free availability of chairs. With cool self-possession this little kernel of floor-dwellers had gazed with boredom at their stiffer, more nervous colleagues. Not for them the plastic briefcase or the shapeless woven basket. Not for them the poised biro and the brand new pad for notes which simply would not lie flat on the knee. Seeing only rabbits or wolves Kelly felt a sinking feeling in her heart.

At the coffee interval it was Audrey who led the conversation. Audrey was the first to call Mike Reeves 'Mike'. Audrey was not afraid to ask where one should fill the kettle. Audrey, a tall, powerful, red-haired girl from Preston, had shown neither timidity nor embarrassment when told by the surly technician (in the tones of one with better things to do) that she would have to fill the two plastic orange-squash jerricans with water from the outside tap and then bring them back to fill the kettle. Kelly O'Kelly would have died rather than be the one upon whom the rest of the group were relying to expedite the mid-morning break. These responsibilities held no terror for Audrey. Arranging her blue-and-white head scarf around the tumbling explosion of her Pre-Raphaelite hair, Audrey had only to nod in a vacant manner which drew attention to her diamond nose-stud and everyone knew that they were in safe hands. Kelly detested her.

She lit a cigarette and tried to calculate whether there would be enough plastic cups to go round. To one side of her, in a close, self-congratulating and self-policing knot, three boys and a girl whom they had decided would 'do' were already laughing, exchanging pieces of useful local information, and giving one another Marlboro cigarettes. 'Chico', an olive-skinned boy with dark, bright eyes and a Mexican belt, was from North London and 'had a band'. He appeared to be the centre of attention. His band were probably going to do some 'gigs' once everything had settled down and the rest of the little group agreed that this would be really great. Beside him was his acolyte, Adrian, from Cardiff. Adrian's brother was in a band, and although Chico had not seen them play he was sure that he knew the name. Lee-Hoi, from Tokyo, completed the male membership of this inner-contingent, and he was extremely interested in David Bowie.

The girl upon whose liquid blue eyes the three boys were all apt to linger was Melanie. Melanie was a short, voluptuous girl of eighteen. She had been a day-girl at a leading public school, but professed herself completely disillusioned with what she had seen there as a repressive and élitist regime. Her Headmistress had definitely been both anti-blacks and anti-gays, and many of Melanie's lesbian friends could testify that there had been little short of a witch hunt at St Mildred's. Melanie herself was not gay although of course many of her best friends were, and it was presently in the understanding and liberal arms of her boyfriend-at-home (Graham) that she now lay to pour out her discontent-ment with the minorities situation and her love. Melanie wore coloured tights and a blue silk dress from a jumble sale which she had shortened. Her pale complexion wafted tantalising breezes of scent from the delicate arch of her neck and shadow of her collar-bone. Her wide, soft mouth was coloured in with a faintly oil-based lipstick (which she applied every morning with a brush), and her straight blonde hair was just growing out from the not-excessive tyranny of the softest of perms. Melanie's special interest was Drama, and she hoped to combine her adoration of Brecht with her even greater veneration for Egon Schiele. Chico was enthusiastic about Schiele also.

Kelly turned away from the depressing joviality of this colourful quartet. She felt conspicuous, loitering, ignored, to one side of them. The trouble, she felt, was that there was not one part of the room in which she would not feel conspicuous. She longed, not for the first time, for in-visibility. When Audrey returned with the two jerricans of water, the whole group of new students moved into a wide semi-circle around the elderly hostess trolley beneath the fuse-boxes on the wall. A bird clattered over one of the skylights, its tiny feet making a scratching noise on the glass. Kelly could see a line of brilliant sunshine along the dark edge of one of the shutters.

The coffee interval lasted for half an hour, and then a little longer, because Mike Reeves thought that they were all doing such a good job of getting to know one another. He moved from person to person, and finally came over to Kelly.

'Kelly,' he said, smiling.

'Hello . . .'

'How are you getting on? This is just an informal group really, just to get everyone together. Have you sorted out your room and registered and everything?'

'Yes. I think so,' Kelly giggled nervously, hating herself.

'I must say that we were all most impressed by your interview portfolio. Some of the portraits were marvellous. Have you been sketching over the holidays?'

Kelly thought about the drawings she had done of Miles Harrier. 'A little,' she said.

'Well you must show me when we all meet tomorrow morning. I want to find out first of all just exactly where everyone is up to, and then . . .' (here he gave a pleasant laugh) '. . . we can take it from there. All right?'

Kelly supposed that it was, but she still felt as though she was being sold something. Rummaging in her bag for her cigarettes she managed to drop everything, and stooping down with flaming cheeks she clumsily retrieved from the floor her photocopied enrolment papers, a little bottle of perfume, half a packet of mentholated sweets and a brand new box of tampons.

★

Life − for some − is first presented as a cornucopia of wonders, and does little over the years to tarnish its initial reputation as a beautiful and benign experience in which we have only to pleasurably explore in order to find yet further cause for gratitude. It is possible that for Audrey, and Chico, and Melanie (and her boyfriend) it was this gorgeous process that the college years were no less a gorgeous aspect of. On the other hand however there were those (and they were many) for whom art college remained synonymous with misery and mental disturbance for the rest of their lives.

Kelly's course and Kelly's hall of residence (Knighton Hall) contained representatives of both these points of view. Within a week or so it became clear that the 'Audrey set' were so boundlessly superior at adjusting themselves to the demands of their situation that the rest of the group were almost grateful to them for supplying such an effective cover to their less-assured efforts.

At Knighton Hall, where personality disorders were asked to coexist with sensible bathing arrangements, it was a different matter. Kelly was fond – architecturally at least – of her new home.

Knighton Hall was a greybrick Edwardian building set at the end of a gravelled drive and overhung on its left-hand side by a spectacular cedar tree. Long french windows opened from the large 'television' room on the ground floor onto a broad lawn. Directly above these ran two further lines of eight sash windows; each window signifying a pleasantly appointed and sized study-bedroom. Knighton Hall had been purpose-built for the old college as a ladies hall of residence, and the thirty or so girls whom it housed were considered particularly lucky to begin their new studies in surroundings which were as convenient as they were reasonably priced. The far side of the house was devoted to a small laundry, and the kitchens, these connecting through a baize screened door to the self-contained flat of the hall warden, Mrs Hemsworth.

From the spacious entrance hall, with its cheerful vases of dried sea thistles and framed map of the Sussex coastline, one turned either left or right into the dining hall or television room respectively. It was only upstairs, within the rooms of the girls themselves, that the air of archaic domesticity was replaced by the headier and more colourful tints of youth. On the first- and second-floor landings, in exactly the same position at the top of the stairs, there was a long window with a crimson cushioned window-seat. Beside each of the window-seats there stood a rosewood side-table, and upon each side-table there was a blue-and-white china bowl containing home-made pot-pourri. Each floor could also boast fire extinguishers (three), and bathrooms (four).

Kelly's room was at the far end of the second-floor corridor and had a view of the garden with the sea beyond. It was longer than it was wide and differed from its neighbours by having a curious feature arch along its outer wall created by the access to the fire escape. It was also Kelly's privilege to be able to get out onto the fire escape and admire the view. Had Kelly been the kind of girl who invited small parties of girls into her room she would certainly have featured the fire escape within the entertainments she had to offer as a hostess.

On the first day Kelly had approached her room just as the sun was setting. The window at the far end of the corridor had been filled with a bronze, mellow light, and as she walked unsteadily towards it with her two heavy suitcases Kelly had noticed an effect like a hovering layer of dust upon the bough of the cedar which was parallel to the sill. For a moment her throat had tightened as she thought of autumn in Twyford and her old school. Wanting to cry, but too weighed down to do so successfully, she had also thought of Harrier, and was filled with love and hate. Resting her suitcases outside the door, halfway between two lives, Kelly remembered the way she had sat beside him in the long, grassy meadow near the Walker-Jones's, and how happy she had been as she watched a distant white steeple catch the last of the light as it pushed defiantly into the purple of a stormy sky.

The door swung open and Kelly peered in. The room would do. Kelly was growing to want her surroundings to be largely a matter of function; the wardrobe would be adequate to house her meagre collection of clothes, and the white wooden dressing table would benefit enormously from the removal of its mirror to a less confrontational position. The bed was narrow, with an overstuffed mattress. A duvet was specified in the notes which Kelly had received from Mrs Hemsworth, and this explained the undersheet and single pillow which were resting beside the headboard. Kelly wondered how many young men had been entertained on this hard cot.

Having shut the door and locked it Kelly then sat down on the cane-seated chair. She smoked a cigarette and wondered where the lavatory was. Eventually she began to unpack, surprising herself at how quickly this was done. Other girls (and she knew that they were there because she could hear their footsteps and laughter and radio-cassette recorders) would be locating the payphone and borrowing blu-tak off one another. Kelly had neither posters nor ornaments. Her transistor radio required new batteries.

Nobody called her and nothing happened, indeed it seemed conceivable that she could avoid all detection indefinitely. A little after eight o'clock she realised that supper had been served an hour ago. She wasn't hungry. The following day she had to report to the Faculty Office with the rest of the group. She would smoke for a while and then go to bed.

It was at about this time that Kelly realised she could get out onto the fire escape. Gingerly climbing between the railings she slid herself upright and peered out over the dark garden. Some traffic was moving along the sea road in the distance, and strings of pale bulbs swung in gentle lines between the ornate blue and white lamp-posts on the promenade. All was quiet, and still. Kelly tried to reconcile the everyday life which was going on a mile away in the town centre with the curious institutional atmosphere of the hall. Doubtless it would soon pass, the strangeness of it, and the two states would become one.

The moon was rising, three-quarters full. Kelly had never seen moonlight on the sea before and was entranced by the effect. A curious grey half-light like fine etching seemed to hang between the sky and the water; and then the deep inkiness of the waves and their invisible splash on the beach. She could see the clouds moving by, quite fast.

Her cigarette went out and she turned to go back inside. On the horizon she could see the lights of an oil tanker, inching imperceptibly towards Holland.

*

A month after the beginning of term Kelly O'Kelly was upset by a succession of tearful outbursts which seemed to suddenly have taken hold of her. After the second of these Mike Reeves escorted her to his little office to try and find out what the trouble was. The tutor, with twelve years' experience of art education behind him, did his best to locate the violence of Kelly's emotion into one of the known areas of student trauma. 'Boyfriend', 'wrong course', and 'home-sickness' failed as suggestions to bring a reassuring little nod from Kelly's bowed head. She sat awkwardly in the armchair facing Mike's desk, looking at her knees and fiddling with a pink tissue between her fingers. Added to her misery was the embarrassment of attracting attention. The telephone rang twice, and the faculty secretary came in for long enough to see that a 'surgery' was taking place. Kelly felt awful.

All that she could sense about her situation was that the minor difficulties of her routine were beginning to turn into horrors. The identities of these horrors were manifold, and a random selection would include a fear of communal dining, Audrey, and an appalling sense of dread which accompanied the approach of each weekend. By mid-afternoon on Fridays, Kelly's hands were a yellowing white colour due to nervousness.

'I think that you should come and have dinner at my house tomorrow evening,' said Mike. 'Try and talk about it with my wife; maybe she can help . . .' This well-meaning suggestion was based on the tutor's suspicion that Kelly's problem might be sexual.

Kelly nodded, and said 'Thank you'. 'How can I possibly tell him,' she thought, 'that that's the last thing I want to do. Why can't they leave me alone?' For the truth of the matter was that Kelly now felt that she had no emotions left – she had given her feelings, with all her determination, to Harrier. He had now rejected them and there was nothing left to say, just loneliness. No further debate was necessary.

As a result of Kelly's dinner with Dr and Mrs Reeves, in their comfortable, untidy family home (the evening marred by the fact that Ruth had made vegetable moussaka and Kelly hated aubergines), it was generally decided that what Kelly needed was a weekend job in Brighton to take her mind off things.

Kelly always got these things wrong.

*

Halfway up a fashionable precinct in the centre of Brighton, just a few hundred metres from the main shopping centre but happily annexed to the older, more elegant portion of the town, stood Hudson's.

Hudson's had been opened in June 1973 by a successful young entrepreneur whose fortune had been made by fulfilling the desire (hitherto dormant) of the population of Chelsea to eat crêpes.

The provision of affordable continental snacks at the shabbier end of the King's Road had swiftly offered the means to create a small chain of 'bistro'-style restaurants. The young entrepreneur made sure that all his new branches were opened in areas of London where residential gentility sat side-by-side with youth-oriented retail outlets which would attract a sympathetic class of customers. Sensing money in the air he saw no reason why his fashionably served and nourishing crêpes should not find favour with the new chic. Very soon Notting Hill, St John's Wood, Islington, Hampstead, Kensington High Street, and (surprisingly) Battersea, were all happy to boast a Hudson's crêperie.

Having cornered the London market with an effortless barrage of buck-wheat, framed theatre posters and short-stemmed freesias in white china *saké* vases, the pancake mogul turned his attention to the quainter provincial centres: Oxford, Cambridge, Bath and Brighton.

The Brighton branch of Hudson's was housed in a cavernous former laundry. Where previously starch and bleach and steam and blue had combined to make the premises seem remote and depressing, there was now a sophisticated cheerfulness of decor and clientele alike. Taking advantage of the variations in floor level, the Hudson's interior designer had created a succession of little platforms and alcoves, thus catering for both the romantic and the flamboyant. The semi-boarded shopfront had been removed to install two huge single panes of glass on either side of the recessed entrance, and the popularity of the two street-facing tables was such that on Saturday nights a doorman was required to regulate the queue of those who demanded them. One couldn't book at Hudson's.

Whitewash, large mahogany-framed mirrors and hanging baskets made cheap, short and effective work of decorating the walls and ceiling. A massive bar provided the centrepiece. Upon its shelves stood row upon row of coloured bottles, and, as if eager to please the lightning-fast demands of the two handsome barmen, their contents were flashed into a variety of drinks ranging from straight house wines to many-hued cocktails of baroque complexity.

The menu, too, was extensive. Tuna fish steaks and fried calamari added a maritime note to the otherwise batter-based tradition of Hudson's. Brown bread ice-cream and pecan pie provided original desserts which were suggestive of glamour. It was all a great success.

It was the policy of Hudson's to employ young, fashionable, and good-looking staff. It was said that being a weekend barman at Hudson's could be considered rather more useful to a student than gaining a first. Audrey, Chico and Melanie were all old hands at Hudson's within a month. Kelly despised the pretence at long-suffering with which these three masked their pleasure at being able to say 'Are you working tonight?' when they left the studio at five.

The benefits of working for Hudson's were immense. The pay was adequate, the tips generous, and the exposure as a local personality considerable. Local boutiques and nightclubs looked first to Hudson's when recruiting their models and dancers. And when it was quiet the staff could all sit around their own table, like a curious brand of nobility, smoking cigarettes and reading magazines.

Kelly O'Kelly, having first walked passed Hudson's twice, got a job five streets away as a Saturday girl in the TrueFit shoe shop.

★

A change of situation does not always guarantee one immunity from the defects of circumstances and personality which may have caused one to seek a change in the first place. Kelly O'Kelly's new era as a TrueFit Saturday girl brought with it little more than a chocolate-brown 'skirt and top' uniform and a small aluminium badge with her name mis-spelt upon it: 'Kally'.

Sometimes, when the shop was quiet, and Richard Taylor (the manager) had gone out 'for a breath of fresh air', Kelly would be left to tidy the stock-room and match up odd pairs of shoes which had fallen from the shelves.

She enjoyed these brief periods of solitude. There were

few customers, either elderly local residents or tired young parents with small children. TrueFit excelled at catering for both these markets so there was very little actual selling to do.

Once alone in the shop Kelly would tidy the shelves and then straighten the display card which stood behind the socks, tights and stockings counter. 'There's nothing pathetic about doing this' she would think to herself, happily. The card displayed a sleek pair of sheer black stockinged legs against a background of candlelit marble. Although the image finished around the upper thighs the graphic artist had cleverly managed to exploit the sheerness of the stockings and the obscurity of the background to some partially erotic effect. Standing before the picture in her chocolate-brown uniform, Kelly tried to make out whether the model was wearing a very short black skirt above her suspenders or nothing at all. The thighs were pressed close together at the top and then the legs were crossed beneath the knee and the toes pointed downwards. Kelly had watched bored men studying the image whilst their wives or girlfriends pushed and wriggled their way with less sensual motion into a new pair of TrueFit 'DayTrek' or 'Night Time' shoes. There was usually a struggle with size to be overcome prior to the first tentative 'walk up and down'; some pinching about the toes, some tightness . . .

Kelly's course work was beginning to disturb some of the tutors. After a week or so she had more or less given up working on preparatory sketching and applied all her time and energy into making body prints. Valerie Arnus blamed it all on the (wrong) assumption that Kelly had been watching old films of Yves Klein pulling blue painted models across canvases stretched on the floor. Kelly did not know who Yves Klein was.

As many of the group were favouring the more Gothic occupation of photographing one another wearing white make-up and startled expressions in the local cemetery, Kelly found that she frequently had the then-quiet painting studio to herself.

Mixing large tins of scarlet and dandelion yellow powder paint, she would carefully roll up her sleeve and then coat her arm with the dripping, vivid colour. Having first prepared on the work surface a taut sheet of absorbent paper, she would then press down onto its virgin surface to make a heavy imprint. The physical sensation of the roughness of the paper being soothed by the liquid cool of the paint on her arms was one which Kelly found deeply satisfying. The resultant images were also most striking, but Kelly found herself restricted by the limits imposed upon her experiments by the open-access of the studio.

Mike Reeves, whilst encouraging her with these prints, also took her to one side to have a little talk about them. It happened on a Tuesday evening, in November.

'I like the purple ones,' he said, by way of starting a conversation, 'but I wonder whether you can take this kind of work any further?'

'Oh, I'm going to . . .'

Mike Reeves paused, holding up a sheet of fluorescent-green handprints. 'I can see the idea you're after Kelly but . . .'

Kelly looked at him, waiting for official disapproval.

'. . . I don't think you're taking it far enough . . .'

Kelly blinked.

'. . . and I don't think that you should take it any further until you've learned more about drawing the body; and you won't learn more about drawing the body until you've done more life drawing . . .'

Kelly nodded and began to shuffle her dried body prints into a rough heap.

'No, now don't get me wrong, don't take it the wrong way. I'm simply saying, "go easy" – don't let this sort of work become its own enemy – that's all . . .'

Kelly nodded sweetly as an exciting plan occurred to her.

'When are the end-of-term shows please?' she asked.

'Well, the work's going up on December 6th and the performance pieces are on the 10th and 11th – why?'

'I'd like to enter a performance piece please, if that's all right?'

'Of course. Anyone can do a performance; but you must have an approved body of drawings as well. You've already done a lot of drawings which are well above first-year standard so I can't see any difficulty in your doing a performance piece . . .'

Kelly smiled – she had a lovely smile – and agreed to pay more attention to her life drawing and not get side-tracked.

*

By the middle of November, with its sudden chilling fogs and short afternoons of clear freezing skies above the sea, Kelly O'Kelly was aware of three main strands twisting into a steel wire around her days.

Firstly, there was the looming threat of the End-of-Term party when Chico's pop group 'The Statements' would play in the Knighton Leisure Centre. Attendance to this was more or less compulsory as the event was being organised by the students to raise money for a departmental video camera.

Secondly, there was the attention being paid to Kelly by Richard Taylor.

His courtship had begun towards the end of October, when Kelly was feeling particularly nostalgic about Harrier. It had been a very quiet Saturday afternoon and Kelly had expected Richard to go out, returning only to help 'do the till' and lock up. Instead he started asking her questions: Where was she living?, What was the art school like?, Did she have a boyfriend? and so on.

'I never saw the point in going to college,' he had said, 'not unless you want to be a doctor or something. I couldn't wait to get out and start earning a bit of money . . .'

Kelly agreed that there was a lot to be said for this point of view. Outside, the lunchtime lull was being muted even further by a tallow-coloured fog. Hardly anyone seemed to be straying up the quiet street where TrueFit stood. Kelly wondered whether the attractive waiters and waitresses at Hudson's were busy. As if reading her thoughts Richard said: 'Do you go to Hudson's much? That's a really student place. But I'll tell you . . .' (and here he leant forward conspiratorially) 'there's a few good-looking girls working in there! Phew!'

'One or two of the girls on my course work there . . .'

'Oh yes? Who are they?'

'Oh you wouldn't know them. Just girls . . .'

'You never know; I might. I like girls . . .'

Kelly smiled weakly and began to rearrange the ladies casuals.

'Me and Mark Farrow from the Hove shop sometimes go to Hudson's. They do great club-sandwiches there. Expensive though. Do you ever go out?'

'Me?'

'No. Her.' (Pointing gesture.) Kelly turned around. Laughter. 'Just testing. No. You're a good-looking girl – no I mean it. You ought to go out . . .'

Richard Taylor was not Kelly's idea of a date. It was all so difficult. She looked at him as he leant over the counter, his face broken into what he assumed was a playful smile. He had a red face, and red hair. He was tall, and thin, and his shoulders were weak and stooped within his regulation brown blazer. His thin legs were encased in pale grey flannel trousers and his long neck with its protruding Adam's apple stretched awkwardly out of his loose-collared shirt. The shirt had rounded collars and had lost a button beneath the neck. The brown tie was awry. He had long fingers and bitten nails. On the middle finger of his right hand he wore a signet ring which was too big. He constantly rotated this ring beneath his knuckle with his thumb.

Kelly did not know where Richard lived, and she had no desire to find out. Feigning a worldly air she said that she had a boyfriend at home who spent a lot of time motor-cross racing at weekends.

Just then a lady came into the shop to return a pair of brown shoes which leaked, even when re-waterproofed. Filling out the customer service slip Kelly could feel Richard's grey eyes running up and down her back, like some frustrated centipede trying to climb out of a yoghurt carton.

Thirdly, there was what Kelly enjoyed doing the most; making her plans for the end-of-term performance piece.

*

Walking back to Knighton Hall from the TrueFit shop, or going into the centre of town to do her shopping, Kelly would be inspired to continue with her own peculiar aesthetic by the sight of slim, flippant girls who had grown stout and humourless with motherhood. She refused to accept, however dully, that life was wretched and meaningless without having first done something which would stick in the gullet of whatever it was that was trying to consume her. Perhaps it was men who were the enemy, or perhaps the sexes were eventually made equal by the consequences of their respective vanities, desires, and stupidities. Perhaps, in the end, it was simply an attitude that one grew out of.

Kelly could not imagine, as she thought about what made people beautiful, that Chico, or Audrey, or Melanie, had ever given much thought to those aspects of existence which did not conform to their figure-flattering and per-sonality-developing codes of narcissism.

One particular afternoon, looking about the town and the promenade, so grey and monotonous in comparison to the glorious gold and blue of high summer, Kelly O'Kelly turned her head towards the hairdressers. She had made an appointment for four o'clock at 'Line One' in the Old Lanes. She had saved up twenty-five pounds for the treatment.

★

Three hours later, just as the tired salon juniors were sweeping up and the six o'clock appointment had long since departed, Kelly O'Kelly paid Michelle (her stylist) and left her a generous tip. Where once there had been an average head of pale blonde hair, self-styled in front of the mirror with nail scissors and a wet comb, there now existed a sensation.

Although some of the boys on Kelly's course had been to punk rock concerts with crude primary colour sprayed onto their fringes, and although henna was of course old hat, none of the people that Kelly knew had as yet undergone a baptism of pure peroxide. Catching sight of herself in a shopfront mirror, Kelly O'Kelly smiled with pleasure at the sight of her luxurious new look, her 'mask'. It had been worth the stomach upset by nervousness; it had been worth the awful fear that she would simply look ridiculous. For three hours Kelly had sat with her eyes screwed up whilst a variety of girls had washed and rinsed and dyed and cut her hair. For three hours she had refused cups of coffee and magazines. Finally, in the last twenty minutes, she had looked at her reflection in the illuminated mirror and seen first of all the triumphant expression of Michelle.

Kelly's hair was now neon-white. Where previously there had been a ragged fringe there was now a neat, boyish side parting. At the back, where her ribbon had used to dangle, there was soft white stubble, gradually thickening towards the crown in perfectly trimmed and shaved little layers.

'I don't know why . . .' Michelle drawled, 'but this look really suits your face. Would you mind if we did a photograph for the salon?'

Kelly said that she would rather they didn't.

'Oh well, if you change your mind just pop in. You'll have to come back in about six weeks to have your roots done and a trim, so see how you feel then – okay?' The 'okay' was pronounced with a cheerful upward turning of the second syllable; part statement, and part question.

Filled with a strange kind of elation Kelly made her way down the wet promenade towards Knighton Hall. The sea was dark and swelling, with long white-peaked waves which raced up towards the tiered shingle. Kelly hurried on, her happiness increasing as her new haircut managed to effortlessly survive the wind and rain. 'A new look!' she kept thinking, 'A new look!'

Above the big hotels the sky was low, the colour of wet gaberdine. The streetlights were steaming. Behind her Kelly could see the pier, with its tiny lights, stretching out into the darkness. As the rain blurred her vision the lights seemed to sparkle like crystals. The few evening fishermen had long packed up their tackle and headed for home. 'Unhappy fishermen,' thought Kelly, 'not to have a wonderful new look.' She would just miss supper and be able to slip indoors unseen.

Knighton Hall was busy that evening. Most of the girls were talking to friends in their rooms (wet pullovers hung to dry over the radiator), or working; heads bowed over graphics projects, or kneeling dismayed before sheets of recalcitrant tissue. Hurrying down the corridor in her dripping raincoat Kelly put a magazine over her head in order to escape the inevitable comments. Just as she was unlocking her door her neighbour, June Woodsterne, came suddenly out of her room.

'Hello Kelly. You're wet!'

'Mmm – it's pouring.'

'See you!'

June had given up any hope of having sisterly little talks with Kelly a long time ago. Instead she went off to see

Angela from Second-Year Fashion downstairs. Her slippers made a slapping noise on the parquet.

All around there was the sound of music being played at sensible volumes.

Once in her room Kelly put on the bedside lamp. She had left her window open and the room was filled with the cold scent of rain. One side of the long floral curtains was damp. She sat on the low straight-backed chair in front of the mirror. Her hair was just as beautiful as she had hoped it would be. Also, it was now short enough to be painted.

Lowering the sash window a little, Kelly closed the curtains. Then she stood up and took her raincoat off before checking that the door was locked. Kelly's room was blessed with a large area of clear floor space. She took off her wet clothes and put on her oldest trousers and a white T-shirt. Then she knelt on the floor and began rummaging under the bed for the two rolls of paper she had removed from the painting studio. Soon she had rolled back the rug and stretched an area of two square metres of paper across the floor. She was pleased by the efficient way that the floorboards took the mapping pins to hold it taut. In her basin she mixed several litres of brilliant crimson paint. By using one-and-a-half times the prescribed quantity she managed to make the colour deeper, and more lustrous, and slightly sticky. Outside the wind was buffeting gusts of rain against the windows. It was getting late. One by one the traces of music had been turned off. All that Kelly could hear was the sound of a conversation somewhere beneath her; low serious voices whose subject was of no interest to her. The orange-shaded lamp sent curious shadows up to the high ceiling; they looked like folds of velvet, or reminded one of grandly flounced ballgowns, hanging from the picture rail. Having looked again at the paper spread out on the floor in front of her, Kelly took off her clothes.

A little after midnight Kelly had finished the backdrops for her performance. Drying herself with a large bath-towel she looked down with satisfaction at the finished images on the floor. There on the paper were three prints of her whole body. Curious mutated shapes denoted the pressure of her stomach, breasts and thighs. Reflecting against the print of her front was the print of her back. Here her shoulderblades, buttocks, and backs of her legs were separated from one another by areas of white paper, creating a cartography of implications. In between these two full-length portraits was a third, overtly sexual, where Kelly had bound her legs and wrists, the trailing cords leaving a whip-like, bloody effect. Looking down at these sparse, alien images, which she had made so simply, Kelly felt that at last she had followed through one of the ideas of daring which Miss Wadham had first suggested to her nearly five years ago.

Having sprayed the images with a fixative, Kelly left them to dry on the floor. She would roll them up loosely into tubes until they were needed. It was ten-past two in the morning. She opened the curtains and pushed up the window. Turning out the light she sat on the sill and smoked a cigarette. The rain had stopped and the clear air was much colder. The following day Kelly would have to face her contemporaries with her new haircut, and she was suddenly troubled by the thought that maybe she looked ridiculous after all. She ran her fingers through her short fringe and decided that she no longer cared what anyone thought. It was a change of appearance which she required at this stage, and further ways to talk without speaking.

Throwing her cigarette end into the wet garden, Kelly lowered the window again and went to bed.

*

On the Saturday of 'The Statements' concert – just four days before Kelly was due to do her performance – she found that she was unusually polite to Richard Taylor. She wondered whether he was lonely, so she enquired after the health of the only one of his friends whose name she knew.

'How's Mark Farrow?'

'Oh. Fine.'

★

The Knighton Leisure Centre was a sports and entertainments venue just a little way down the road from the hall of the same name. It had been built recently; a two-storey concrete oblong with a glass-walled swimming pool at one end and a concert hall at the other. In the main building there was a private health club, a sauna, an aerobics room, two squash courts and a bar. All of these different areas were connected by broad, carpet-tiled corridors which smelt of chlorine.

The whole complex stood in a landscaped park, and was reached by a smooth access road which meandered around on itself beneath tall sodium streetlights. There was a large carpark to one side of the swimming pool and from there the verge dropped sharply away into a dark expanse of newly laid turf. When the students began to arrive for the end-of-term concert it was raining hard and the night smelt of wet leaves.

Kelly O'Kelly, feeling sick, began to change her clothes in readiness for the big evening. She hated Chico with a passion, and had no interest at all in his pop group. Apathetically she began to pull on her best clothes – a short black skirt and a white blouse which had to be held shut with a brooch. Having no presentable jacket she would have to wear her raincoat over the top.

She locked her door and began to walk down the echoing corridor towards the stairs. Ahead of her there was a gaggle of happy young people, the leading male of which was confidently carrying a large bottle of cider.

'Ooh Pete!' said a girl, roguishly, 'we'll have to carry you home!'

Pete made a noise which implied that that was his intention.

'Oh Christ,' said Kelly, and turning on her heel made her way quickly back to her room, let herself in and locked the door.

★

Shortly before the first evening of performance pieces was due to take place, Mike Reeves informed the group that a man called Ray Green from the local theatre group was coming to watch the work.

'He runs quite an important little fringe outfit,' said Mike, 'and he does a lot for the local avant-garde.'

Everyone was duly on the look out for Ray.

Kelly's piece, somewhat to her surprise – was scheduled to be the very last. The whole event was sold out due to the smallness of the studio and the number of friends whom the participants had invited. In a frenetic atmosphere of drama and crisis the performance studio was made ready, the technical assistant briefed as to his duties, and a small xeroxed handsheet produced to identify each work against its creator.

The quality was mixed.

On the first evening Kelly found that she was digging her fingernails into her palms with embarrassment, and then feeling her eyes go rigid with boredom as she watched people pat coloured balloons at one another whilst their friends fiddled with old radios.

In some cases it seemed as though communication between the performers involved in group pieces had broken down entirely. During a short work entitled 'Death Factory', one performer had dramatically intoned the phrase 'I am Cunt', only to be informed by an irritated voice in the darkness that he wasn't.

With a nervousness which made her oblivious to further

panic, Kelly O'Kelly was surprised that her own piece, 'Kally', had drawn such a crowd. Someone had seen her in deep consultation with a bearded youth from the College Mountaineering Society and this had doubtless provoked curiosity. Added to this was the fact that since Kelly had transformed her image so radically there were many people who were beginning to regard her as some new breed of important person. Even Audrey had begun to notice her, and was keen to recruit the dramatically short-haired girl into the little circle of fashion aristocrats. Kelly made herself unavailable, and this, of course, made her more sought-after.

The studio doors were locked during the interval before Kelly was due to perform. An excited crowd gathered outside, some sceptical, and others enthusiastic. The general opinion was that this was Kelly's big night.

As the audience filed in, a loose-knit phalanx headed by Mike Reeves and the rather selfconscious-looking Ray Green (a short, balding man with a shifty expression and a tan leather jacket), their first impression of 'Kally' was that of pitch darkness.

Humorists noted that this Stygian conceit was possibly all that the work consisted of, but once seating had been arranged, and voices lowered, and half-finished cups of white wine placed gingerly between the legs of stack chairs, there was a gradual flush of golden light, akin to a sunrise, just above the centre stage. There was no soundtrack, and no other performers. Peering into the glow, and trying to adjust their eyes in order to discern the shape hanging there, all the audience could hear in the silence was a swinging, creaking sound, like that of leather straps.

The lights went up a little more, pushing out into the darkness with a soft white edge. There was a sudden gasp from the people in the front row, and those behind craned their heads to try and see.

Swaying slightly in a carefully concealed harness

(arranged with the expert help of 'Climbing Soc.'), Kelly O'Kelly, painted gold from head to toe, was hanging high above the stage from a hook in the back wall. She was at least three metres from the ground. Fastened to the wall around her, crudely fly-postered, were the crimson body prints in their curiously twisted and sexual positions. A silence filled the performance studio as all eyes were irresistibly drawn towards Kelly's face. She was wearing her TrueFit uniform, which she had spraypainted gold, and a pair of sparkling golden shoes, *lamé* encrusted with *diamanté*. All of her visible body – legs, hands, face and hair – was also painted gold. Her head was slightly to one side and her mouth (beautifully outlined in gold lipstick) was set into an expressionless line. Blue shadows fell down one side of her face and across her golden neck. Her hands and feet were bound with golden rope, the ragged ends of which swayed in the light.

'A priceless work of art,' said Valerie Arnus, mesmerised.

'A thing of beauty,' said Ray Green, wiping his glasses.

'The eyes . . .' someone said. 'They really do follow you around the room, just like a painting . . .'

To understand that was to understand everything.

For half an hour Kelly hung from the wall of the studio surrounded by the amused, the unsettled and the lustful. And then, when the people were beginning to file out, she hung there for another hour, nearly alone, in the semi-darkness.

Ray Green was the last to leave. Finally Mike Reeves led him away.

'Kelly doesn't want anyone to see her getting down,' he whispered.

'How can she get down – she's a painting,' said Ray, but left anyway.

A little later Ray tracked Kelly down at Knighton Hall. He could scarcely believe that the girl in front of him was the thing he had watched for nearly an hour.

'That was an excellent piece you did,' he said, 'I hope you can do it for us at the fringe festival in the spring . . .'

Kelly said that she probably would.

★

But this was the only interest that Kelly received in her performance. She did repeat the work for Ray, but her heart was no longer in it.

Kelly O'Kelly remained in Brighton for another three years. She never had a boyfriend and she did little to attract attention. For her final degree show she planned four large paintings of Miles Harrier based on some old snapshots which she had of him. Bronchitis prevented their completion, so she simply left, and was finally awarded a pass degree on the strength of her course work.

Kelly was due to see Miles Harrier once more, but as she left for a series of dull jobs in Reading the only things which distinguished her in her own eyes were the thought that she might one day make a living out of hanging off walls and her steadily tarnishing head of white hair.

FOUR

The Imperfections of Stella

It would appear factitious to suggest that Miles Harrier was in possession of looks and charm of such a kind that they conquered wherever they turned, but it is in fact true to say that Kelly O'Kelly, Lucinda Fortune and Stella Walker-Jones (three such very different kinds of person) were all united by his courting of them. Of the three it was Stella who would prove to be his grandest passion, and of all three it is perhaps inevitable to state that it was Stella who caused him the deepest distress.

Girls, as a race, elude the simple classification into 'types' so favoured by beer-hall analysts throughout the ages. There is no such thing as 'the dumb blonde' or 'the tough brunette', and the day has yet to come when any man could settle with impunity at the commencement of an affair and make a prediction of its outcome based on such an evaluation. Love, 'the old dance', begins largely as a question of appearances and usually ends as a question of attitudes. The intervening period (sometimes termed 'halcyon') is distinguished by the manner in which lovers discover that mutual exploration repays each delight with a doubt, and, more often than not, each vow with a condition.

At love's outset however, it is appearance which holds sway, or beauty, and when one speaks of the power of love (particularly with reference to the young), one is, in most cases, speaking of the power of beauty. To know that Stella Walker-Jones was beautiful is fundamental to achieving any real understanding of her. To know that she was one of

Lucinda Fortune's oldest friends is fundamental to achieving any real understanding of Miles Harrier.

With regard to Stella it is impossible to say how such beauty comes about. As a child she required no special attentions of the kind one might lavish on a rare plant or particularly delicate item of glassware, and up until her twelfth birthday her looks could be termed 'ordinary' with greater truth than they could be called 'remarkable'. It was shortly after her twelfth birthday, whilst holidaying with her parents and brother by the sea, at Lyme Regis, that this pretty but unspectacular little girl in brown shorts and tank-top had a nasty accident of the kind which initially made her family worry for the future of her looks.

Stella had always been a lively child. The contents of her toy cupboard were most used to occupying extensive areas of floor space elsewhere in the family home, and her con-siderable collection of soft toys had a degree of mobility that many of their real-life originators would find hard to match. Stella was one who 'played hard', and the slightest occasion for excitement was always met with enthusiasm and exploited to the full. Bicycle rides, fishing, climbing trees (the Walker-Jones were lucky enough to possess an orchard), and garden games of Cowboys and Indians were enjoyed as much by Stella as were her other pastimes of playing with dolls, model horses and the family kitten. In this much she was a very typical little girl.

The unpleasantness at Lyme was due to Stella's enthusiasm to enjoy herself.

Lyme Regis is not a dangerous town, and none of its featured amusements, from grubbing for ammonites in the shadow of the black cliff-faces, to playing crazy golf on the uppermost garden terrace overlooking the little harbour, could be said to require excessive parental supervision. The beaches too were devoid of hazard, except in the places where thoughtless sea-anglers had left surprisingly large fish-heads to rot, and so it was that Stella and her brother were allowed to play quite freely for the first four days of their holiday.

Of course the main feature of Lyme Regis is its Cobb; a short, man-made promontory, rising some fifteen metres in height over the distance of its length, which stretches around the harbour like a protective elbow before terminating in a romantic collection of rocks at its furthest point in the open sea. The Cobb has existed for many hundreds of years, added to over time and never losing its attraction for the tourist. The sunsets viewed from its height are best seen as the facing cliffs around the coastline turn the colour of purple heather in the twilight, and the sea which separates the viewer from his prospect becomes a sheet of metallic blue. For the romantic there is much to fixate his ecstasy when first confronted with this simple but effective meeting of land and sea, and at high tide, when the wind is up, the waves break with a force and drama which could satisfy the most demanding of imaginations. There is also an Aquarium on the Cobb, and it was returning from this that Stella had her accident. The conger-eel (it was a metre-and-a-half in length and enjoyed the status of an old and respected resident of Lyme) had fascinated Stella, and even though her brother James had preferred the sea-mice it was the eel that absorbed Stella's thoughts on the walk back around the Cobb to the tea place. She had hung over its long tank for nearly twenty minutes, watching the flatness of its eyes and rejoicing in the sight of it squeezing through a length of pipe. She wondered whether it yearned for the open sea, or whether, in some curious kind of way, it simply yearned for a longer length of pipe.

Stella and James made their way around the Cobb, walking, as children will, too close to its sea-facing edge. The tide was coming in, and already there were black patches on the sides of the sea-wall which marked the heavier slapping of the waves. Stella, suddenly squeamish with thoughts of the eel, decided – in a kind of panic – to run quickly down the rest of the slope. What she didn't see in her excitement was a low bollard, with a rope tied taut about it, and scarcely had she realised that she had stubbed her toe through her sandal than she lost her balance completely, let out a piercing scream and fell into the sea. James, seeing the accident, began to run and shout for help.

The local paper was swift to report the speed with which a woman working on her boat nearby had dived into the water and rescued young Stella. The little girl was only in the water for a matter of seconds and was saved largely by the fact that her tripping had twisted her feet first into the deeper water. Stella's parents were quickly called, and by the time that they arrived she was sitting wrapped in a blanket, fully conscious, and waiting for the doctor.

The real injury had come not from the fall but from her panic on feeling her rescuer's arm beneath her chin. Flailing her arms in terror she banged her head badly on the side of the boat and cut herself deeply across her left eyebrow and lower forehead. Such wounds bleed heavily, and Stella was taken directly to the doctor's front-room surgery where she was given immediate stitches in her face. From there Stella was taken back to the hotel and given a warm, shallow bath by her mother. At first she appeared feverish, and silent, this giving rise to further concern, but then she began to cry and with this emotion soon calmed down. In her mind's eye she kept on seeing the eel tank, and the grey sea rushing up at her. She had felt sure that she was going to die. The Walker-Jones continued the remaining two days of their holiday, possibly feeling that Stella's sense of trauma would be even further compounded if turned into an 'event' by coming home early. Most of the time Stella stayed with her mother, and the sight of her small, suntanned face with its sticking plaster and stitches caused Mrs Walker-Jones no small amount of tears.

Stella would sit beside her in the hotel gardens, watching the shadows lengthening off the conifers and listening to the seagulls. The depth of the shock which she had received was only just beginning.

Stella would think, particularly as she was falling to sleep, of the long smooth body of the conger-eel, now quite malevolent, and imagine the sensation of it against her body in the water. Her rescuer's kind arm became the eel in nightmares, and it was some months before the whole event had been displaced as her foremost preoccupation by the passage of time and new distractions.

★

The autumn following the Walker-Jones's disastrous holiday in Lyme saw the inauguration of a change in both Stella's personality and her looks. The transformation of a rather ordinary little girl with a penchant for the boisterous is not a unique occurrence in itself, but with Stella the process was both swift and dramatic.

Initially however, the change took the form of a deep silence. This silence began on the windy evening in mid-September when Stella had her stitches taken out. The cut above her eye had healed, but there remained as a reminder of it a crooked line, which turned in time from scarlet to white. This scar began just above Stella's left eyelid and terminated, with a slant to the left, on her upper cheek. Her eye, miraculously, had not been damaged. Although the doctor had said that Stella could cover the scar with light make-up should she so choose, her mother was swift to point out that no amount of foundation or colour would disguise the slight elongation and sharpness that the cut itself had caused to Stella's left eye. Whilst offered in a tone of cheerful practicality, this comment caused the girl a great deal of distress, and it is possible that cosmetic concerns were as much at the root of her ensuing silence as anything else.

With the silence came shyness. Where Stella had once

been the first to proffer new toys for inspection by the most casual of callers, she would now withdraw to her room at the slightest hint of visitors. Her room, once a battleground of leisure pursuits, was now a delicately feminine boudoir. Its decoration had been the treat she most requested as recompense for her spoiled holiday. The walls were stripped of their colourful, cartoon-covered wallpaper, and the many pictures and ornaments which they had sheltered were either thrown away or put in a box in the attic. Stella chose the softest of pinks ('Babyrose') as paint for the walls; and a new carpet, curtains and bedspread were selected to match. She also had a new white dressing table with a little vanity mirror to place in front of the long, leaded window, and where once the toy cupboard had spilled its contents into the centre of the room there now stood a demure white wardrobe with her clothes and shoes stored neatly inside; jumpers and woollens to the left, dresses to the right.

All of this took place in under a month.

At school her scar brought with it a degree of fame, particularly with the brothers of her friends.

Stella's teachers were swift to notice the change in one of their naughtier pupils. Whilst relieved to find her easier to manage they were distressed by the distance her personality had covered in the opposite direction. Blushes, tears, shyness and silence had become the currency of Stella's behaviour, and in some cases this timidity caused more irritation to the authorities than had her previous, louder inclinations.

Worst of all there were those who began to take Stella's reticence as evidence of a secretive nature, and this made the girl feel guilty for things that she had not done whilst also causing her to feel immense shame for thoughts that she could almost believe those around her could guess. In this much, puberty was a nightmare.

Coupled with Stella's retreat into herself was the sudden development of her body. She grew tall, and slender. Her face lost its childish roundness, and her fair hair (which she had always been told would darken) began to turn gold. Her eyes (which were brown) deepened into a dark, liquid hazel, and were offset by china-perfect whites. Her scar, which drew immediate attention to her face, became as an imperfection the agent of glamour. She developed a fine bone structure, and her skin was smooth and brown. Her shoulders were broad and her waist narrow, and at fourteen she looked sixteen. Her advanced physique and immense prettiness began to draw jealous hostility from some of her contemporaries. In answer to this envious surveillance Stella decided to make up for her nervousness by being not only the prettiest but also the most fashionable girl in her circle. In this she succeeded. Her wardrobe and make-up collection were as well chosen as they were precocious. The problem with her position was that the more she developed an image and a reputation, the more hotly she was afraid of 'being found out'. She did not know what it was that she was afraid of being found out about.

★

The world inhabited by the Walker-Jones was a curious mixture of county gentility and suburban snobbishness. Mr Walker-Jones was a successful Temple lawyer whose skill at advising men slightly richer than he on what they should do to become even richer had gained him increasing personal wealth. With these riches he had moved to a large house and three acres on the outskirts of Henley-on-Thames, and it was from this pleasant situation that he commuted most days (first-class) to London in the company of Richard Fortune, father of Lucinda.

The Walker-Jones's large house stood near to (but not intimately so) several other large houses in a small and exclusive residential area which was carefully wooded with deciduous trees and traversed by quiet private roads. From the speeding breadth of a nearby dual-carriageway, the traveller fixed on reaching this affluent Arcady was asked to plunge down a tiny slip-road overhung with gracious lime trees and bordered by lush fields where grazed the sizeable population of locally owned ponies. A small parade of shops in the old 'owner-managed' style so valued by the house-wives of the district, found picturesque conclusion in the half-timbered opulence of the 'Coat & Coachman' public house. From here the little road became three, the left fork becoming 'Bushy Lane' as it followed the gentle slope of a wooded hill, the right fork swooping over a low bridge under which ran a small but swiftly flowing river, and the central option leading into the copious carpark of the quaint Victorian railway station. The railway station was pretty enough to warrant frequent use in the filming of period drama whilst the service which it ran to London was gauged to be both fast and regular. It was precisely this combination of scenery and convenience that the elders of the district were most used to reminding one another was 'what they were paying for'.

This was essentially correct. Cynics existed who claimed that the area was little more than a prison, so lacking was it in the wider, more vulgar services, but they were swiftly silenced by the authority with which the friendliness of the shopkeepers was extolled and the controlled beauty of the environment pointed out.

The Walker-Jones lived at 'The Leas', a house at the top of Bushy Lane which lacked only a meadow to qualify as a small estate.

It was indeed a fine house. Built in 1906 to imply 'squire' whilst affirming 'businessman', 'The Leas' had six bed-rooms, four bathrooms and a long drawing room with a view from the hillside to the treetops denoting the verge of the dual-carriageway. Several skilfully designed nooks and crannies added an impression of eccentricity to this otherwise perfectly sane building. The size of the house was nearer to 'grand' than 'domestic' and here and there the architecture was flicked by the brush of the monumental. Its three red-bricked gables contained inexplicable arrow-slits, and the garden wall connecting the front of the house to the double garage was adorned with two enormous lead urns on either side of the railinged gate. The house had aged well however, and now blended with the landscape in a manner which made it appear much older than it really was.

Stella's room was the smallest (looking out over the garden), and her brother James lodged down the corridor. They each had their own bathroom, as did their parents, who occupied the master bedroom on the other side of the house, overlooking the drive and front lawn.

In the reception and dining rooms fine antiques mingled with reproductions of same, and the overall effect was one of low-shaded lamps, heavy curtains and pungent leather. This look demanded (but did not receive) servants, and took to children not well at all.

Mrs Walker-Jones was house-proud, and united with her husband to convey (whilst not carrying out) a general code of strictness. This seldom created problems because the children were happiest playing out of doors, either in the garden or down by the little river, but at the onset of adolescence there was a marked stiffening of the parental countenance and new rules were introduced to limit the potential for teenage entertainment. As James went off to Eton at around the same time that Stella withdrew, this stiffening went largely unattended and it is possible that Mr and Mrs Walker-Jones felt rather disappointed at the lack of effect their regime had had upon daily life.

The Black Hand Gang had been an early invention of Stella's, created when she and Lucinda and James and Miles had first played together as children. The adventures of the gang, whilst aspiring to the excitement of those encountered in children's fiction, had been largely commonplace and endemic to the Walker-Jones's locale. The conversion of an abandoned pill-box into a secret headquarters (no less secret for its outlook onto the sixteenth green of the local golf course), the discovery of an old boathouse which turned out to belong to a neighbour, and the gang's suspicion that a retired bachelor living nearby was a master criminal, had all contributed to the activities of the Black Hand Gang. Viewed nostalgically from their teenage years, the Black Hand Gang still did not seem that silly to the four children; rather, they simply abandoned the name.

Lucinda Fortune was the youngest, and she was the poor unfortunate whom the scholarly James had decided was psychic. A seance ensued, and a craze for Ouija, but nothing happened except for Lucinda feeling frightened even as she rejoiced in the honour of being attributed with special powers.

Stella and Lucinda had long been friends, but whilst initially it was Lucinda who had always appeared to be on the verge of tears, by the time that she had had her nasty accident it was Stella who came across as the more sensitive and emotional of the two. Miles (except when called abroad by his mysterious family) became a regular holiday visitor at 'The Leas', and the two girls always connected the end of term with his arrival. Miles was kind and had wonderful manners. He was also good at arranging games and had just enough money allowed him to fund occasional treats for the gang as a whole. He bought an air-rifle, a junior-sized motorbike, and, for Stella in particular, he bought a small aquarium. This was no fairground bowl of goldfish but rather a proper tank, with heated water, pumps, and lights. Mr and Mrs Walker-Jones, not wishing to question the young aristocrat's generosity, allowed Stella to keep the tank in her room, and after the boys had returned to school in the autumn she would sit beside it in the teatime darkness and watch the two brightest fish – one scarlet and one blue – shepherding the shoal of neons. Stella, mesmerised by the colour and movement of these exquisite fish, could somehow never place them as relatives of the dreaded conger-eel of summers past. Lucinda helped her with the maintenance of the aquarium, and each time Miles came to stay the gang would go up to London to choose another fish.

The tropical-fish stockist ('Underwater World') was housed in a sprawling maze of dark sheds near the Edgware Road. After a year or two 'buying a fish' became a regular feature of the holidays and once the children were approaching their mid-teens it served as a good excuse for a general shopping trip in central London.

By the time she was fifteen Stella was beginning to receive a great deal of attention from boys. It seemed that every boy known to the gang was wild to go out with her. Stella usually agreed to see maybe one or two of the most persistent suitors each term. These lucky youths would receive about four weekend 'dates' (more if they did not attempt heavily sexual overtures) and then be dropped, sometimes without a second thought and sometimes after a certain degree of soul-searching. Some people rather unkindly said that Stella was a bit 'fast'. This provoked some bitterness on the part of the discarded, but Stella never encouraged, with either words or gestures, any serious commitment. She felt (quite rightly) that if a boy could not control himself in her presence then it was not incumbent upon her to silence the lion of desire by putting her head in its mouth.

On one or two occasions over as many years, Stella had felt moved enough by a companion to enjoy a certain amount of kissing. Both of these sessions ended in embarrassment and disaster. With the first boy (Jeremy, or 'Jem'), Stella had stretched out her long legs in mid-kiss in order to stop her foot from going to sleep. Her skirt rose of its own accord to her thigh and the next thing she realised Jeremy's eyes had screwed up tight – as if in agony – and a curious succession of jerking motions were disturbing his lower body. Stella was completely aware of what had happened.

As she felt the boy's grip on her arm relax and his gradual repositioning of himself take on the feel of one whose pen has leaked, she gazed at the swerving neons and felt as though she had forgotten to let the dog out.

On the second occasion, this time with a supposed man of experience called Stewart (he was eighteen), she had been forced to use harsh words.

*

Stella, despite being slightly senior, ended up by following a similar academic course to Lucinda. She took her O-levels early and then, whilst Lucinda was preparing for hers, attended an expensive secretarial college in Reading called Stoughton's. Here, with twenty other girls whose attitudes ranged from exasperation to deep shame, she was prepared to enter the more exclusive end of Administrative and Personal Assistant work. This process was combined with learning the rudiments of deportment, elocution and conference planning. She gained her diploma the same year that Lucinda passed her O-levels and left school. Neither of them wished to continue studying, and nobody encouraged them to do so.

At the end of their last respective summer terms, Stella and Lucinda sat in Cluso's Cafe and discussed the forthcoming holidays over quiche.

Stella and James were going to the Italian lakes with their parents. Lucinda and her parents were due to spend one week in Greece and three in Oban. Harrier would join the Walker-Jones on their return to 'The Leas' in early August. As Stella sipped her apple juice, a youthful goddess in cotton skirt and T-shirt, she felt that her approaching vacation would do little to dispel the staleness which she had sensed in her life of late. Lucinda, looking the other way at a dark print on the cafe wall entitled 'Selbourne; from the Hanger', was smoking a cigarette. In the silence which appeared to be the echo of a greater silence, Stella reasoned that at least Italy would give her a chance to sunbathe. It must also be noted that Stella's shyness was making her immensely vain.

★

The attractions of Italy are well-known to her NATO allies, and the region of Lombardy, with its spectacular lakeland scenery, is no less attractive than the rest. The Walker-Jones arrived at Lake Como during a heatwave, and from the moment that they stood grouped around their luggage in the unfamiliar glare, their faces revealing that curious mixture of suspicion and anticipation which attends any new arrival in a strange place, it seemed destined that the lovely Stella was due to attract attention. Cars hooted, scooters swerved, and a knot of loafers who were congregated around the hydrofoil stop all rushed to assist her with her luggage. Mr Walker-Jones swiftly dispelled the carnival atmosphere by saying 'Thank you, Thank you' in a firm voice whilst transferring his family into the waiting taxi which was to take them the length of the lake to the pretty little town of Bellagio.

Bellagio is a relatively quiet spot on the side of Lake Como. The hills around it are reputed to be as high as the water which washes its motor-launch steps is deep, but to the casual tourist this pleasing statistic is but dry academic dust in comparison to the richness of the colours, the iridescence of the light and the serenity of the view. There are those (regular visitors who can recall the pre-war purity of the place) who now say that a degree of the town's natural charm has been contaminated by the growth of tourism, but there remains the pretty cloistered promenade, and the steep cool alleys between the buildings, and for those with a fondness for flowers, Latin bustle and the drinking of coffee or grenadine out of doors, there is much to please. On arrival at Bellagio the Walker-Jones moved into their hotel just as the clamp of heat which had accompanied the siesta hours was loosening in the golden light of late afternoon. The lake was sparkling with the light of a million diamonds, the dry earth in the geranium pots was black with recent watering, and the shops and cafes were reopening their shutters in anticipation of the brisk business of evening.

The Walker-Jones were staying at the Hotel Bellagio, an austere, lake-facing mansion whose services to the Anglo-German tourist were residual from the heyday of the Grand Tour. It occupied an entire block at the northern end of the promenade, thus commanding extensive views of the lake both east and west; but despite its size and position the Hotel Bellagio was but a bourgeois lodge in comparison to the magnificence and splendour of the famous Villa Serbelloni Hotel whose gateway it faced. The Serbelloni, whilst not beyond Mr Walker-Jones's pocket, had been considered too much of an extravagance for a standard family holiday. Besides, Serbelloni's gardens and swimming pool could be used by residents of the Bellagio on presentation to the porter of their key.

Stella was indifferent to the grandeur of their neighbour. She liked the worn stone stairs of the Bellagio, and the curious undulations of its marble corridors; at the end of each was a rusted balcony balustrade quite overgrown with fluorescent green creepers and paper-thin white flowers.

The Hotel Bellagio was comprised of two parts, equally dusty, and bridged by a corridor with large window panes. The elderly glass in these windows was thick, and mottled, and the view through them was distorted, as though someone were pouring jugs of cold water down them from above. As she paced behind the porter to her room, suddenly feeling the self-consciousness of one being directed by a stranger, Stella saw the glittering lake through these windows and the shadows of the mountains beyond, flicking in perspective with the density of the glass.

Stella's wing of the hotel was dark and quiet. At the corner of each corridor there was a brass light bracket where three yellow bulbs were constantly burning at a low wattage. As the only daylight to reach these corridors came from the balcony windows at their ends – and even this was a greenish half-light, filtered through foliage – the dim glow cast by these bulbs was the only direct illumination. Stella's room was halfway down the corridor, the darkest point, and the atmosphere around it was church-like: cool and faintly aromatic. As the porter swung open the door Stella was relieved to be met by the fresh air and sunshine which poured in through the recently opened shutters. She heard the floorboards squeak beneath her feet, thanked the porter in an uncertain European murmur, and then she was alone.

The room was big and high-ceilinged, with off-white walls and a varnished wooden floor. A tall window with thick green shutters (now neatly folded back) was directly facing the bed. The bed itself was enormous, a luxury which Stella had not enjoyed before, and it was only the singular pillow which made her forbear from checking with her mother that they weren't being charged for a double. The furniture, though mahogany, and antique, was sparse; a wardrobe with a creaking door and a mountainous chest of drawers. Beside the window there was a little stool and next to the bed a tiny cabinet. The light over the bed was switched on and off by use of a brass dove attached to the end of a chain. The rest of the accommodation comprised a small tiled bathroom with a complicated showering arrangement which looked like an old-fashioned telephone. The bathroom had no windows at all but was floored with marble, the cold sensation of which Stella found most pleasing to her hot feet.

Like all good explorers Stella made first to the tall window in order to appraise the view. An ubiquitous portion of lake rewarded her concern.

Stella's intense femininity was soon pervading the atmosphere of the room. By the time that her brother came to collect her for dinner, looking somewhat uncomfortable in a new pair of trousers and his school blazer, the air was sweet and slightly stinging with the scent of hairspray, the steam in the bathroom was distinctly herbalised, and the marble shelf which ran above the iron radiator was a parade-ground of cosmetics.

Stella was just putting the finishing touches of pearlised pink nail varnish to her toes when James entered the room. On the floor beside her was a deep and orderly stack of fashion magazines which she had bought the moment the family touched Italian soil.

'Bit of a barn isn't it?' said James.

'Oh −' (eyes glazed with concentration) 'I think it's lovely . . .'

'I can't shave − the plug won't fit in the socket . . . I say, have you seen any of the other guests? They're gruesome. I ran into a squad of them making for the bar. They were all twice Grannie's age at least . . .'

'Finished.'

Stella gave a last sideways shake to her hair and flicked a rogue mote of mascara off the end of one of her long eyelashes. She was already a flattering honey colour, and her dress, although buttoned up the front, was designed to give further sunshine full access to her legs.

'Mother will have a fit when she sees that dress,' said James.

'She helped me choose it,' said Stella.

Brother and sister made their way through the maze of corridors, which were sometimes dark and sometimes burst upon with sudden patches of evening sunlight. Soon they were down in the purple twilight of the neo-Gothic lounge where their parents were struggling to keep afloat in velvet cushioned chairs of immense depth. They smiled brightly at the approach of their children.

'Well! This is a place isn't it?' said Mr Walker-Jones.
James and Stella agreed that it undeniably was.

★

Several days passed, uneventful save for the intensity of the
heat. Twelve times daily the hydrofoil sped from one end
of the lake to the other, collecting and disgorging passengers
at each of its little stops; Cadenabbia, Argegno, Brienno,
Laglio, Como . . . Hardier souls windsurfed, their journeys
shortened by the scarcity of wind.

Pliny's villa was visited and duly admired. The hydrangea
were out in the gardens of the Villa Carlotta. Coach parties
were organised to Venice and Milan, the participants returning exhausted at midnight and clutching little paper bags of
postcards which rustled in the darkness of the hotel corridors, disturbing fitful sleepers.

On their third afternoon the Walker-Jones went to Como
to see the church and the shops. The visit culminated in an
ice-cream tea at a little pavement cafe overlooking the square.
The *gelati* were extravagant concoctions of cream and fruit
and coloured syrup, their apices sprinkled with crystalline
sugar and glacé cherries. It was traditional for the recipients
of these monstrous confections to emit a little gasp of self-
reproach when first the waiter delivered them. The waiters,
being themselves no strangers to tradition, would answer the
gasps with a modest smile of triumph, a touch of the personal
which the tourists valued highly as a humorous garnish to
the otherwise mechanical nature of the transaction.

Eventually the heat drove Mr and Mrs Walker-Jones to
spending their days seated in the shade of the terrace sipping
iced drinks. Stella made good use of the four different
swimming costumes which she had brought with her and
sunbathed for hours beside the swimming pool of the Villa
Serbelloni. The waiters on duty there took turns at serving
her side of the terrace.

James, tired and nauseous with the climate, roamed the cooler areas of the Hotel Bellagio in search of distraction. He discovered some elderly bound collections of the *Transatlantic Quarterly* and amused himself by reading the archaic adverts for tropical cruises and liver pills. He began an errant volume of Proust. Finally, on discovering an old Monopoly set, he sat alone for hours in the hotel lounge, a rather pathetic figure, gleefully charging himself double rent for owning both Park Lane and Mayfair.

★

Despite her interest in fashion and glamour, Stella had never considered attempting a career in modelling. Sometimes she attributed the impossibility of such a thing to her scar (a feature with which she had grown to live but seldom, if ever, forgot), and sometimes to the fact that modelling − like ascending a hitherto-unclimbed Himalayan peak − was simply beyond the reach of common humanity. In her dress and appearance Stella always aimed for perfection, courting an ambiguity between figure-flattering fashion and the subtly erotic. The speed and severity with which she redirected the interest which boys took in her 'sexiness' towards the obscure yet alluring qualities of dress which were demanded by 'fashion' − a purely feminine concern − served only to interest them further. And thus, whilst whatever Stella wore was worn with regard to the shape of her body beneath it, she never seemed to come across as vulgar or promiscuous. In this manner Stella's look − or rather, Stella − suggested complete sexuality; gusts of erotic inference made all the more appealing as her natural beauty was revealed by the suggested complicity of what covered it had with being removed. In short, Stella looked like the ecstatic frustration so necessary to pure romance.

During her second week at Bellagio, Stella settled into a daily routine of sunbathing by the pool at the Villa Serbelloni. The intense heat had cleared the terrace of all but the most dedicated of sun-worshippers. The pool beside her sparkled gold above the turquoise of its base, and the sky above her was an undisturbed azure. In the formal gardens spread out before the hotel the shrubs and flowers were dry and browned, the foliage of the more shaded regions being comprised of dusty ivy and thick purple leaves which drooped over the edges of the little paths. Every now and then a waiter would pass by with a tray of iced drinks, the glasses tinkling sweetly in the silence.

Stella's determination to achieve an all-over tan just managed to outweigh her natural modesty, and she would sunbathe in the briefest of bikinis, with a tube of expensive tanning cream to one side of her and an iced lemon soda to the other. Thus equipped she reached a trance-like condition during the savage heat of morning and alternately swam and lay on her stomach during the afternoon.

One day, shortly after lunch, Stella's attention was drawn lazily to a certain amount of bustle on the terrace above her. She twisted over on her side to see what was going on. Several small vans and a white estate car had drawn up in front of the Serbelloni, and now a suave-looking youth in black jeans and black T-shirt was busily arranging tripods, reflective aluminium sheets and racks of clothes protected by polythene sheets. The clothes were swiftly wheeled out of the sun into the gloom of the hotel foyer. On the terrace, newspapers and books were lowered to knees, and several middle-aged English couples craned their necks to see what would happen next.

Fairly soon a short man wearing a baggy beige suit and three tall girls were installing themselves around a makeshift arrangement of mirrors, cosmetics and photographic equipment. It was, the residents all brightly reasoned, a chance to see some fashion photography.

Stella looked at the models from her vantage point beside the pool with interest. They were all dark, and skinny, and had a transferably international look about them. Their prettiness was uniform: long legs, long necks, and a slightly tired haughtiness which snapped into a pose during each run of photographs. The photographer, obviously something of a celebrity, worked quickly and silently, his rhythm disturbed only by interventions from the make-up girl, changes of costume, and occasional smiled or barked directions to the assistant. The models worked with cool precision. Stella noticed that one of them had a parasol with *Grazia/Mondadori* printed upon it.

In the meantime Stella was extremely thirsty, and so, waiting until what appeared to be a convenient break in the shooting, she slipped on her T-shirt and sandals to go and order a drink. Just as she was passing by the photographer a lizard ran over her foot, and scarcely before she had screamed she heard the whirring of a motor-shutter and discovered that she had been photographed. The photographer drew his inspiration from the chanced-upon. His little troupe all smiled at Stella, as if to imply that she was about to receive a sprinkling of gold dust from the master's magical touch. He approached her with outstretched hand, his first Italian greeting being swiftly transferred into perfect American. His name was Remo Giovetti, he was taking photographs for *Grazia* magazine of Milan (a copy was immediately offered), and he thought that Stella had one of the most photogenic 'charismas' he had ever seen. Mrs Walker-Jones was swiftly on the scene, defenceless before such charm and politeness.

Addressing Stella's mother more than Stella, Remo asked if Stella could be permitted to model some new garments his magazine was featuring. There would be a fee (of course) and a chaperone (it went without saying), and he would be most grateful. Mr Walker-Jones was duly consulted and a brief manly interview ensued, terminating in Mr Walker-Jones stiffly shaking the Italian's hand and saying that it was up to Stella. James, fractious with the heat, made comments about cheap romantic fiction.

Stella, more or less without words, said that she would try. The three models began to stop looking at her.

That evening, surrounded by lights and a small audience of local people and tourists, Stella was photographed wearing a variety of exquisite Japanese suits. This took place in the little public gardens overlooking the lake.

The intervening hours had been spent with Francesca, the make-up girl, who completely restyled Stella's hair in her room at the Bellagio. They talked about fashion and their different lives, Francesca speaking in admirable, if limited, English. She was surprised to hear that Stella was going to be a secretary. She told her about the beauty course which she had taken in Florence. She asked about the scar. 'It's fabulous,' she said, her face close to Stella's as she worked with a thick powder brush. 'It's . . . perfect . . .'

She asked if Stella had a boyfriend.

'Oh, no,' replied Stella with a laugh, her back stiffening for a second.

After the photography Remo and Francesca sat for an hour with Stella and her mother over coffee. Mrs Walker-Jones was just very slightly short with the Italians, as though annoyed that they had discovered something which hitherto only she had been aware of.

Before leaving Remo gave Stella his card with the name and number of the London Mondadori office upon it.

'Adrian Jones is the contact there. He's a nice man – I'll call him, he may be able to find you good work.'

Promising to send on copies of the issue of *Grazia* in which Stella would appear, the Italians disappeared into the night.

The lamps were casting a mauve hue over the lower branches of the little trees beside the lake. The night was clear, and sweetly scented. Stella's mother thought that it was time they were all in bed.

★

Three weeks later, towards the end of August, Kelly O'Kelly and The Honourable Miles Harrier were sitting on the edge of an overgrown copse in the open country halfway between Twyford and the Walker-Jones's. Kelly and Harrier had met ten days previously at Susan Henshaw's seventeenth.

Their relationship was at a curious stage. Kelly, sitting now cross-legged in grey canvas trousers and a black pull-over with a v-neck, was hopelessly in love with Harrier. Harrier, lying on his back three feet away from her and looking dependable in fawn corduroys and a collarless shirt, was enjoying the present but uncertain about the future. Kelly made no demands upon the future at all. She loved to be with Miles – what else would she stay for? She loved his face and his laughter; she loved the way that he was so totally different to the other boys she knew.

Harrier was completely unforthcoming about his family. He had a younger brother and his parents lived abroad most of the time. They had a house in Yorkshire. (Kelly pictured something along the lines of her aunt's house in Hove – a four-bedroomed detached with pebbledash and a big garden.)

Of Eton too he would say little.

'Oh – it's all right I suppose. I quite like it anyway. It's a large and ancient public school for boys in the Thames Valley. Sometimes we wear funny hats . . .'

Kelly giggled, and told him about Miss Wadham.

Sometimes when they were walking Harrier would put his arm around Kelly's shoulder. When they parted he would give her a tight hug and kiss her, lingering for a moment before letting her go. Then he would say something funny. If they were outside Kelly's house he would say 'Don't get lost on the way home.' Or if she was about to get on the bus: 'Remember to change at Crewe.'

However slender the joke Kelly would always treasure it on the way home and remember all the details of the day they had just spent together. This made her look forward doubly to the next time they would meet.

Once or twice they had kissed passionately, Kelly feeling herself slide from within herself with pleasure, her arms tightening around Harrier and her mouth growing softer and more vulnerable to his. Harrier never tried to take this side of their relationship any further. Sometimes this frustrated Kelly but her love for him made her glad at whatever he did and trust in his judgement. Kelly O'Kelly, with completely sincere feelings for her beloved, had already given him more of herself than she could ever have done in bed; in her heart she had given herself totally to Harrier.

As they sat beside the little copse, the field of long grass before them went light and dark with gusts of warm rain. The sky was the colour of slate, but on the far horizon there was a crooked line of sunshine trying to break through onto the wet earth. Behind them was an impenetrable undergrowth of brown, sharp-thorned brambles, fallen branches and tall clumps of stinging nettles. The plan had been to picnic beside the river, a mile away, but the weather had forced them to shelter.

The countryside was quiet, out of earshot of the dual-carriageway. The leaves were dripping but the ground where they sat felt warm. 'Tell me about Stella — why wasn't she at Susan's party?'

'Stella? Oh, Stella's always somewhere. Awfully popular girl you know, but never really . . . what's the word? . . . "Settled" possibly.'

'How do you mean?'

'Well, I only know her as James's sister. I know that sounds awful but it's rather as though she had one life which is me and James and so forth and another which is completely separate. I mean, we are her friends but none of us have really got a clue how she spends a lot of her time . . .' Miles paused, and watched the approaching bar of sunshine comb the top of the grass and make it glisten in the middle distance.

He continued, 'I suppose what I mean is boyfriends and so on . . .'

'She's terribly pretty isn't she? My brother was saying that everyone in his year lusts after her madly . . .'

'Yes, she's very pretty. She got asked to model whilst they were on holiday. James said they scarcely recognised her when she was all dolled up – I think she rather enjoyed it. Would you like to model, Kelly?'

'Don't be stupid –'

'Well why not – you're just as good as Stella . . .'

'Look at the rain . . .'

A brief cloudburst was drenching the field in front of them. Behind it the sun was shining brightly, turning the grass to gold.

'It's like it's only raining in one little bit – how odd,' said Miles.

'Isn't it lovely,' said Kelly, and rested her arm on his shoulder. 'You're lovely,' she added, in a murmur.

'I don't think she has got a boyfriend – Stella,' said Miles after a moment. 'When you ask she says it's because of her scar and makes Man-in-the-Iron-Mask jokes and so on . . .'

'Has she got a scar – where?'

'Above her eye. She cut herself quite badly when she was little . . .'

'Is it hideous? It can't be if she models.'

'It's rather distinguished actually. But it makes her look like she's looking at you in a very cool way when she isn't really.'

'What's she doing now?'

'She's just finished a secretarial course. And I think she's been offered some more modelling work as well, but her father wants her to take a steady job as well – look it's easing off. Let's make a run for the next field . . .'

And so hastily putting the remains of their picnic and the rug into a bag, Miles grabbed Kelly's hand and they sprinted off through the wet grass. Kelly laughed breathlessly as their trousers got soaked, and the clouds above them began to separate; white continents divided by blue summer sea.

★

Five months after this conversation Kelly O'Kelly was watching the dark sea swell up and down between the rusted pillars of the old pier at Brighton. It was late January, and the town would freeze overnight.

She watched the waves for a while. They began as dark bars out to sea, pushing forward beneath the surface before rearing up at the very last moment. They looked malevolent, and ugly.

Then she walked into the town. In the darkened window of an antiques shop, pistols, maps, cutlasses and an ivory globe were tipped by the light of a streetlamp. Kelly remembered a habit of her earliest childhood. She had used to kiss all the objects around her in her bedroom before going to sleep, rejecting none and favouring all, compelled by infant sentimentality. This memory mixed with knowledge about the present. Harrier had failed to get into Oxford and was, a postcard informed her, in France. The friendliness of the card had been worse than silence.

Kelly felt sure that she no longer had any real love to give to anything. She had given it all to Harrier.

Although the colours of certain details – random, glanced-upon things of no significance – were sometimes too vivid for her to bear, the world which Kelly now saw was black, and dull. Her months without Harrier had become a meaningless orbit around a distant vein of light which receded daily.

★

The following summer was the last that the Black Hand Gang would spend together at 'The Leas'. The scent of change – part excitement and part nostalgia – was affecting all the young people.

Harrier and James had both left Eton after the entrance examinations to Oxford the previous Christmas. Harrier had failed so badly that his father spent the entire spring lecturing him on what he ought to do next. It was really of little consequence, but the upshot of all the discussion was that Harrier should be 'apprenticed' to a friend of his father's who owned several large printing companies. The part-time duties there would be interspersed with managing the lesser administration of the family's property in England. For Harrier it was as though little had changed; he would simply live in London most of the time as opposed to at school. He had always felt as though he was waiting for some light to be turned on in his life, and that he had not yet found the switch. He had thought for a little while that Kelly O'Kelly might know something of its whereabouts, but eventually, with a numbness which shocked him, he had realised that she didn't.

James, it was generally thought, was becoming rather peculiar. He had suddenly transformed from a capable student into one whose name the masters would dwell upon, as if to infer 'bright'. From 'bright' he had risen to 'exceptional', and been taken under the wing of several teachers on the Classics side. He gained a place at Balliol which he would take up in the autumn.

Stella and Lucinda, slightly younger than the boys, looked on askance at the world outside of their immediate plans to get jobs and move to London together.

In the end they convinced their respective parents of the benefits to be gained by making this move. And on condition that they both found secure positions the Fortunes and the Walker-Jones would combine to help buy them a small flat in London. As Mr Walker-Jones remarked to Mr Fortune on the train: 'Such an investment with the property market as it stands would be no bad thing.'

A flat in Pimlico was found and bought. Stella, temping as a receptionist when not modelling for the 'Zero Degree' agency which Adrian Jones had recommended her to, earned slightly more than Lucinda, who was working as a floor assistant at Sotheby's, this being preferable to typing all day.

Stella had been not a little disappointed that her modelling career had failed to continue at the international level at which it had begun. She discovered from those she worked with that the majority of models spent their time demonstrating perfume in department stores or twirling in separates for massive mail-order catalogues. But Stella did get quite a lot of work, particularly for poses which required perfect legs, or backs. As yet however no avant-gardist had made full use of the beauty which Remo had detected in her scar.

Six months later the families sold the flat in Pimlico for a larger one in the Gray's Inn Road.

Lucinda, attractive fern to Stella's bouquet, began the seemingly endless task of searching for a job slightly more lucrative and interesting than the one which she had already. Some months after this she gained her position with Roebuck StJohn Maitland.

Stella had no boyfriend. Lucinda had one or two half-hearted affairs with well-bred young men who laughed too easily and whose eyes, like those of a portrait, would always follow Stella around the room whenever she happened to be in.

Thus pursued but not involved, Stella Walker-Jones began her excursion into darkness.

FIVE

'Joy Division'

The teens turn into the twenties and the fordable streams which kept youth's meadows lush grow swifter and broader until, in some vague way which weds surprise with fear, we discover that we have become more dubious about attempting the crossings from one area of life to another. We ridicule the surprise, and justify the fear by calling it sense, or prudence, but still we blunder on, ever seeking change and pursuing new desires, weighed down yearly by those habits of mind and prejudices of temperament which we wear as clumsily as an ill-fitting suit of clothes. With time we grow used to this costume, excusing its pull and bulk, until one day we say, in a rather defensive manner, that it fits us as well as any other.

Miles Harrier, by the time that he began his dalliance with Lucinda Fortune, was beginning to feel rather comfortable in his bewilderment with life. Born privileged, and never having had to face the idea (let alone the reality) of material survival, his complacency was perhaps understandable. Lucinda Fortune however, believing herself to be in love with Harrier and unaware that he had grown to test his emotions empirically, more or less just waiting to see what would happen next, was retaining the keen edge of life by sharpening it on passion.

Shortly after their dinner at Kettner's, Lucinda called Harrier at his office from her office.

'I just rang to say "I love you".'

This much had already been inferred on the telephone the previous evening and so Harrier simply swung around in his padded leather desk chair to face the window and smiled, receiver cradled beneath his chin.

'Thank you.'

'Do you have any plans for this evening because if not I think we ought to . . .'

The plan is immaterial. It was delightful and expensive and based on all the requirements most necessary to a romantic evening.

After they had rung off Harrier faced his desk again and frowned as he sipped his coffee, not looking up as he drank.

The romantic evening found Harrier and Lucinda, arms around one another, standing on the river walk outside the City of London School. With his face close to hers, Harrier was running his fingers through Lucinda's hair, every so often feeling her soft kiss above his collar. She inhaled his aftershave and slipped her hand between the buttons of his shirt, pressing her cool palm against his chest. He could feel her whole body resting lightly against him.

A tug drifted by in mid-river, silently hauling two barges. Its wash slapped gently against the embankment. The hot July night amplified the sound of these little waves and they seemed oddly disconnected from their source in mid-stream, already moving down towards Tower Bridge.

Harrier tightened his grip around Lucinda's stomach and felt the waistband of her skirt brush his wrist. She drew her arms around his neck and kissed him for a long time, her eyes closed and her mouth lingering on his. The sultry air wrapped around them and the tug sounded its siren.

'I think we should go somewhere and drink coffee,' said Harrier once the kiss was over and they had stared for a moment at the expressionless face of Bankside Power Station.

'Absolutely,' said Lucinda.

And they headed up the broad steps away from the river and started walking towards Smithfield.

The all-night cafes at Smithfield Market are ideal for

lovers in the first flush of love because they combine picturesque seediness with the romance of being open at two o'clock in the morning. All inclinations towards the cinematic are gratified within their shabbiness, and as lovers seek a loving world the messy task of meat-handling and the meat-handlers for whom the cafes were created become colourful and complicit with the scene. Trysts and confessions can be shyly murmured across thick beakers of weak tea as outside the lorries reverse and the porters call, following their nightly routine of dragging carcasses and frozen joints into the gloomy caverns of the market.

Harrier and Lucinda exchanged several such trysts and confessions over their hot drinks that night, and the upshot was their departure together for Harrier's small house in Chelsea.

Whilst they were waiting for a taxi Lucinda felt some dampness through the soles of her flat summer shoes. Later she saw the red discoloration on their white lining and realised she had been standing in blood.

★

It was unfortunate for Lucinda Fortune that without her knowing it her affair with Harrier coincided directly with his general complacency about life. His passions (as much as his emotions) had become mechanical, and whilst Lucinda may well have looked upon their relationship and seen something as unique as a four-leaf clover, Harrier – if pressed – would have had to admit, eventually, to seeing nothing more remarkable than a flurry of short-lived snowdrops or a bed of reliable alpines. The depth of his emotional slumber was extreme.

But this is not to say that he did not enjoy being with Lucinda. He found her pretty and charming. A recent addition to this condition was the fact that he enjoyed making love with her, but were any intimate friend to extract an honest version of his feelings about this coupling, deplorable words like 'nice' and 'adequate' would probably have featured high in his analysis. Is it so easy, however, to condemn a person thus caught in a routine of passions? Harrier's awareness of his feelings flickered in and out of range like a weak radio transmission late at night. There were some days when he felt an immense optimism about their future, and pieced together a mutual happiness made up from the way Lucinda looked and what they were about to eat. His thoughts, and worse, his emotions, were always informed more by circumstance than sentiment. Consequently his happiness never rang true; it was thin, and strangely elliptical, and appeared to alter in volume according to how it was seen.

The worst of Harrier's 'doubts' – if doubts they can be called – occurred at night, when he and Lucinda were in bed.

'It's so nice just to sleep beside someone,' Lucinda would sometimes say, and this, of course, is a statement that many would consider it bestial to disagree with. Harrier would nod, feigning exhaustion, and then lie awake for hours, unable to get comfortable and watching the curtains bat gently against the partially open window. After an hour or so his legs would begin to ache, and he would start fidgeting, furious with insomnia and aware of how solitary one feels when one watches another sleep.

On other occasions their day would finish with sex, but whilst Lucinda appeared to slip into a post-coital sleep of regular breathing and a luxurious stretching of limbs, Harrier, enervated as opposed to exhausted by their exertions, would frequently get up and go to watch the television in the kitchen, a haunted figure, with bath-robe, cup of tea and cigarette.

Despite all this, he began to believe himself to be in love with Lucinda. He shared with her the appropriation of coincidences as proof that a benign supernatural had blessed their relationship – moreover, they held one or two small dinner parties for their friends.

When they were about to entertain in this manner Harrier's heart sank slightly as Lucinda, happily repositioning the cruets, would say 'Katie and Hans are coming – they're really interesting.'

And then the evening would begin in earnest, domesticity vying with informed wit for supremacy as the overall mood.

Seated on the two broad sofas in Harrier's drawing room overlooking Walton Street, their condition hesitant between relaxed and overly polite, the group of diners would drink their gins and their sherries, discuss their lives and times, and then sit down to eat – witty pea soup, poached salmon and salad, the pause, cheese and sorbets. Couples affectionately poked fun at their partners, humorously raising their eyes to heaven during the little performances of disagreement and criticism which they were putting on to bond their relationship even closer whilst appearing to say 'Look! We are not dependent upon one another.'

Re-seated on the sofas they would later drink coffee, and more than one of these evenings concluded with one guest saying:

'Next time you must come and see our flat.'

And everyone would agree that this would be lovely.

It was during one such after-dinner conversation that a friend of Lucinda's read out an interesting item from the evening paper. It was a small piece, sandwiched between a competition and an article entitled 'Commuters win chance to run their own railway.' It was headlined: 'Planets going backwards cause chaos.'

Apparently astronomers were confused by the sudden reversal of certain heavenly orbits. There were, it was true, various reasons why this phenomenon should be seen to occur, but the pith of the story was a claim by astrologers that such a breach of harmony was causing untold confusion and disruption down on earth. The houses of the Zodiac were in complete disarray and, because one or two of the less benevolent planets were flatly refusing to enter into any form of concordance, all manner of terrible consequences were befalling an unprepared world. Business deals were falling through, letters were getting lost, a lake in Central Africa had mysteriously drained of its contents thus causing a drought, and the Stock Exchange was at odds with itself from dawn until dusk. Moreover, in some distant part of the galaxy, an entire rash of brand new stars had suddenly made an appearance so bountiful that observatories were at a loss to give names to them all. No one was predicting quite how long this cosmic anarchy was going to last, but informed opinion suggested a month.

The usual discussion about astrology followed the reading of this piece, with people displaying amazement that Hans, for instance, was a Gemini.

Amidst mutual goodwill, thanks and farewells, the party broke up just before midnight. As they were seeing off the guests on this particular evening, Lucinda reminded them all of her forthcoming party, at Kuzumi's, just over a week away.

★

Shortly before Lucinda's birthday, Harrier, Lucinda and Stella all went down to 'The Leas' to stay for the weekend. This visit was to prove not only significant, but also fateful.

Harrier and Stella, upon being reacquainted by their mutual old friend Lucinda Fortune, made a deep impression on one another. If one believes in Destiny, then it would seem that Destiny was at work when first the children, now grown old, approached one another for the first time after so long, self-conscious in the face of so much familiarity and so much change. Stella saw Harrier and thought 'He is the one. He is solid, and a man to trust and love. Also, he belongs to another, and it can never be.' And when Harrier saw Stella he thought 'Here is my heart's desire; here is the most beautiful girl in the world. But I belong to another, and it can never be.' This is what the two young people were really thinking as they greeted one another with smiles and formality. Harrier said 'How nice to see you again,' and Stella said 'It seems like so long . . .' And after that they tried to suppress all other thoughts, and deny the sudden relationship which had sprung up between them on first sight. But this hidden relationship, having announced itself, silently, and under the worst possible circumstances, would not go away. As Harrier and Lucinda saw more of one another, so Harrier found ways to chat for a few minutes with Stella every time he went to the girls' flat. And as his visits became more frequent so Stella became anxious to ensure that she was in when he called – hardly realising as she did so that she was beginning to prepare for his calls. When Lucinda said 'Oh Miles is calling for me at about eight,' Stella would smile, and nod, and then feel her heart beating faster. Sometimes she would go and change, pretending that she was going out herself later and thus she would look exquisite when Harrier called for his girlfriend. If Harrier and Stella were left together for a few minutes at any time, they would become slightly playful, as though luxuriating in a private language which was only theirs on the rarest of occasions. Once Stella said, 'Oh I must show Miles the aquarium – I've still got it you know . . .' and the two of them went off to her bedroom, and stood side by side in the semi-darkness, laughing and smiling at the new generation of colourful fish which darted about in the tank.

In the space of three weeks Harrier had thus started seeing one girl and fallen in love with another. He fell asleep beside Lucinda thinking of Stella, relaxed with the former and disturbed by a rich and mysterious excitement when he considered the latter.

Harrier and Stella never admitted their feelings to one

another and thus neither knew what the other was thinking. And so their silent relationship became stronger, and so both regarded it with a deep sense of poetry, all the more potent for being so clandestine.

And so Lucinda, happily in love with Harrier, and trusting her two friends completely, was both deceived and mocked by the birth of this unspoken love affair which was taking place in front of her. Why did neither Harrier nor Stella speak out? It would appear that they were too afraid, or too intoxicated with fantasy. Perhaps both of them were afraid of hurting Lucinda's feelings, but such genteel considerations could only be a mask for some deeper fear, and some deeper sense of luxury.

On that first weekend in August, as the three young people drove towards their childhood home in the early evening, they were full of the heroics common to urbanites paying a call on the provinces, and their conversation was full of laughter and plans. Turning down the sliproad which led to Bushy Lane they all commented upon how dark the sky was.

'It's going to pour,' said Harrier.

'And you would have a flashy open-topped car,' returned Lucinda.

'Make her get out and walk,' chimed in Stella.

'She only does it to tease,' replied Harrier.

Approaching the parade of shops, Harrier slowed down and turned off the car stereo. The sudden silence was strange, and the air seemed too thick to breathe. Down by the little river a deep plantation of stinging nettles and foxgloves were overhanging the water. They seemed fleshy and stupefied, the violent bells of the foxgloves drooping into a morass of furred foliage. The river gurgled between the stones on its bed, and the strands of weed which twitched in the current looked fluorescent in the twilight. A mighty crash of thunder echoed through the stillness, and soon big spots of rain were falling on the dusty windscreen of Harrier's car.

Laughing, Lucinda made a ghost noise.

The following day, Saturday, a steady rain had set in. The view to the dual-carriageway was obscured by mist, and down at the 'Coat & Coachman' people pulled jackets over their heads as they ran from the car to the bar. In the afternoon Lucinda had arranged to go shopping with her mother, and so Harrier and Stella were left alone. They located an umbrella and some boots and went for a walk.

Beneath their controlled conversation they felt guilty and light-hearted, neither making reference to their feelings. As they walked down Bushy Lane they had to keep to the centre of the road so as to avoid the two fast-flowing streams of water which were flooding either gutter. Above them the trees were dripping, and all around the countryside was grey, and sodden. They did not talk very much.

They began to walk over to the church, St Dunstan's, which stood out white against its graveyard and was surrounded by tall fir trees halfway up a grassy hill on the other side of the village. St Dunstan's was a small church, much patronised by the local community, and the remaining Norman masonry of its porch and squat tower was an historic feature of the parish. The rest of the church was eighteenth-century and heavily restored, the simple stained glass in the nave and chancel hardly letting in any light at all as the building backed (as though ashamed of itself) into the small wood directly behind it. Inside the church it was always cold and dark, whatever the time of year. The copper weathercocks, heavily stained with verdigris, would reputedly sing to one another and the Glory of God when the world was about to end. Stella was just remembering this legend when Harrier said 'Are you coming to Lucinda's party?' This question was somewhat gasped as the two of them made their way up the steep little path towards the church, both pausing to allow one another to pass by dripping brambles. 'I don't know,' she replied, walking unsteadily as the big boots which she had borrowed wobbled around the black ski-pants which encased her slender legs. 'If I possibly can I will, but I'm supposed to be going to Manchester to do some awful fashion show in a hotel. I may be back. You'll be going of course . . .?'

'Oh yes — I said I would. It ought to be rather fun. I gather they're having turns — I'm not sure what, fire-eaters and Thai boxers and so forth . . .'

'It sounds super . . .'

By now they had reached the graveyard. All around them the white tombstones clustered like freshly sprouted mushrooms in the wet grass. Beside recent black marble headstones, with little jars of flowers beneath them, older, ornate stone caskets were weathering yet another down-pour. One particular grave had a gruesome epitaph carved upon it: 'Here lies Jane Mortimer, aged 46 years, whose heart burst . . .'

Over on the far side of the place, just beneath the trees, a length of raw, copper-brown earth still decked with flowers and damp-blackened ribbons denoted a recent burial. The colours were garish against the wet earth, and the individual raindrops clinging to the long grass.

'It's odd to think that someone was buried so recently,' said Harrier. 'Somehow one doesn't feel that graves ought to be new . . .'

Stella nodded. Looking down she knelt to right a fallen jamjar which held a spray of flowers. There was a line of green mildew around the inside of the glass. Wiping her hair out of her eyes she shivered. Beneath her old raincoat she was wearing a soft black polo-neck. Harrier suddenly wanted a cigarette, and was delighted when Stella asked for one too. He hadn't seen her smoke before. Some smoke got into her eyes, and made them shine.

'Look down there,' she said.

On the road a wedding party was assembling. Holding their hats down with the flats of their hands, brightly dressed women were stepping out of cars whilst men in morning suits produced umbrellas and made jokes about the weather. Pale blue dresses, patent handbags, and the trimmed silk head-dresses of the bridesmaids, who were laughing and self-conscious in apricot-bodiced satin, made a sudden rash of colour in the rain.

Harrier and Stella began to walk away from the church again, and as they did so the sound of a carriage pulled their faces up to watch. It was the bride and her father, humorously perched in a pony-and-trap as they sheltered their finery beneath a golfing umbrella. Stella and Harrier stood to one side to allow them to pass. 'I'm sure that was Susan Henshaw,' said Stella, her attention suddenly fixed on the passing carriage.

But it was too late to tell. The little carriage, painted, polished and hung with artificial flowers had now reached the path to the church, and its occupants were climbing carefully, as if from a boat, onto the road.

As Stella and Harrier made their way back up Bushy Lane the sky seemed to lower even further, and the wind flurried the lower leaves of the trees. Down at the church, carriage and driver awaited the return procession. The patient pony stood quite still in the pouring rain, his head lowered, and as the rivulets of water trickled down the decorations on his harness he shook his mane from time to time, as if in irritation.

★

Whilst Harrier had been so preoccupied with his affairs of the heart he had completely forgotten about the unpleasant young man who had disturbed his evening with Lucinda at the Spanish bar. The young man, Chris Patterson, former lover of record producer Douglas Stanshaw, had also forgotten about Harrier. Whilst Harrier, Lucinda and Stella were dining with Mr and Mrs Walker-Jones at 'The Leas' on the Saturday night of their visit there, Chris was out in the West End with his friend David.

'I'm going to fucking kill him — that's what,' Chris shouted again, whilst nodding to himself, above the noise of the music in Adam's discotheque on the Charing Cross Road. For several hours now, his bombast fuelled on lager and pernod, Chris had been boasting about his plan to do away with his ex-boyfriend. David was beginning to weary of this dramatic tirade, and so he leant back in the corner of the booth they were sharing and began to watch the dancers. So far Chris had been paying for his attention with drinks.

Adam's was neither fashionable nor well-patronised. It was a cheap, dingy place, usually more empty than full, and run at a loss by its obscure management. The small dance-floor was overhung with a lattice of red and green lights, and the flashing beams which came from these were somehow lost in the crepuscular middle ground at which they were aimed. The bar and dance-floor were one simple oblong, surrounded on three sides by torn and cigarette-burned booths. The booths were dark, and musty, illuminated by orange lights which shone up fans of dirty chiffon which were stretched behind them over silver textured wallpaper. The club smelt of stale lager and burning. The bar had a pad of studded vinyl running along its front, and behind it there was a long mirror embossed with pictures of Hollywood stars which reflected the bottles of spirits and red ice-buckets. From a little counter in the corner, usually dark behind a closed grill, there was a place where one could sometimes buy hamburgers.

Chris had first been picked up in Adam's. That had been three years ago, much of which had been spent living with, and off, Douglas Stanshaw. Subsequent to their row in the Spanish bar, Chris had now given up all hope of support from Douglas, and it seemed taunting to him, now used to better places, that his first unfunded evenings should be spent at Adam's.

'Oh fuck, it's punk night,' said David as the music suddenly became faster and several dishevelled figures in pointed boots and ragged leather jackets began to jump up and down and shout choruses at one another.

'I hate this shit,' he continued, 'it reminds me of my shitty older brother – let's go to the pub.'

'We've only just got here and we've paid.'

'Drink's cheaper at the pub.'

'Fuck off then.'

'Look at the state of that –' shrieked David, pointing at a short girl in torn black tights and a dirty plastic mini-skirt. Her hair was black and her eyes had waxy lines drawn about them. She was standing on the dance-floor, waving a lager bottle, and snarling towards an imaginary audience as she mimed to a record.

'What a dog. Jesus . . .'

Chris wasn't interested. 'There's this bloke,' he was saying, 'and he's one of shitface's druggy mates only they don't get on. Did I tell you? He's got mates in the I R A and he was telling me he's kept guns for them and everything . . .'

David sighed. 'Oh God you're so hard . . .' he drawled, 'what are you going to do? Shoot him?' Chris looked dark and mysterious.

'I fucking would. What am I supposed to do now he's ponced off?'

'What about the money he gave you?'

'That's not the fucking point – I really hate him . . .'

'So fuck off and kill him then,' said David, 'I'm getting out of this poxy place before the smell kills me – and if you'll believe that a mate of Douglas Stanshaw's is in the I R fucking A you'll fucking believe anything . . .'

★

The druggy mate with whom shitface no longer got on was in fact none other than Ray Green, erstwhile entrepreneur within Brighton's avant-garde and now removed to

London. Ray Green's tragedy was the indifference of the public towards advanced non-commercial art. For a little while, in the late nineteen seventies, it had seemed probable that Ray was cornering a potentially lucrative slice of the entertainment market halfway between performance art and punk-rock music. Affecting a position of critical and entrepreneurial superiority, Ray had spent six months cultivating and booking various young acts and showing them in a makeshift theatre space called 'The Shed' in Brighton's Old Lanes.

He had one or two successes – with pop groups – but due largely to a lack of business acumen (and capital) he swiftly lost these fledgling stars to shrewd talent scouts from London-based record companies. Bitterness followed fast on the heels of disappointment, and as the people who sought Ray's backing became more and more obviously unsound as commercial propositions, he gradually turned to video-marketing (and small-time drug dealing) as a means of income. Finally he had a severe warning from the police about his activities, and although he was not brought to court his brush with the authorities was disturbing enough to make him give up his life beside the seaside and move to London. In London he lived with one foot in the underworld and the other floundering uncertainly above an endless stream of 'projects' – none of which ever seemed to work. It was only a matter of time (and somehow one could tell this from his grey face and trembling hands) before he would lose his balance entirely and disappear down one of those unmarked cracks which are so prevalent in the capital and out of which very few ever climb.

At the time that Chris Patterson had met him Ray was working the evening shifts behind the till at the 'Lots O' Fun' bookshop off Brewer Street in Soho. One way or another he earned enough there to rent a small bed-sitting room in Lewisham. Like Chris. Ray was much given to exaggerated stories of the violent and the illicit. It was one such story of Ray's that Chris had believed in, or wanted to believe in – about holding and obtaining guns for terrorists.

One must not underestimate how desperately Chris Patterson wanted to believe in Ray's ability to have someone killed. It is highly probable that in his heart of hearts Chris was dimly aware that Ray Green was talking nonsense when he crashed his glass down onto the bar with authority and said (affecting the cold indifference of one used to contracting international killers): 'Three hundred quid son – three hundred would have it taken care of . . .'

To not believe in Ray as a practising gangster would be for Chris to no longer have hope in anything at all, for once the lie of one loser is challenged then the many lies which support the many losers will fracture and crumble like so many eggshells. For this reason most of Chris Patterson's friends pretended to believe in one another's lies. For Chris to seek out Ray Green and ask for Douglas to be killed was therefore an act of faith.

Chris found Ray behind the counter at 'Lots O' Fun'. He was smoking a thin cigar and reading a paperback copy of *Room at the Top*. Ray looked up, saw Chris, and put his book away. He was pleased to have someone to talk to.

'Alright?'

'You?'

A young man in a beige raincoat carrying a slim briefcase walked briskly through the curtain of primary-coloured plastic ribbons at the entrance of the shop. He seemed surprised at the lack of customers and the meagre stock. He began a decisive perusal of the magazines. They were all shrinkwrapped in cellophane.

'Special offer this evening, Sir,' said Ray, 'any three for eight pounds.'

The young man nodded without looking at him.

'Been busy?' asked Chris, lighting a cigarette.

'Off my feet,' lied Ray.

The young man who had been looking at the magazines turned on his heel and left the shop.

'Pervert,' said Ray. They both laughed.

With his heart beating fast Chris brought the conversation quickly around to his request. 'Listen – you know you once said about having someone done . . .'

'Eh?'

'When we met a while back – you were saying about guns and that . . .'

Chris swallowed, lowered his voice and continued, 'Well I've got two hundred quid here and I want someone hurt . . .'

His eyes narrowed and he showed Ray a corner of the roll of notes in his jeans pocket. Ray suddenly looked hard at him, and then motioned him into the little room behind the counter. This room was brightly lit, with a powerful strip-light which hung above the sink and water-heater. There was a shard of pink soap on the draining board and a calendar with puppies on it on the wall. On the little table there was a brown teapot, a cold, half-finished mug of tea, and a packet of bourbon biscuits.

'Right . . .' said Ray slowly, scenting a fool and his money.

'Well –' (and now Chris felt important, and confident) 'I can't tell you too much but Douglas is trying to get me done on a drugs charge – and it's rubbish, he's simply trying to get rid of me . . .' Ray looked unconvinced, but nodded encouragingly.

'He's already had me beaten up,' continued Chris, clutching his shoulder as if to prove the point, 'and I want him sorted out . . .' Ray shifted uneasily on his chair, trying to work out the precise reality of the situation. Chris, fearing a lack of support, began to embellish his story. 'He's trying to get you done as well,' he babbled. 'He's told some people that you're selling heroin and . . .' Ray fought back the urge to laugh. He was now quite certain that Chris was talking nonsense. 'Bastard,' he murmured instead, 'fucking bastard – how did you find this out then?' and he began to nibble a bourbon biscuit.

'Followed, wasn't I? Beaten up – everything . . .'

Ray made a quick mental calculation. If he went along with the story and agreed to take the money offered to have Douglas 'hurt', then he could see no way in which he could either lose or endanger himself. There were no witnesses, he had absolutely no intention of harming Douglas in any way (besides which he did not have the slightest idea how such an assault could be brought about), and if anyone raised the issue later he would simply say that Chris was mad. He had in fact already decided earlier in the conversation that Chris must be mad to part with such a sum of money on such a ludicrous proposition. Two hundred pounds would get Ray to Paris, and in Paris there was a friend he wanted to see. Leaning forward he said 'Okay Chris, I can see you're in a fix. We've got to do something to the bastard – but killing . . .'

'Maiming then,' said Chris.

'I know what you mean. And I know the people . . .' And he nodded, in a hard, cunning kind of way. This sinister acknowledgement made Chris swell with pride. He felt like a Gang Baron, delegating contract thuggery to a trusted henchman. He gave Ray all his money. Ray counted it and said, 'Now listen, there's this flash party happening next week in Knightsbridge; an old contact of mine is helping with the entertainment. I'll make sure that Douglas goes along to that and we'll do it there, either when he's coming in or going out. Here's a card that'll get you in. You just watch. No more trouble from Douglas . . .'

And that is how Chris Patterson paid two hundred pounds for an invitation to a party at which he would neither be wanted nor even know anyone.

★

It was true that someone on the fringes of Kuzumi's PR team remembered Kelly O'Kelly's 'hanging off the wall' performance. It was also true that investigation at their old college had thrown up a telephone number which finally led to Ray Green as Kelly's 'agent'. Kuzumi decided that such a performance would be just the thing to decorate the party she was holding with Lucinda and the team from Roebuck StJohn Maitland. Thus it was also true that for sixty pounds (Ray kept another thirty) and her travelling expenses, Kelly O'Kelly had agreed to come down from Reading and hang off Kuzumi's wall for the evening. About Chris Patterson she knew nothing. She also knew nothing of the fact that for the first time in nearly ten years she would see, from her vantage point high above the fashionable crowd, her one and only true love – The Honourable Miles Harrier.

★

Lucinda Fortune's birthday dawned bright and golden half-way through the second week of August. Stella woke her, triumphantly bearing breakfast-on-a-tray, with Greek yoghurt, and cereal, and a little vase of freesias.

'Look at all your cards!' she said.

At work Lucinda's friends all said that they would try to come along to her party at Kuzumi's that evening. Those who wouldn't be able to attend stopped beside her desk to combine their best wishes with their explanations.

At lunchtime Harrier took Lucinda to L'Escargot. They faced one another over the spotless cloth and held hands from time to time across the table. Harrier gave her a beautiful scarf and a pair of silver earrings inlaid with a design of jet. It is possible that a vague sense of guilt had inspired him to such extravagance. On the card he wrote 'With much love, Miles Harrier', a formality which delighted Lucinda.

Teatime at Roebuck StJohn Maitland was filled with further hilarity and celebrations. A large box of cakes from

Fortnum & Mason was circulated around the little office, and two bottles of champagne. By the time that the cakes had been eaten and the champagne drunk, and Lucinda had received and given thanks for her present – a record token and a large bunch of lilies – it was time to go home.

She had arranged to meet Harrier outside Harrods at a quarter past six. First, she would go home to the Gray's Inn Road, and change. It was a beautiful evening. Making her way through the crowds and carefully shielding her lilies against the push of pedestrians less happy than she, Lucinda rejoiced to the warmth of the sun against her face and the softness of the breeze against her arms.

Kelly O'Kelly travelled down to Paddington that same afternoon. The train was dark, and half–empty. The elderly carriages had compartments, and a corridor which smelt of stale cigarette smoke. Passing through the light industrial hinterland which insulates the line heading into London, Kelly watched the brilliant sunshine reflecting off opened factory windows and the windscreens of parked cars. A line of cherry trees beside a carpark flashed by, and a tall aluminium tower with SasCo written on it. The train rumbled across points, and an old lady negotiating her way down the corridor fell against the side of Kelly's compartment. Unhurt, she moved on, seeking the buffet.

On the seat beside her Kelly had a small bag containing costume, hooks, greasepaint and safety harness. She felt – as was usual to her of late – morose. Her days had become so thin that she barely sensed their passing.

She had a vague plan to undertake a teacher-training course.

★

Douglas Stanshaw had lunched in a Spanish seafood restaurant off Charlotte Street with his friend Tosh Myers and two elderly 'single girls'. Affecting the casual weariness of veteran jet-setters, the two girls had talked about pop-music celebrities in tones which implied an intimate knowledge of them.

'I said to Rod – I said . . .'

and

'Bill's a real laugh . . .'

The girls wore fringed suede mini-skirts and high-heeled cowboy boots. They had long fingernails and, approaching middle age, the skin around their knuckles was loose.

Tosh wore a blue shirt with Dick Tracy motifs printed on it. His hair was receding at the front and long and permed at the back. His face was fat, and ruddy, and the lines about his many chins deepened into a network of black semi-circles as he called the waitress 'love' and ordered champagne.

Douglas was happy in such company. It made him feel part of the successful aristocracy who could dip in and out of the eternal party whenever they chose.

They all listened with respect when Tosh described the luxuries which had been made available to guests by a senior record executive at his villa in Cannes.

In his coat pocket Douglas had an invitation to the party at Kuzumi's that evening. When Ray had passed it on they had had a 'good laugh' about Chris Patterson's little visit to 'Lots O' Fun'.

*

At a quarter past six that evening the sky over Harrods was pale blue and soaring. The rush-hour traffic crawled in what seemed to Lucinda a good-humoured confusion; blonde ladies with large square sunglasses tried to hail distant taxis by wagging snakeskin purses at them; commuters jostled with tourists around the newsstands by the tube station. Between the towering fronts of the department stores which caught the full blow of the declining sun, the side-streets were cool and shaded. The smaller shops seemed livelier away from the main thoroughfare, as if untainted by commerce, and whilst Lucinda was waiting for Harrier she watched a pretty girl with mounds of brown hair arranging wicker chairs and satin cushions beside a window display of heavy necklaces. The girl looked like a gypsy princess tidying a caravan — haughty, remote, and graceful. Lucinda stood with her feet pressed together, her hands folded in front of her and her new scarf spread proudly over her shoulders. She was wearing her best navy-blue skirt, a new white shirt and a pair of flat blue shoes which had an intricate design of stitchwork and tiny bows upon them. Around her neck she was wearing her parents' present, a fine string of antique pearls.

It was a shame that Stella would not, after all, be able to come to the party.

When Harrier arrived he kissed Lucinda on both cheeks, took her hand and said 'Ready?' She nodded happily. After they had walked a few paces he added 'No Stella?'

On the pavement outside Kuzumi's new shop there was already a small crowd of party-goers who had sought the cool of the street in preference to the heat of the throng who were mingling inside. The company was made up of friends of Lucinda's who were there to celebrate her birthday, and a much larger quantity of assembled contacts and colleagues who were there because it was a fashionable early-evening party and champagne was being served. Reaching the edge of the little crowd outside, Lucinda was suddenly pounced upon by a girl who shrieked her name and then dragged her off to be introduced to 'some people'. Lucinda hadn't seen this girl for some time.

The gathering sucked Harrier and Lucinda into its bosom. The centre of the party was marked by a waiter holding a large silver tray upon which were standing tall frothing glasses of champagne, and shorter, less-spectacular glasses of mineral water and peach juice. The shop had been left virtually empty, its stock of garments being kept in storage until this celebration was over. The walls were bare concrete, with small chromium light-fittings. Concrete shelving – now adorned with white vases containing exquisite sprays of orchids – ran along the length of the walls. Halfway into the shop a hand-made rosewood staircase, broad and steep, descended into the equally empty basement. In the basement there were further party-goers, another waiter with another tray of champagne, and a smiling, bearded young man who was plucking oriental melodies from a harp.

Harrier met a colleague from the world of business publishing and, having lost Lucinda for the time being, engaged in speculations about the future of salesforce software.

In a gaudy knot of leather and dark glasses, Douglas Stanshaw, Ray Green and an up-and-coming music publicist were standing in one corner roaring with laughter. Their commotion caused several heads to turn, partly in concern and partly to share the joke. Nobody knew who the red-faced, angry, rather common-looking boy who began to elbow his way through the crowd towards the doors could possibly be. It was, of course, Chris Patterson, and his mind was blank with fury. He knew now that Ray had completely taken him in, and there was nothing he could do about it. When he reached the street and the smiling throng on the pavement the world seemed to be made of cardboard. A drowning sensation overcame him as he walked towards the traffic. A car hooted and its driver shouted angrily. One or two people who were watching this eccentric exit pulled faces of amazement at one another. Chris disappeared around a corner into the sunset with a terrible pain behind his eyes.

'Simply high as a kite,' murmured someone.

'I don't know where they find the money,' replied another.

For the time being London had closed once more over the head of the would-be assassin.

★

Hanging from the wall, high above the crowd, with her golden feet dangling towards the chasm created by the staircase, Kelly O'Kelly was considered by many to 'really make' the occasion. At first people took her for a mannequin, so still and controlled was her pose. Her face and hair were painted gold, as were her arms and hands and legs. She was wearing a gold lamé evening dress of archaic design, and fastened onto the wall behind her, spreading out in a luxurious span to either side, were two enormous wings made of real feathers painted gold. The wings had been made by Kuzumi, and they were (wittily enough) the only article of clothing on sale in the shop that night.

The only hint that Kelly gave to the crowd of being as human as they was to blink her eyes from time to time. On one occasion, catching a man staring at her, she suddenly smiled her brilliant smile. His reaction brought a new crowd of people to the head of the stairs to look at her. She was hanging from the highest point on the wall above the stairwell. It had taken several hours for a builder to drill and plug the brickwork to securely take the hooks for her safety harness.

As she looked down into the crowd at the men who were looking up at her, Kelly wondered into whose arms she would choose to fall if she felt she really had to. None of the upward-turned faces appealed to her. She stirred in her harness, exciting new attention.

Her golden arms were slender, the muscles on her shoulders were smooth and shadowed. Twisting her head, her golden neck took on the arch and grace of a statue. Kelly O'Kelly had never looked more beautiful.

It is difficult to assess quite what happened next.

It was Harrier who saw her first.

He was uncertain initially that it really was Kelly. The idea seemed so strange. He looked, despite himself, at the shape of her body beneath the tight *lamé* of her dress. And then he looked at her mouth, with its broad, soft curve. It had to be Kelly. He smiled to himself as to what was the correct mode of address under the circumstances. He walked down two steps so that he was directly beneath her, and then Lucinda rushed up. She was slightly drunk and laughing at a joke which she had just heard. Slipping her arms around Harrier's neck, she kissed his ear and whispered 'I love you' before moving to stand on the step beneath him and gaze up at his eyes, her arms around his waist.

Kelly O'Kelly recognised Harrier at the moment Lucinda went up to kiss him. A curious dizziness overcame her, accompanied by a tender pain in her chest. The roar of the party buzzed in her ears as she stared down at her only love. Each one of Harrier's features cut into her as she saw them again for the first time after so long. She had remembered him so clearly. He was wearing a black suit, white shirt and red tie. On his finger was the signet ring which she had once tried on and found so big. He looked slightly taller, but not much, and he had grown well into his features with age. Worst of all, Kelly looked down and saw him as her husband.

Life can be cruel and heartless and the machinery with which we attempt to function within it so frequently lacking to the task. If suicide is the act of madness then we can only assume that for a second or two Kelly O'Kelly went insane. Her momentary insanity however, must also have been mingled with determination.

Pushing her feet against the wall behind her and leaning away from her wings, Kelly made the straps of her harness tight, snapped open the buckles which had held her in safety and plummeted down the height of the building into the edge of the crowd below.

Lucinda Fortune, whom she hit, was killed outright.

At first people thought it was a stunt. Kelly O'Kelly had neither screamed nor waved as she fell. Some guests looked up and simply saw the pair of wings where the 'mannequin' had been. Some, turning suddenly at the sound of a horrified gasp, had seen a twisting gold shape flash by the concrete walls. Others, deep in conversation away from the incident, were unaware that anything had happened at all. Amongst these were the caterers, who had just begun to serve the canapés.

For Harrier the situation had not yet become clear. He had heard the gasp, stepped instinctively back, and then felt Lucinda snatch away from him. At first he looked over to the other side of the basement, expecting to see her standing there, smiling with him at something. Then he heard a noise; a heavy thud and a crack. A little way away from him the two girls were lying close together at the foot of the stairs. There was a cut down the side of Lucinda's face and a pool of blood was slowly widening around her neck and head, black against the floorboards and red upon her skirt. Her eyes were closed, the lids faintly blue. A lock of hair had fallen across her face, knocked out of place and covering her nose. She was on her side, her knees drawn up to her stomach, and she looked as though she was about to suck her thumb.

Harrier stepped forward, quite numb. A woman rushed past him and knelt beside Lucinda. From the way she was loosening buttons and feeling for a pulse he assumed she was a doctor, or a nurse. The stranger left Lucinda and moved quickly to Kelly. After a moment she said, 'She's still alive – get an ambulance, please, now . . .'

Kelly's neck was broken. Her legs were stretched out and her gold dress had ripped beneath the arms. She lay half on her back, silent. Her eyelids were flickering.

A woman nearby burst into tears and pressed herself against the person next to her. 'Oh God,' she kept saying, 'Oh God.' Her boyfriend started murmuring something about how soon an ambulance would arrive.

News of the incident was quickly reaching the rest of the party. It spread like ripples in a pond. People came crowding up to see, bringing their friends with them. Some of the guests, assuming that someone had simply fainted, were trying to keep the party spirit up by telling jokes. Nearer to the scene an emotional young man was rushing among the crowd and roughly pushing people back the way that he had seen policemen do on television. In one or two cases he got pushed back in return by angry bystanders, and so he started shouting details of the tragedy at them in order to gain obedience.

'Simon!' someone shouted. 'Simon —? If anyone sees Simon could they tell him to move his car – the ambulance won't be able to get through; Simon . . .'

As the realisation that one, of the girls was dead filtered through, the crowd gradually quietened. A hushed argument about rigor mortis was taken up by two men at the top of the stairs, their voices scientific, and connoisseur-like. 'I think you'll find that in most cases . . .'

'Shut up,' said a girl beside them.

Trying to be useful, a friend of Kuzumi's had rung Lucinda's flat to try and contact Stella. She got the answer-phone, and then didn't know whether to leave a message.

Harrier knelt down between the two girls.

'Is she with you?' said the stranger who was kneeling next to Kelly. Harrier mouthed something but couldn't speak properly. 'They both are really . . .' he said quickly, and then his voice gave way again. He knew that Lucinda was dead. He looked pleadingly into the eyes of the woman kneeling next to Kelly. The woman wouldn't look at him.

★

Kelly O'Kelly died before the ambulance could reach her. The bodies were carried out on folding stretchers under scarlet blankets. Police arrived and cleared out all of the party-goers except for a few immediate witnesses. Their radios crackled addresses and code numbers in the hushed atmosphere.

A young sergeant spoke gently to Harrier and Kuzumi. He was friendly, and took down details in a matter-of-fact manner, running over points several times. His speech seemed to be completely disconnected to the event.

Kuzumi was taken home, hysterical.

Someone stood with Harrier on the pavement, offering him all manner of assistance. Harrier couldn't really hear him, but thanked him and accepted cigarettes and a drink. The only drink was champagne. The friend had to open a new bottle.

Pedestrians and traffic slowed down as they passed by the shop, wondering what had happened. It was getting dark; there was nothing else to be done.

As Harrier stood on the pavement, deep in shock, a white saloon car with four young people in it drove slowly by. The windows were wound down and the car radio was playing loudly. Harrier saw the faces of two girls in the back of the car, and heard the blaring music, jubilant and melodic. The chorus reached his ears, swelling to crescendo, and then the car moved on again, gathering speed in the dusk.

PART TWO

'*The Power of Love*'

ONE

*'I once returned from a party of which I
was the life and soul; wit poured from
my lips, everyone laughed and admired
me – but I went away – and the dash
should be as long as the earth's orbit* ——

———————— *and wanted to shoot myself.'*

[Kierkegaard]

The death of Lucinda Fortune and Kelly O'Kelly left those
who witnessed it and those who subsequently came to
grieve for the tragedy no resources upon which to fall back
in order to make the event less disturbing – or at least more
comprehensible. The horror reached out with an icy touch
to all who had known the girls – real, and unpredictable,
calling up a hundred connecting sadnesses and laying over
them all a blanket of shock, as undeniable as snow.

For the first two days after the incident, Miles Harrier
existed in contradictory states: one hour would find him
calm, running through the sequence of events which had
led up to the tragedy, and positioning each fresh memory
into a manageable chain of impressions which he could then
balance between the two dear lives he was trying to reconcile
with death; the next would fall upon him like a venomous
shower of uncontrollable emotion – tears, helplessness and
guilt jostled in his mind without respite, like birds trapped
within a room.

Harrier suffered his losses alone, and he suffered horribly. He sent brief letters of condolence to both the Fortunes and the O'Kellys, but he knew even as he wrote them just how impotent their expressions of sympathy would be. The darkness was too great.

The funerals were to take place within a day of one another, at churches in adjoining parishes. Kelly O'Kelly was to be cremated near her home after a small private service; Lucinda would be buried at St Dunstan's. It so fell that Kelly O'Kelly was the first of the girls to be thus sent on ahead.

Harrier was not invited to the private service. Indeed, Mr and Mrs O'Kelly had scarcely been aware of their late daughter's relation to him. He did however attend the cremation, in a little red-brick chapel at the heart of a sprawling cemetery which was separated from the dual-carriageway by a high concrete wall.

On the day of the cremation the sky spread in monotonous whiteness above the low horizon as far as the eye could see. Across the road from the cemetery gates there was a short row of semi-detached houses with cars parked on the verge in front of them. Outside the gates themselves a young boy was selling bouquets of red and yellow carnations from a stand of wooden boxes overhung with a sheet of imitation grass.

Never having sought after friends, Kelly had few who could attend her funeral. Aunts, uncles and cousins, more bewildered than sad, stood in mute shock as the bearers brought in the coffin. The young man from the undertakers stood respectfully to one side of the immediate family, with a neatly furled umbrella over his arm.

As the coffin was rested in front of the mourners, Harrier tried to realise that it contained the body of Kelly O'Kelly. In a clear voice the young vicar pronounced the Blessing and a prayer. The faint noise of machinery lay beneath his words as the coffin slid slowly out of view behind a purple curtain. Harrier noticed that the curtain was frayed around the bottom.

After the service Kelly's parents stood outside to receive and thank all those who had attended.

'I'm so sorry,' said Harrier, when his turn came.

Kelly's parents nodded and smiled at him in the same mechanical way that they had done with those in the line before him.

At the back of the chapel there was a little 'Garden of Rest', like a shallow concrete pool drained of its water, and here were displayed the flowers which had been sent. Harrier saw his own tribute, a bunch of white freesias and fern. They looked strange surrounded by all the other flowers, as though they had been left there by mistake.

He turned to walk back down the broad grey road to the cemetery gates. Looking over his shoulder he saw a sudden wisp of smoke come from the crematorium chimney. The wisp turned into a ribbon and the ribbon became like silk, drifting unnoticed above the earth. It quickly disappeared into the white sky.

And then Harrier thought of Lucinda's funeral the following day, just a few miles away, on the green hillside.

In his heart he felt like a bigamist.

*

Miles Harrier had never had cause to question the sanctity of funerals. Moreover, his experience of them was limited. There had been one or two elderly relations, distant, childhood ancients from one branch of the family or another whom he had seen interred within family vaults amidst much solemnity and display of formal bearing, but never before had he been to the funeral of a friend. He was shocked by his inability to grasp the reality behind the ceremony, and the correct dispositions of grief or reflection refused to come. But there was a more disturbing development to be accounted for, and that was the manner in which his suffering at such a loss took on a transcendental quality. When his suffering became transcendental it somehow ceased to be suffering and became metaphor; a selfishness of the spirit which could neither be avoided nor redirected back towards those for whom he was mourning. The deaths made his mind light, and this lightness — he could compare it to nothing more than the slight fever which heralds influenza — seemed to double, blasphemously, as the pawn of romance, or the agent of love.

In this manner Miles Harrier approached Lucinda Fortune's funeral with all the sense of guilt traditionally ascribed to an unfaithful husband taking his wife flowers in hospital. He tried to believe that he had no reason to feel thus, but even as he made the ascent up the path towards St Dunstan's in the summer sunshine he felt that the eyes of all the other mourners were upon him, and pronouncing him unworthy to be among their number.

The funeral was to take place at eleven o'clock in the morning. From a quarter to eleven the church bell had been tolling a steady chime; the sadness of its sound mingled with the breeze in the treetops and drifted with the woodsmoke which overhung the little residential valley.

There were many people present in the churchyard, moving towards the freshly dug grave in small family groups. The mourners walked with short steps, halfway between a formal procession and a stroll. Some walked with eyes lowered, barely acknowledging subdued greetings. Others looked purposefully ahead, as if trying to deny death, or explain their faith, by confronting the scene directly.

Harrier saw James — whom he had not seen for some years — standing beside Stella and Mr and Mrs Walker-Jones, but they were on the other side of the grave from him, too far away to join.

The vicar stood with his prayer book, hands folded in

front of his fluttering black-and-white robes, waiting to begin the service. He was middle-aged, with silver hair and glasses; a popular local figure whose attitude was precisely that which his parishioners required of him. He was both dignified and comforting, cheerful at christenings and solemn at funerals. He coached the young towards Confirmation and counselled those about to be wed. He lived alone, and he had been deeply shocked on hearing the tragic and unusual circumstances which surrounded the death of Lucinda.

The burial seemed far more terrible than the cremation which had preceded it. The sunlight shining onto the coffin appeared to be forced away unkindly by its lowering into the ground. It was as though Lucinda was being abandoned by all those present, and that now she would be lonely, remaining forever, cold and friendless, in the little graveyard away from her home.

For an instant Harrier felt himself wanting to cry out, and have Lucinda reclaimed from the earth; that it was all a mistake, that he at least would never leave her . . .

★

Over the course of the following week the lightness which had taken Harrier over began to intensify. During the long days, with their curiously protracted sunsets, the two deaths began to grow closer, and become one, and as their darknesses pressed together so a ray of white light was squeezed between them, obscuring the memory of the graveside scene with its glare.

Excusing himself from work and unable to remain for long periods of time in his house, Harrier went for long walks, often staying out from morning until late at night. He felt weightless, and unattached, neither needing, nor wanting, to speak. He would return home exhausted, and then sit smoking for hours on the sofa in the drawing room.

His sense of unreality was acute. As the days passed by he began to realise that a terrible need had arisen inside him, one so strong and lacking in compassion for all that had taken place that he felt horrified by its presence. The truth of this need finally made itself clear as he walked through Vauxhall one night. There was a massive scattering of stars, and a warm breeze was blowing off the river. The night was quiet, and as Harrier felt the warmth wrap around him and watched the cars glide noiselessly beneath the lights, he was suddenly possessed of a deep sense of happiness. He was free to fall in love with Stella. The deaths had brought them together.

She had stared into the black oblong with expressionless eyes, pale with grief. As she bowed her head her golden hair had fallen in a lustrous wave about her neck. Some loose strands had fallen against her cheek, and she had gently stroked them behind her ear. Her eyes had seemed like black velvet, registering an unselfconscious gravity, full of sorrow, and beauty. And then Harrier's thoughts moved on, and he remembered how her lips had been painted the palest of pinks, and how against the pallor of her skin their shape had seemed to be one of trembling softness. She had worn a dark grey suit, buttoned up to the neck and belted at the waist, its severe cut flattering her body.

Harrier tried to turn his thoughts away from this image of Stella. He tried to think of Lucinda's body in the coffin, and of Kelly's ashes, grotesque in some meaningless jar . . . It was no use, the light had snapped on in his mind, and all that he could dwell upon, or take with him as he walked, was the thought of Stella's beauty; young, alive, and unbearably desirable. The distance between Harrier and Stella Walker-Jones was no more and no less than the width of two graves.

★

After Lucinda's funeral Stella remained with her parents at

'The Leas'. She wept a great deal, and asked her father to tell Mr Fortune that she would really rather not stay on at the flat in London. She wondered how Harrier was coping, but was afraid to ring him up.

In the midst of her misery the modelling agency telephoned with some offer of work. Stella turned them down on the grounds of ill health. There were, agreed the girl from the agency, a lot of nasty things going around.

★

Of all the people who had been at Kuzumi's party, the one who had anticipated a death – or at least a nasty accident – was Chris Patterson. It was perhaps ironic that embarrassment and anger had therefore driven him away from the scene of the tragedy before the tragedy could happen. It was also doubly ironic that when the Grim Reaper had struck he had shown not the slightest interest in Douglas Stanshaw, but rather – for reasons best known to Destiny as opposed to Vengeance – made off with two girls whom Chris had never heard of. Having been cheated of sensation by this turn-out of events, Chris Patterson was left with just over nine pounds cash in his pockets and nowhere to sleep.

Initially, his fury on leaving the party pursued only by mocking laughter had rendered him insensible to the reality of his plight. Turning towards South Kensington tube station he had located the nearest off-licence and bought a half-bottle of whisky. As he wished above all else to distance himself from the scene of his humiliation (he was by now possessed of pure hatred for the whole of the Royal Borough of Kensington & Chelsea), Chris then boarded the tube for Leicester Square and sat with his bottle, sometimes nursing it upon his lap and sometimes taking greedy swigs. The few people travelling with him in the carriage did their best not to catch his eye. When they thought he wasn't looking, however, or when they lowered their eyes from the tableaux of adverts directly above his head, they did look at him, and then they looked with disgust and disdain.

It was not simply the fact that Douglas had survived the evening, it was the fact that Ray had obviously betrayed the deal in the lowest possible way – by treating it as a joke. Lurching towards the doors of the train at Leicester Square, Chris shoved his way roughly through the boarding passengers.

'Look out,' said someone.

'Fuck yourself,' replied Chris.

And so even as a girl whom he had never heard of was falling to her death in another part of London, Chris was standing once more at the junction of Leicester Square and the Charing Cross Road, watching the passers-by. The usual crowds were crossing and re-crossing the road; the same shops were selling the same cigarettes, and ready-made sandwiches, and postcards. Behind and between the cinemas, evening pedestrians were strolling in their shirtsleeves, holding hands with girls, and calling ahead to separated members of their parties to be sure not to miss the restaurants they were looking for.

Chinatown bustled with brilliance, its decorated precincts heavily overhung with the hot, sweet smell of cooking. Towards Shaftesbury Avenue a traffic jam was forming, and at Cambridge Circus someone screamed as a motorbike jumped the lights.

Chris walked pointlessly towards Soho, with his bottle in his pocket. He looked at some cafes but wasn't hungry. The pavements were crowded with people all on their way somewhere. One could tell that they had money by the unconcerned way that they walked; the world – assumed Chris – was their oyster. He despised all of them.

As he drank the whisky his hatred intensified. He decided to go to 'Lots O'Fun' and wreck it. On arriving there he saw two large men sitting behind the counter. He loitered in the entrance for a while.

'Any three for ten pounds,' said the man closest to the shelves. 'Special offer tonight.'

Chris left, his courage drained, and wondered whether David would be at Adam's.

Chris had never been a pleasant person – his earliest non-sexual fantasies had been to do with a kind of glamourised bullying – and two years of living off someone too weak and too afraid of loneliness to protest against exploitation had made him believe that anyone could be exploited. Written into this belief was the supposition that should objections be raised to the process of exploitation, then threats tinged with violence were the best means to expedite obedience. Ray's treachery had now altered this formula. Now, believing himself alone and betrayed, Chris determined to turn outlaw. The drawback to his scheme – and the one which he did not want to face – was that in order to survive in London one must have both money and a direction. Chris had neither of these things, so he went to Adam's discotheque to see if David was there.

★

David was not at Adam's nor at 'The Spice of Life' pub, nor waiting outside Heaven for someone to slip him in. This discouraged Chris.

Having walked back up Villiers Street – that dark gutter beside the old Charing Cross Hotel where it seems the homeless are swept like so much human effluent – Chris stopped beside the Strand and bought himself a baked potato with some chilli sauce in it. The potato wouldn't keep still in its polystyrene box as Chris tried drunkenly to fork bits of it into his mouth. When he did obtain a mouthful it burnt him, and then a man walked quickly by and knocked the whole meal out of his hands. Potato, box, and filling lay face down on the pavement, the brick-red chilli sauce steaming beside Chris's foot. Disgusted, he looked up at the stars, seeking cleaner air. The black bulk of the station stood out against the indigo of the night sky. The rest of the city would carry on, living its life, but the only reality for Chris was four pounds in cash and a few half-remembered telephone numbers. Feeling sick he sat on a bench and put his head between his knees. A man wearing a blackened and vile-smelling coat came and sat down next to him. His trousers flapped above his thin and injured ankles, his shoes were white with urine stains. With an incoherent, jocular mumble, he stretched out his hand for the bottle in Chris's pocket. Feeling faint, Chris let the man take it.

'Got a cigarette?' said the man. 'Smoke?'

'Fuck off,' said Chris, and walking unsteadily made his way in search of a quieter bench. He tried to boost himself with the thought that at least he had finished most of the whisky before the tramp could take it.

★

Whilst Chris was feeling unwell on the bench beside Charing Cross station, Ray Green and Douglas Stanshaw were sitting together over a Vietnamese meal, discussing the dramas of the evening. 'That was really terrible – I mean, like shocking . . .' said Ray, bending forward to bite into a spring roll.

'Yeah – he looked really silly; his face . . .' replied Douglas, pensively stirring a piece of basil into some sauce. His appetite had deserted him; he felt guilty about Chris and sickened with shock by the accident which had followed.

'I meant those girls . . .'

'Did one of them really die? I didn't see properly . . .'

'Some guy told me they both did. There was blood everywhere downstairs; the thing is . . .' (and here Ray paused, as if the thought had only just occurred to him) 'I knew the girl who was hanging off the wall, I mean, technically I was her agent. Hadn't seen her for years though; it was just a one-off kind of thing . . .'

'Why did she fall?'

'She jumped on purpose. Loads of people said they saw her undo the belt thing . . .'

'She must have been on something – thought she could fly perhaps . . .'

'I don't know . . .'

They sat silently for a moment, sipping their lager and watching the waiter place hot-plates between them. The restaurant was hot and busy.

'Braised prawn,' said the waiter, lifting the lid off a dish to show them, 'chilli beef; chicken and lemon grass . . .' he continued. The steaming dishes of food looked enormous to Douglas. He knew he wasn't going to eat anything. 'Special rice,' finished the waiter. 'Enjoy your meal.'

'Two more lagers as well,' said Ray. 'What do you think Chris'll do?' he added.

'Oh – stay with his mate David I suppose. He spent half the time with him anyway – thought I didn't know. That's what really makes me mad . . .' (Douglas had long ago slipped into the habit of using Americanisms to express sentiments or ideas he felt self-conscious about.) 'I mean, like, I knew things were all over – we always ended up having a fight, but this last few months it was just terrible. He went from bad to worse. Like, if we went out he was acting like a spoiled child and if I told him to fuck off he acted like he was a maniac or something . . .'

'I reckon he's got a screw loose,' said Ray.

'No – he's all right, really. He's very young . . .'

'Yeah – he's young,' agreed Ray apathetically. He was trying to gauge when would be the best time to ask Douglas for a loan.

But Ray never got the chance to ask Douglas for a loan. Douglas had been feeling nauseous ever since they first entered the restaurant. He hadn't really wanted to come anyway. Now, slightly drunk and experiencing sharp, stabbing pains in his stomach, he knew he was going to be ill. He went off to the toilets. In the toilets there were two little boys and a little girl. They seemed to be playing a game.

'Excuse me,' said Douglas, and he locked himself in a cubicle.

Fifteen minutes later he returned to the table looking white.

'Oh – I'd better go – feel wrecked.'.

'Is everything satisfactory?' asked the manager.

Giving Ray some money towards the meal, Douglas set off in search of fresh air.

The night was humid. He walked slowly down Kensington High Street with his metal attaché case dangling limply by his side. A row of white mannequins awaiting new outfits were standing in a shop window, their armless and headless bodies caught in brilliant light. Douglas thought about Chris, and about the young music publicist who had come to Kuzumi's. Douglas would soon be forty-seven. A young boy slid past him on a skateboard. He was wearing expensive baggy jeans and a large, snow-white T-shirt which he wore untucked. He had greased-back black hair and a tan. Douglas smiled. It was the kind of thing he liked to see. Chris had seemed like that to him once, when they first met. He'd been so impressed by all the pop stars that Douglas knew, or affected to know. The evening after they had seen David Bowie drinking with some friends in a club they had had the most exciting and satisfying sex. It had all been fine – and then Chris had started to become irritable, and impossible to please. Nothing was ever right then. Initially, Douglas had believed that if he stayed on his best behaviour – in other words, done, worn and said only the things which he knew Chris liked to do, see and hear – then everything would be all right. It wasn't. His best efforts resulted only in mockery or a fight. And all the time Chris had seemed to become more beautiful. He exchanged his provincial awe and awkwardness for a certain metropolitan style, even wearing suits (which Douglas bought) from all the best places, rock'n'roll places, in the King's Road.

Douglas wondered where Chris was now. He missed him.

In the window of a sportswear shop across the street there was a giant tennis ball containing a television set; on the screen a brown hand was clutching a racket, practising strokes, again and again. It would carry on doing this until dawn, when the time-switch went off.

★

The time has come to speak of James Walker-Jones, that obscure figure residing at Whitehall Court Mansions.

By the time that his beautiful sister's best friend was so tragically killed, James Walker-Jones was nearly twenty-eight years old, a graduate of Balliol College, Oxford, and the only member of the little group of childhood friends who paused to consider whether Lucinda Fortune had been struck down by accident or murdered by a work of art – it was the sort of ethical conundrum which he enjoyed.

Upon leaving Eton, James had experienced several differ-ent kinds of ambition. When he was twelve he had been happy to play the role of the slightly surly elder brother, yet was in truth warm-hearted, and affected a chauvinism which he was far from possessing. He enjoyed the games of his sister and her friends, even though he considered it good form not to. At fifteen he was merely full of Eton. He became the full-time schoolboy, with time only for fixtures, college gossip and the rarefied and self-referential webs of intrigue and school controversy which held the attention of his immediate circle.

At this time he was unbearable to his sister, and it was only when he made firm friends with Harrier and discovered that Harrier rather liked Stella and Lucinda that he began to reappraise the family circle with a new eye.

And then Harrier met Kelly O'Kelly, and James felt let down. He saw the world of girlfriends and parties begin to intrude more and more into what he had hitherto assumed to be a sacred male preserve of Eton snobbery and Eton men, and so he turned to books. At seventeen he began to wolf down the A–level Classics syllabus in a manner which his contemporaries found rather sweaty and bourgeois ('Oh James – you're so . . . keen . . .' people would sigh, suspicious of his fervour). Then he went all out to become a member of Pop as soon as possible. He loved the school traditions, and the niceties of uniform and dress code, and he found it an immense sadness that the divisions which had once reigned between rival houses and the ranks of the school hierarchy were slowly beginning to close into a kind of general modernist bonhomie. He was doubly distressed that his aristocratic friend seemed quite prepared to look forward only to a time when he could ask various home-counties and suburban beauties to go skiing with him without the inconvenience of returning to school. Harrier regarded Eton as an unavoidable sojourn between eras of greater comfort.

It was therefore with a certain degree of bitterness that James left Eton for Oxford, determined to choose his friends more carefully.

At Oxford he caught aesthetics in much the same way as others might develop a skin complaint. His being itched with the desire to understand perfect form, and 'meaning'. He sought for truth by underlining things in books, and when this failed to stimulate he would go and consider a fragment of Greek pottery, or a piece of Roman frieze. Truth remained elusive, but James began to find a new ambition – that of being the celibate aesthete, the connoisseur of beauty; the one who would sit at the dinner table, acting twice his age, and carefully press his fingertips together before making some shrewd and ironic comment (murmured whilst staring at the Stilton) about the minutiae of some artistic point.

He detested the contemporary with a passion. His sole desire was to become a Fellow, and then a don, and spend his life relaying his cold enthusiasm for Palladio to a lecture hall full of tweed-jacketed students, some of whom he would dine with later, in a correct, manly environment of Jacobean panelling and candlelight. He wasn't clever enough to become a Fellow, and the students in tweed jackets were more interested in careers in the City and girls than debating the history of perspective, so he went down with a creditable Second and wondered what to do next.

In a rather self-conscious way he tried to ape Harrier once more and become a 'man-about-town'. This failed. He found plenty of girls who aroused his feelings but none who shared his interests in the Classical. It was a sad irony that the one girl (her name was Diana and she was struggling with her Masters at Birkbeck) with whom he did enjoy an hour's conversation at a British Museum sherry party was already engaged to an expert in Etruscan funeral rites. Bowing to a superior talent, James abandoned the search for sex.

He became one of those rather pathetic figures who can always be seen in the foyers of concert halls and museums; those who invariably carry a plastic bag, with a copy of *The Times* in it, and some leaflets from the London Coliseum. In raincoats and college scarves, this legion of the lost consume cheap pasta before the opera, and harbour silent grudges against those who have less need to take Dvořák, or Turner's watercolours, too seriously. They consume culture also, in ordered slices, working by day at jobs they detest, and spending their lonely nights finally trying to get to grips with Italian, or ringing reviews in the listings magazines. These scholars are frequently asexual, managing a social life which makes no allowance for partners. Some are possibly homosexual, others not; either way it is of no importance – art has replaced the flesh.

James Walker-Jones got a job classifying doctoral theses in one of the London University libraries. He also managed to find what he called 'good digs' with a rich Etonian friend of similar dusty interests. The friend was called

Charles Hayworth (James would still call him 'Hayworth Maximus'), and together they held dinner parties. The only thing which held James back from fulfilling his desire to be a leisured man of culture was the fact that he had to work, and he got around this by pretending out of office hours that he didn't. He would wheel his bicycle down Jermyn Street, pausing to buy cheese, and then he would go over to the 'proper' delicatessen in Brewer Street to buy olives and coffee. It was a compromise for a man with such eighteenth-century ambitions, but cynics could point out that it was a fairly comfortable compromise. What with the opera, and the Park Lane antiques fairs, and the after-dinner conversations comparing the Prado to the Vatican Library, he got by.

Of all the things which James found hard to understand, his sister was the hardest. Whilst being quite naturally insensitive to the aura of her beauty, James found Stella's chosen way of life quite impossible to appreciate. He would see her sometimes in adverts, pouting through a mist of typographical devices or lying sensually across the bonnet of a car wearing a swimming costume. He alone had predicted that Miles Harrier would one day fall in love with her.

'They complement,' he said, making a compressing gesture with his hands, 'they – sympathise . . . externally . . .'

James shared his sister's good looks, but he was swiftly putting on weight. He was of medium build, with a pale, strong face. His jaw was square and solid, and his eyebrows expressive, winged with tufts of golden hair. His naturally curling hair was clipped into a sensible county trim, and his blue eyes expressed masculine self-assurance, whilst also watering slightly. His hands were rather slight in proportion to the rest of his body, and whilst he was beginning to look plump as opposed to 'well-filled-out', his legs were decidedly thin.

Although James could quite easily have been called 'handsome', the overall image of his looks seemed to deny sexuality in exactly the same way as his sister's body did nothing but express it.

When Lucinda died, James was sorry for his sister because he knew how difficult she found it to make 'real friends'. Other than this it was the aesthetics of the tragedy which engaged him: the battle 'between art and life'; and from his position on the sidelines it was possibly quite easy to see the war of form and feelings as a largely bloodless conflict.

★

Two months after Lucinda's funeral, towards the end of October, Harrier decided to invite James and Stella Walker-Jones to his house for dinner. It was Stella whom he really wanted to see. Over the weeks he had frequently looked at the telephone, and rehearsed the dialling of her number, but he had always been defeated by the warm sensation of nervousness in his stomach which accompanied his thoughts about her. He believed himself to be in love with her, more than this, he had determined to marry her, and he was frightened by the scale of his ambition. As he rolled the concept around in his mind he knew that the whole idea was barbed with unbearable comparisons and potholed with unmanageable memories. He wondered – not for the first time – whether he was simply shallow.

But something, a demon perhaps, drove him on, strengthening his determination, structuring the scene, rehearsing the conversation, and offering a tantalising array of outcomes. In the end Harrier decided to advance masked, and so he dialled James's number, aiming for the romantic via the social.

James, a socialite of sorts, was enthusiastic about the dinner party.

'I think it's a marvellous idea,' he said. 'It'll help to clear the atmosphere a bit. I mean we've all got to face one another sooner or later, and I know that Stella's just been staying with mother and father . . . do you want me to ask her or will you do it?'

'It's all right thank you – I'll speak to her. If there are any problems I'll get back to you . . .'

'Righty-oh; well, see you on the sixteenth, then . . .'

When Stella was called to the telephone by her mother, her voice sounded distant and slightly frightened.

'Hello . . .?'

'Stella – Miles . . .'

'Oh, hello – how are you . . .?' The question was asked with genuine concern, for in the depths of Stella's sadness she had thought frequently of Harrier and wondered how he was coping with the appalling situation into which Fate had plunged him. Harrier had guessed this concern.

'Oh – I'm fine.' (He had determined that the best way for him to address the past when speaking with Stella was to simply never mention it.)

'And you?' he asked.

'Well . . .' Her tone implied that the question was best left unanswered.

'I know, there's nothing one can say . . .'

There was a pause.

'Mmm –' said Stella, thinking Harrier terribly brave.

Harrier strengthened the tone of his voice, introducing a practical edge to his suggestion.

'Listen, I've just got off the phone to James, and we . . .' (the 'we' was a lie which inaugurated an epoch)' . . . were thinking that it would be a good thing to all meet up for dinner; I mean we've got to face one another sooner or later, and so I was going to suggest that the two of you come here for dinner on November sixteenth . . .? Would you be free? Would you like to come . . .?' (And here Harrier made his voice sound cheerful and appealing.) Stella paused for a second (she was thinking about what to wear), and then said that she would like to come. She accepted the invitation in tones of gratitude which suggested that she felt herself lucky to be invited. This, whilst filling Harrier with joy, also made him feel that he was dealing with a complete stranger, or someone entirely vulnerable to whatever strategy of entertainment he might offer.

'You're down with your parents yes? So you'll get the train to Paddington? Why don't I collect you from the station at about six and then we'll come back here – James is coming for about seven-thirty, so we can eat all the crudités or something . . .' (The little joke seemed to close his mind to the precise nature of the situation which he had conjured up.)

The arrangements were thus confirmed. Stella would look forward to coming; she thanked Harrier again for the invitation.

It must now be said that Stella was by no means unaware of the rearranging of positions which the dinner party would create. She had spent the last twelve years of her life being asked out by one man or another, and her experience in dealing with these requests had left her with little gullibility as regards the coarser workings of the male mind. She knew that the dinner party was a sociable overture in minor key to the broader notes of seduction, but then, she had been secretly in love with the Honourable Miles Harrier for the past three months, and nothing that could follow his dinner party would equal the jealousy which she had felt for the girls more assured than she who had, at one time or another, 'been out' with him. She assumed Miles Harrier's past conquests to be legion; this was not true – Harrier had had but two girlfriends. The peculiarity of his situation was that the first had killed the second, thus realising a figure of speech which has punctuated many less spectacular genealogies of love.

★

November the sixteenth was a Saturday. In the parks the

trees were losing their leaves, and although the sky was blue a strong wind was roaring. Bright sunshine bathed the white terraces of Chelsea, and by mid-afternoon long orange shadows were falling across Belgrave Square. Harrier spent the morning happily arranging his dinner party. He bought a chocolate mousse cake from South Audley Street, and collected the terrine of crab which he had had prepared locally. He bought two bottles of fine Chablis, and as a nod to James invested in some collectable port. Then he bought flowers, and bottles of mineral water, and made sure that his dinner table was polished and buffed to a reproachless lustre. He also recalled the dinner parties which he had held with Lucinda. He wondered whether he was remembering them fondly, like a well-adjusted widower, or whether he was far from regretting their absence, like a man recently divorced, enjoying the freedom to recast himself as a libertine. He tried to be honest with himself and failed; the light and the dark refused to resolve.

Soon it was time to go and pick up Stella.

Stella had spent the afternoon in extensive preparations for the success of her evening. She did not know quite what sort of success it was that she was hoping for.

She bathed, and did her hair. She tended to her face with the most subtle of cosmetics. She selected a fine suit, in a blue which looked black with the finest of pinstripes, and a white shirt. And then she put on new shoes, in black suede, the heels of which she knew adjusted her to exactly the height she wanted to be. At the last moment her courage deserted her, and she imagined herself being caught in a downpour, and she sat on her bed to cry.

Without warning the crying grew worse, and her sobs attracted her mother, who came and sat beside her, holding her hand and saying nothing.

'It will do you good to get out,' said Mrs Walker-Jones. 'You can't just hide up here all the time . . .' Stella nodded, and wiped her nose without saying anything.

'I look so terrible,' she said.

'You've always said that – you know it's not true. You look lovely. Would you like Daddy to run you to the station?'

Stella nodded.

'Give our love to Miles,' said Mr Walker-Jones, as he dropped his daughter by the picturesque little railway station. 'Poor fellow – he must have had quite a rotten time of it . . .'

At the station Harrier greeted Stella with a frank handshake to imply the birth of a new era, and a kiss on both cheeks to acknowledge intimacy. Conversing politely they then drove on towards the house in Chelsea which Harrier had prepared so skilfully for their pleasure.

*

At a quarter to seven, wearing a dark blue suit, college tie and black topcoat, James Walker-Jones set out from Whitehall Court Mansions (so conveniently hidden between the Ministry of Defence and the river) and set out across St James's Park with a firm stride. He tapped the ground with his tightly rolled umbrella as he walked along, but tinged this rather military bearing with a touch of the aesthete; a man receptive to both art and nature, on solid ground with the Old Masters and quite possibly fluent in Italian. Luckily for James, no one who passed by him in the darkness would have possibly guessed that he was an assistant librarian.

Walking down Buckingham Palace Road towards the dirtier streets around Victoria Station, he tut-tutted inwardly at the sight of a bedraggled youth begging for change. 'Probably spend it on drugs,' he thought, as he pressed a pound coin into the boy's hand. James was not insensitive to the plight of the homeless, but he regarded their misfortune with a patrician sense of responsibility towards the poor which was an echo of Victorian philanthropy. At Oxford he had once thundered on the subject, seeing himself as a descendant of the great social reformers: 'Neither political wing is correct on this subject,' he had concluded. 'Politics is a game played by the well-fed to ensure that the hungry remain numerous enough to be argued about . . .' He had been proud of this minor tirade, but for fear of losing face with the classicists and art historians he had been sure not to say too much about it. Instead he always gave generously to charities because he liked to give – moreover, it was the 'drama' (sometimes it seemed like a romance, sometimes less so) of destitution which touched him. He did wonder, though, at the increasing number of beggars that he came across, and it worried him.

However, feeling that he had paid for the luxury of his evening in advance, James Walker-Jones arrived at Miles Harrier's house punctually at seven-thirty.

*

A pretty face is little more than banal, yet its form becomes a truth to one who believes it beautiful. When questioned about the nature of this truth, the lover may well answer that he has found a beauty which is the residence of bliss, and that this, at least, is a truth he believes inviolable. Questioned further about the nature of the bliss, the lover can only refer one back to the beauty, and this he does rather helplessly, as if dealing with the partially witted. It is a powerful constellation of emotions, kept alive by desire, and at the outset it will permit no impediment.

By the time that James arrived for dinner, Harrier had spent just over an hour drinking in Stella's prettiness and believing it to be beauty. She had shown a great interest in his home, moving from room to room on the 'guided tour' with a respectful admiration for what she saw that made her enthusiasms – breaking, as they did, through immense reserve – seem all the more intimate and precious. Her attitude was that of one privileged to visit, and this, of course, was flattering. When she singled out various features for special comment she did so in a way that made Harrier feel as though he was getting closer to her. She appeared to want him to take the lead in the planning of her visit; she presumed nothing, and agreed to all his suggestions – where they should sit, what they should drink, whether it was time to take one thing out of the fridge and put another into the oven. In all this there was the suggestion of a greater complicity, yet on the surface there was an innocence which denied the existence of deeper forces being at work. She seemed to give pre-prepared answers to his questions, like an obedient child, and this made her moments of spontaneity appear to be of a far higher value than those formulated and practised witticisms so effortlessly offered up by the more socially self-assured. When she pointed to her scar, and made a humorous reference to its origin, Harrier felt as though he was being permitted a glimpse of heaven. Every degree that she relaxed he regarded as an honour; every slight loosening of her reserve (placing her drink on the floor beside her as opposed to holding it in her lap) he found as exciting as a lapse of modesty. Innocence and gravity made themselves far more effective agents of Stella's beauty than any particularly alluring or daring clothes she might have worn.

And so Harrier pressed on. He had wanted this situation to come about, had planned it with precision, and now he gave himself over to slipping beneath its surface.

Stella too was contributing to the supremacy of the moment. Her love for Harrier had hitherto been academic, a benign fairy-story against which to compare the fragility of her daily life. Beneath her reserve she had determined to cut loose from the fear, distaste, or indifference with which she had regarded other potential lovers. In a sense, the Honourable Miles Harrier was already on probation within Stella's scheme of things – a fallible male, pitted against the flawless double of himself who had triumphed over all adversity in Stella's fantasies.

The entrance of James did little to subdue their subtle idyll. He shook hands with both of them – a formality which gave rise to their first shared private joke – and then he plumped himself down on the sofa to begin running through the agenda of conversational topics which he had drawn up during his walk.

The first of these touched accidentally upon Lucinda. He had not meant to make this error, but having launched enthusiastically into a list of operas which he had recently seen, the story of Don Giovanni was raised and out of that some observations on the supernatural.

'Of course, I always maintained . . .' (and by now he was expansive with magisterial rhetoric) '. . . that our own Lucinda was possessed of the gift of premonition; the ability to foresee, and that this was both her blessing and her curse . . .'

His voice trailed away and he looked embarrassed. A second later his apologies were adding further layers of pain and awkwardness to the already crowded moment. 'I say – I'm frightfully sorry, I didn't think – I mean, I didn't mean . . .'

'That's all right,' said Harrier, 'I'm sure Lucinda wouldn't mind . . .' And having thus extracted a cheerful forgiveness from the recently deceased which was as bogus as it was unlikely, Harrier steered the conversation back to the subject of theatre, commenting *en route* that he had not attended anything like the number of performances that he had meant to. Stella, now sitting on the floor with her back resting against the sofa, gave a nod of agreement.

James began talking about the difficulties of staging contemporary productions of Classical drama.

'Take Aristophanes for example . . .' And so they took Aristophanes, and quietly sat down to dinner with him.

Satire, maintained James, had become corrupt, exchanging artistry for low punches and well-observed detail for ludicrous sensation. Harrier disagreed, he thought that violent satire was the sign of a healthy state.

'Take *Private Eye* for example . . .'

And so the two young men discussed *Private Eye*, first finding fault with inaccurate journalism and then quoting particular favourites from its contents because they enjoyed to hear them spoken.

Stella smiled with them, and laughed at their recitations. She had little interest in either satire or the state but she knew the men were enjoying their conversation so she let them continue. All the time she was observing them with an attention to detail which neither suspected. She thought her brother entertaining, but could still detect the schoolboy in him, playing the grown-up and relishing eccentric opinions secondhand. Harrier was more graceful. His style of speech was breathless, and slightly clipped; a voice which seemed to flatten the ends of sentences into delightful assumptions. He would frequently finish a statement with the words 'Don't you agree?' and this interrogative ending would be spoken with coercive charm, as if expressing concern that one might disagree whilst registering pleasure that one felt the same way. Stella began to think that Harrier's voice was the magnet which made him so attractive.

The hours passed in elegant procession, neither dragging their feet nor rushing; time made ordered progress, respectful of conversation and digestion alike. The four thin, white candles gave just the correct amount of ambience, and course followed course in a delicious but unobtrusive pageant of tastes and colours. When it was time for the port all three of the diners were in that pleasant condition wherein good humour and warmth coexist with intelligent lucidity. It is the aim of all dinner parties to achieve this balance, but few succeed, and it must be said that Harrier himself was proud of the outcome which he had supposedly brought about to the evening. He privately attributed this success to Stella, whom he saw as the presiding genius of the occasion, but he was far too polite to say such a thing out loud.

Just after midnight the party broke up, Stella leaving with James to stay at Whitehall Court Mansions.

'Well I have enjoyed myself Miles,' said James, as he hunched his arms into his overcoat. 'We musn't leave it so long next time; call me for lunch – I know you're a man of leisure . . . ' (The little joke was, at all events, a good note to conclude upon.)

'Absolutely,' said Harrier. 'And Stella – we must go and see that play . . .'

'I'd love to . . .'

'How are you fixed? Do you want to arrange it now?' And before she could answer he went to collect his diary.

'What about . . . the twenty-second; wait a moment, that's next Friday – no, that's all right for me – what about you?' But the preliminaries had been unnecessary; for Stella was not working at the moment, and any time was convenient for her.

'I'm afraid I wouldn't be able to put you up,' chipped in James. 'You see, we have our debating group on Fridays, and it's our turn to do the wine . . .'

'Oh . . .' murmured Stella. Harrier was thrilled to detect genuine disappointment in her voice. 'Well, there's plenty of room here,' he said, as though chancing upon a happy solution. 'You don't sleepwalk or anything do you . . .?'

'No.' (Laughter.)

'Well, that's fixed then . . .'

'All right – I'll bring my bag !'

'Splendid.'

And so Harrier and Stella continued to follow the course which they had both determined to pursue no little time ago, when the world had seemed rather different.

★

'The Master Builder', at the National Theatre, had never seemed less interesting.

During the interval Harrier and Stella sat outside on one of the terraces (leaning slightly against one another now), and delightfully agreed to miss the harrowing conclusion of the piece in favour of having the 'river-view' restaurant to themselves for an hour. Bounding happily down the stairs, Harrier went to have a word with the head waiter about bringing forward their table reservation. Fortune was on their side; nothing could be more easy. They would get the best table by the window – with a view of the river, and the lights of the north bank, and the faraway traffic, like a glacier of diamonds, drifting towards Blackfriars.

Having been the first to be seated in the restaurant, Harrier and Stella were also the last to leave. It had been a happy meal, with jokes, and humorous self-effacement, shy encouragements, and ventured philosophies, all of which, from both of them, combined to create the best possible version of themselves.

A little after eleven o'clock, Stella said to Harrier: 'I think that you're the most wonderful person I've ever met.' Neither agreeing, nor disagreeing, Harrier kissed her.

And that – so the cynic might say – was that, only it wasn't, for beneath the seeming resolution of their embrace lay a host of assumptions, and upon such assumptions are false hopes built and the steady course of lives redirected.

TWO

The Best Thing

Whilst the Honourable Miles Harrier and the beautiful Stella Walker-Jones were approaching their love affair during the crisp autumn days, so too was Chris Patterson enjoying a certain frisson of mood by mistaking his homelessness for independence.

September had been a mild month, belying the sudden chill of October, and whilst the lease upon summer appeared to continue so Chris was given cruel encouragements that his destitution would merely be temporary – only to have these hopes contradicted ten days later.

At first it was David who had seen no difficulties at all in Chris sleeping at his house for a few weeks, 'just until he got himself sorted out'. And then David met an American marine engineer who didn't like 'Chris hanging around all the time', and a violent scene ensued which left Chris and David on bad terms and an unpleasant taste in the mouths of everyone concerned.

Towards the end of September, Chris was homeless once more, but with just enough money to stay in the cheapest of hostels. Being full of the heroics, to say nothing of colourful and complex schemes of revenge, Chris awoke to each new autumn day with a certain sense of purpose. The novelty of this sensation distracted him from his aims, and so by the middle of October (the weather turning colder now) he was living from day to day on the streets again. This process had been gradual, but irreversible. The whirlpool had caught him up, first holding him down and then pushing him under. If he could have spent one week, with some support, trying to sort his situation out, then maybe he would have struggled through. But he never managed to reach the week; something always tripped him up, either through bad luck or his own mismanagement. And then there were the acute depressions and self-consuming hatreds he underwent. These were succeeded by a desire for oblivion, and then the priority was to find alcohol, or better still drugs, and these left him even less able to cope.

His clothes — he had a pale blue suit, a T-shirt and a maroon pullover — were filthy. In a British Airways bag which Douglas had once given him he had a toothbrush (he would wash in public toilets), and some socks and underwear which he had stolen from David's American. He also had a thin sleeping-bag which he carried rolled up. The problem was that he could never dry his clothes even if he found somewhere to wash them. He carried them and wore them damp; he caught bad colds; he developed a painful rash on the insides of his legs which made it sore and awkward to walk.

He suffered acute diarrhoea and spent a week in soiled agony, locking himself in toilets for hours until someone moved him on, thinking that he was up to no good. After this he bought a bottle of kaolin and morphine mixture, and then, discovering that in large quantities the substance helped him to sleep, he made himself even more ill by drinking too much of it.

In a matter of weeks he discovered that he had joined the ranks of the supposedly irreclaimable. He slept under the concert halls of the South Bank, or beneath Charing Cross, or inside the trains which were left in sidings beside Victoria Station.

On one occasion, pathetically, he went to a large department store to see if there was casual work. He didn't know who to speak to, so he wandered around a while beneath the watchful eyes of assistants and store detectives. One man whom he recognised from his nightclubbing days — a bitter and sarcastic person who worked in the luggage department – mimed the gesture of flushing a toilet as he walked by, wrinkling his nose in disgust. It was only the fact that he knew he would be arrested which stopped Chris from attacking his critic. He left the store filled with shame and hatred. He hated looking shabby and unclean; he hated the assumption of the general public that he was in some way from a different planet to them.

But he might just as well have been. With neither money nor direction, London wanted nothing to do with the likes of Chris, and so he recast the city as a map of survival – where one might best beg for money, where one might sleep unmolested, and where one might possibly be able to drink in peace.

Sometimes he simply flopped down in the hope that someone might pick him up – no one did, and he was afraid of drawing the attention of the police. In six months he would maybe not care anymore, but after only four weeks he was still possessed of a certain degree of fight, or hope.

One day he stole a box of records from outside a secondhand shop in Kentish Town. He managed to sell these for twenty pounds at another secondhand shop, but only after a great deal of questioning from the man behind the counter. His hatred of questions had grown intense. He wanted to be left alone. As October moved slowly towards November he began to think he was going mad. At the centre of this madness were Douglas and Ray, laughing at him. With slow relish Chris would fantasise about their deaths, curled up in a doorway or sitting over the remainder of a cup of coffee in any cafe which would serve him. His thoughts began to return to violence.

Eventually, after a sleepless night spent watching the rain pour mercilessly down across the street from where he was sitting, Chris determined to find Ray. In the logic of three o'clock in the morning it had seemed that there was every chance that Ray would give him at least some of his money back.

As soon as it was light and the street was beginning to fill with traffic again (Chris was near Farringdon), he made his way to Soho. 'Lots O'Fun' was closed. There was nobody to ask.

With the bit of change he had saved, Chris bought himself ten cigarettes and a cup of tea. Then he returned to his post outside the shop and waited. The rain grew heavier; people kept coming in and out of the doorway in which he was waiting.

To pass the time he went into a nearby amusement arcade and felt in all the winnings trays of the machines for loose coins. Finally he felt something in the Derby Races game. It was a token, useless, said the assistant, except to play another game of Derby Races with. Nodding, Chris went over to the machine. He heard a tapping on the glass of the change booth behind him. 'Broken,' mouthed the assistant. Chris went back to 'Lots O'Fun'.

The shop was open now, its curtain of plastic ribbons billowing in the wind.

Inside there was a woman unpacking a cardboard box. Chris wandered up to her, his heart sinking.

'Is Ray Green here please?'

'Who?'

'Ray Green – short bloke – glasses . . .'

'I don't know; maybe later . . .'

'Can you tell him Chris called . . .'

'I'll tell him, if I see him.'

Not once did the woman look at Chris. He left the shop, suddenly tired. Passing by the magazine racks he read the labels on the packets: 'Lesbo Action', 'Straight and Gay', 'Close-up Oral', 'Mixed Man/Woman Group'. The thought of sex made Chris feel ill.

As he made his way up Wardour Street, with nothing but shelter in mind, Chris suddenly felt himself collide with someone on the pavement. It was Douglas.

They stood and stared at one another for a moment, neither knowing what to say.

'Chris?'

'Yeah –'

'You look terrible – I thought you were back in Plymouth . . .'

'No, listen, I . . .'

'Do you need any money?'

'Yes.'

'Well here you are . . .' Douglas gave Chris a twenty-pound note, his hands shaking as he passed it over. 'If I were you I'd spend it on a ticket home. You're in a right mess, and you've only got yourself to blame – what was all that shit about with Ray . . .?'

Chris shrugged. He desperately wanted to ask Douglas to take him back, if only for a few days, but he couldn't shape the words. It is conceivable that Douglas, seeing the pitiful state into which his former friend had fallen, would have agreed to this request, but then a thin young man in dark glasses (the very same music publicist with whom Douglas had attended Kuzumi's party) appeared by his side and laid a hand on his elbow. The young man had high cheekbones, and a face the colour of steel. He was wearing a baggy black suit and had a greased ponytail dangling over his collar.

'Hey Doug – they'll be waiting . . .' And then, seeing Chris, he gave Douglas a look of surprise, widening his eyes in mock horror as if to suggest the serenity of their lives was under threat. He turned his back on Chris. 'And you left the TV on this morning,' he continued, as if to distract Douglas, 'you're always half dead in the mornings . . .' Douglas nodded at the stranger, patting his hand. And then he turned to Chris again, half-apologetically.

'Sorry – big meeting . . .'

'Who's that bloke?'

'Oh – that was Erik.'

'Is he with you?'

'Well, sort of; we've been working together – new album . . .'

Erik, who had been regarding Chris with increasing distaste, suddenly broke back into the conversation. 'Yes I am with him, and I've heard all about you so just back off — some of us have got work to do . . .'

'What's the band?' asked Chris.

'Some independent hoi-polloi made good,' said Erik. '"The Statements"; not perhaps quite your scene n'est ce pas, now fuck off . . .'

'All right, all right . . .' said Douglas, and then Erik motioned him towards the StarSound studios beside them.

'Just go home — all right,' said Douglas, looking at Chris.

'It really would be the best thing . . .' finished Erik, nastily.

'Where's Ray?' asked Chris.

'Paris,' said Douglas, turning to leave.

★

That night there was a dense fog across central London. It was the last day of November, and down Regent Street and Oxford Street the first Christmas lights hung silently between the buildings, their pink and white shapes softened in the mist. The fog had begun at noon, and office workers, hurrying from their desks to queue for sandwiches, had felt a sudden seasonal thrill as the whiteness obscured the streets.

Amongst these was James Walker-Jones, striding through Bloomsbury with a copy of Leonardo da Vinci's *Notebooks* stuffed in his overcoat pocket. He was on his way to his favourite cafe, to meet Stella for lunch. Stella, who had spent the morning modelling a skirt, was full of excitement.

She met her brother on the pavement outside the Tavistock Cafe, near to the British Museum. Even to James she looked lovely, her face glowing and her eyes shining. Men turned to look at her as they walked past, their hands deep in their pockets. James knew that she had 'news' even before she spoke. 'I say, look at this fog,' he began, kissing his sister on both cheeks the way that he had seen Harrier do it. 'The British Museum, had lost its charm,' he added, wittily. But Stella didn't know the song so she missed the reference. Leaving the studio in King's Cross she had been so cold that she had been forced to buy a thicker pair of tights, but her day had been so exciting that she had almost forgotten the weather.

Brother and sister sat down, Stella slipping off her coat to reveal a tartan jumper and black mini-skirt.

'Gracious – where did you find that?' exclaimed James, pointing at the jumper. 'Och aye,' he added, humorously.

'It was fabulously expensive – if you don't mind – but listen . . .'

And then the waitress came up, biro poised over pad. Stella ordered a cottage cheese salad and a glass of apple juice; James had his usual roast beef sandwich.

'You're not going to believe this, but I've been offered the most fabulous job . . .' said Stella. Her voice was low, and thrilled, as though scared of the responsibility that her statement bore. Despite her excitement she spoke softly, with her usual reserve.

'Heavens – doing what?'

'Well . . .' (and now she seemed particularly reticent, as if frightened that her brother would disapprove). 'It's to work on television . . .'

James paused over his coffee, quite taken aback. Knowing his sister's shyness he was truly puzzled by the thought of her working before the cameras. He set down his cup again, and straightened the tight knot of his silk tie.

'Gracious!'

Stella leant forward, her palms flat on the table. She had prepared every word of her announcement, rehearsing answers to suggested difficulties, and negotiating turns of phrase to overcome potential objections. She had never stopped to think that her family and friends might really be pleased for her. She was always afraid of being 'found out', and this fear had grown over the years to shape her conversation.

'You see I did some work last year for a film company,' she continued. 'Do you remember? The sportswear video? You laughed because I had to wear a bobble hat . . .?' James nodded, an indulgent nod of the kind one might give to a child explaining his or her favourite toy. 'Well, the man who directed that,' she continued, 'has been commissioned by some big European cable television company to make a whole series – on fashion – and he wants me to be one of the main models – every week!'

James chewed his beef sandwich. He was pleased for his sister, but she was already speaking of a world which he could not understand. Outside the fog was thickening – one could hardly see across the street. The pillared front of the British Museum was an obscure, ghostly outline of itself, the black railings before it swathed in damp mist. Dark figures hurried past the cafe windows, curious shadows which seemed to move silently between the traffic.

'This is terrific news Stella – is it definite?'

'They're putting a proper letter in the post today, and then I have to go and sign the contract . . . I'm going to do it.'

'I suppose the money is good?'

'It's marvellous – I could take six months off if I wanted to . . .' (And here Stella began one of her speeches of justification, the rationale of which was wasted on James.)

'The only thing is . . .' (and Stella had saved this detail until the end) 'that the studios are based in the Midlands, so I'll have to go up there, I mean buy a house and everything. They'll help with it all . . .'

'Where in the Midlands exactly . . .?'

'Telford – it's a new town.'

★

If James took the news in – which he did, with a kind of benign half-awareness that characterised his view of all subjects which didn't really interest him – then at least he took it calmly, and with genuine pleasure at his sister's good fortune.

With Harrier it was a different matter.

Taking the kiss at the National Theatre as the official opening of their affair, Harrier and Stella had been 'going out together' (or 'in love', depending on their mood when the subject was under discussion) for just over a week.

But what a week it had been! Working from the principle of physical beauty (by which one must in this case mean the beginning of their sexual relationship), Harrier had felt his belief in Stella as both truth and bliss confirmed.

She had given herself readily – and he had been eager to receive. Their love-making had begun during the twilight of the day which followed their visit to the theatre. In the semi-darkness of the drawing room where they had sat so nervously the week before, their initial caresses had swiftly transformed into an epic of desire – lasting until dawn. By the time that the light of early morning had taken over from the shadows of early evening, Harrier and Stella had touched upon all forms of physical exploration from the wildly pornographic to the most tender of sentimentalities. Lying on the sofa, watching Harrier sleep, Stella had then looked at the brightening windows. A blackbird was singing nearby. Stella wanted Harrier to feel that no woman could ever give him as much satisfaction as she had done. She had made her body, and her expression, and her gestures, all pursue an intense and imaginative course of action. During several climaxes she had felt herself lose control, and longed to lose it further, until her mind and body were one ecstatic sensation – but somehow this abandon never happened. This made her increase her exertions – for exertions her movements had become: efforts of strength, willed and inspired by the need to recreate her celibate desires into a form which would keep Harrier with her. Stella loved Harrier deeply – or as deeply as their circumstances would permit – but she knew, as she had always known, for ten years or more, that her body could take no lasting pleasure in physical love. She had known this when, as a teenager, the reality of a boy's body against hers had seemed disturbing, and frightful. Initial desire was there, and no shortage of feelings, but nothing would make the sensation of flesh against flesh come right.

When she paused to analyse the situation, she was filled first with confusion, and then dread. As a model she was aware of her power over men, and sometimes she hated herself for being desirable even as she rejoiced in the beauty she possessed. At first she had determined to overcome her fear – she considered seeking counsel on the subject – and then she grew up to control whatever relationships she got into so that the fears would not arise. This made her calculating, and lonely. Finally she began to seek out examples of men who had mistreated their partners, hoping in this to find justification for her plight.

Above all, she dreaded loneliness, and that was how she had begun to think of Harrier as her lover. Now he was her lover, and she was terrified that he would leave her if he realised that she could not, with all the love in the world, enjoy making love with him. Out of such situations are tragedies made, the proportions of the tragedy being relegated to the obscure reaches of 'domestic unhappiness' by the manner in which 'frigidity' is made to slip without complaint into a catalogue of presumed disorders. From this point on, ugliness takes over, bringing the personal into the public or clinical eye, a place where love will not sit. Stella's love for Harrier was real, and she determined to make herself maintain the physical aspect of her passion, whatever the cost in pain.

For Harrier, the night had left a sensual warmth.

Anticipating his demands over the following days, Stella

made herself as desirable and willing a lover as anyone could dream of. Thus the warmth continued – she constructing a routine wherein both their needs would be satisfied, and he regarding their situation as one of highest bliss. With the news about Telford, a faint draught began to blow on the scene, barely noticeable as yet, but curiously persistent as the harbinger of a deeper chill.

★

Having told James her news at lunchtime, Stella then went on to see Harrier in the evening. Making her way towards Walton Street in the late afternoon she attempted to rehearse the scene, but there was the fog, dense and distracting, and Chelsea is a confusing place.

Walking past Harrods, the window displays looked like open caskets, candle-lit, with a dowdy, bronze light. The evergreen and gold so dear to the appearance of the world's most famous department store seemed cold, and funereal; the mannequins, decked in seasonal browns and crimsons, were standing beside extravagant displays of dried flowers, pendulous icicles, holly-trimmed backgammon boards and snowcapped globes. They were all viewed through a distorting mist. There was neither comfort nor cheer in the presence of these scenes, but rather a dreary sadness, as if the principle performers in the festive tableaux were addressing the world from beyond the grave. Stella shivered as she walked by, wondering at how quiet the streets were, and worrying about the impact of her news upon Harrier.

He received her, as ever, with smiles and kisses and laughter. Before she arrived he had managed to create an intimate and domestic scene; a log fire crackled in the grate, the heavy velvet curtains were drawn in voluptuous folds, and upon the dinner table a bottle of claret stood breathing in anticipation of a simple, but delectable, dinner.

Taking Stella's coat, Harrier slipped an arm around her

waist and pressed himself against her back to kiss her neck.
She laughed slightly, freeing herself from his grasp.

'Have you had a fabulous day?' he asked, 'terrible fog,
but awfully picturesque – don't you think so?'

'I met James for lunch –'

'Was he well? He usually is. I must, must, must have that
lunch with him sometime. He'll be thinking I've forgotten
. . .'

(And now Harrier was relishing the prerogative of being
a couple; discussing diaries, and pouring drinks.)

'And what else did you do?' he continued, 'it was skirts
this morning, wasn't it?'

'Miles . . .'

And so Stella told Harrier about the director of the
sportswear commercial, and about the wonderful opportunity, and the super salary.

He listened with a smile which disguised immense unease.
He nodded a lot, and said 'But that's wonderful', yet all the
time he was sure that Stella was trying to tell him something
more fundamental to their relationship. In the end the strain
was too much for him, and sitting down beside her, and
taking her hand in his, he asked her frankly whether she felt
it would be better for them to stop seeing one another.

'Oh I knew you'd think that!' she exclaimed, clasping
his hand even tighter, 'of course not . . . I do love you
you know, and I don't think I could bear to lose you – it's
just a question of my work; I can't carry on doing little
bits here and there and hoping that my luck will last out
. . .'

'Do you have to work?'

'I need to work – I really do. If I just sit around – even if I
was seeing you – I know I'd feel awful.'

The situation, despite Harrier trying to hold it in perspective, seemed to have taken on a new tint. The 'even if I was
seeing you' part of her statement worried him particularly.
For his own part he believed that he could quite happily do

nothing but see Stella all day. His reasoning, and this belief, were false.

'Where is . . . Telford, exactly?'

'You mean in relation to Sloane Square?' laughed Stella, hoping to make humour facilitate understanding. The little joke didn't work. In his heart Harrier felt that Stella was welcoming the opportunity to see less of him.

'I simply wondered,' he said coldly.

'It's in the Midlands darling – near Coventry I think . . .'

'Coventry!' The name exploded from his lips as though she had spoken a forbidden word.

She slipped her arm around his shoulder, and rested her face against his. The firelight played merrily around the room, darting in and out of corners. A portrait of one of Harrier's ancestors, a flippant young flapper, peered into the dark room with an amused smile. The lovers faced one another, and then kissed. Harrier felt far from comforted by the embrace, but as he looked at Stella's face, and saw her dark eyes smiling at him, he knew that he could not oppose her decision.

'Well, I suppose that it will do me good to get out of town from time to time,' he said.

'Of course it will darling,' replied Stella, and taking him by the hand she led him into the kitchen, to prepare salad, and to make mature, farsighted plans as to how they would benefit by this sudden alteration in their circumstances.

★

Discussion may possibly sire inspiration, or fixate the wandering mind upon a solution to its problems, but these things will not simply come when asked. There is so much to be solved: the unhappy love affair, the bad-tempered colleagues, the daily round of confrontations which seem to test the individual in hope of crushing him completely – the conflict is endless. Thus cynicism offers itself as one solution, and distractions present themselves as another. Faced with this tangle it would seem that to live in the thought of things as opposed to their reality (daily procrastinating further) is an ideal solution to the problem of a poorly lit life. This is as much the inclination of the lazy and the unimaginative as it is of the poet or the philosopher — indeed, the gap between these two classes of person is more slender than we might like to think, and the particles which drift in front of the one are much the same as those which get in the eyes of the other. It is the way one perceives the particles which counts, and perception is a difficult business, having as much to do with faith as it does with intellect. Thus it was that Harrier and Stella sought a solution to their problem by dining and discussing; all the while making light-hearted and facetious comments about life in Telford, whilst outside the fog thickened, and began to freeze.

It thickened in Walton Street, turning the pretty terraces of white houses into a dank Venetian canal, and it thickened across Sloane Square, and Lowndes Square, muffling the yellow windows and silently curling about the leafless trees. It brooded over Hyde Park, where the cheerful beginnings of the paths were turned into brief grey spaces which pressed on unseen into an interior darkness. It hung in the canopy of the bandstand, and clung to the lamps. Crossing Park Lane, the fog shrouded the big hotels, and then it passed on through Mayfair, darkening corners and hanging at the ends of cul-de-sacs like a ghost. The fog covered the whole of London, and at Oxford Circus, like everything else, it went in all directions.

James Walker-Jones, making his way down St Martin's Lane, approved of the fog. He found it dramatic, well-suited to his idea of the city, and as he tried to perceive the curb around Trafalgar Square he inhaled with pleasure, scenting the Victorian.

Chris Patterson's face was reddened by the brake-light of a taxi as he attempted to cross the Tottenham Court Road on his way to the Albery Court Hotel in St Pancras. He too found the fog appealing, summoning up a thousand memories of film-noir stalkings and killings, detectives shot down, cars stolen, and jealous lovers avenged. With the money which Douglas had given him, Chris was going to spend a warm night at the Albery Court, the cheapest of cheap hotels.

In a curious way many insecure people were comforted by the phenomenon of not being able to see.

★

The night manager at the Albery Court Hotel had heard every possible tale of misfortune and injustice, but despite this wealth of experience he was neither colourful nor philosophical. His job was to extract in advance the price of a room from any person who might require one. This was the only house rule – that the guest must pay in advance. Rates were cheap because the hotel was both dirty and insecure.

The Albery Court was an early and much-treasured find for Chris. It stood in a curious maze of streets at St Pancras, the windows of its west-facing rooms having an upward outlook towards the fairy-tale spires and minarets of the towering railway station. With nearly ninety rooms on four floors, opening like cabins off perfectly straight yet imperfectly lit corridors, the Albery Court combined the functions of a clandestine meeting house with the ambience of a morgue. In this much it was the urban romantic's dream of sleazy living, but it would require a suitably hardened urban romantic to cope with the inoperative toilets which exhaled raw sewage, the coffin-wide beds with stained nylon oversheets and a single blanket, the light switches which spat blue sparks when operated, and the constant litany of shouts, fights, screams and arguments which filled the air from midnight until dawn. Chris Patterson was neither worried about such conditions nor in a position to choose, so for him the use of a room and some warm water was a wonderful thing.

Having paid the night manager and watched him stretch wearily for a key off the piece of hardboard fastened to the wall behind his head (all the while following the action on a small television screen on the desk before him), Chris made his way up to room forty-six. The room was on the second floor, away from immediate disturbance, and close to a bathroom. The light in the bathroom did not work but there was hot water – a gush of steam followed by a cough of scalding spray testified to this. Taking advantage of the situation, Chris locked himself in the bathroom and ran a deep bath. As soon as his eyes had grown accustomed to the darkness he felt in his bag for the small bottle of vodka he had bought earlier, and gave himself up to a relaxing soak. The frosted glass in the narrow window was turned into a hundred flickering fires by the condensation, the fog, and the streetlight outside. For the first time in many weeks Chris began to feel happy.

It was good to feel the hot water against his skin, to wriggle his toes beneath a trickle from the hot tap and swirl the heat about his body. He found a soft white lump of soap, and after some initial tests began to lather himself. Outside in the corridor he heard footsteps, and tensed himself in anticipation of an intruder – but the footsteps passed by his door, and he was left in peace once more.

The darkness – it was a mixture of orange and black – felt comforting and soporific. Chris had had other baths during his months of homelessness, but none as good as this. His anxieties began to soften, and he thought only about the heat of the bath, and the density of the fog outside, swirling about the station. He was unbelievably tired, with an exhaustion of mind and body which lay just beneath the surface of light-headedness. As his breathing grew more regular and his eyelids began to weigh heavily, he thought about going home to Plymouth, as Douglas had suggested. Perhaps Douglas was right in the end – anything had to be better than spending winter on the streets. Thus thinking about Douglas, and Erik, and of the little greenhouse which stood behind the Pattersons' house on the outskirts of Plymouth, Chris fell asleep in the bath.

★

He woke at dawn, chilled to the bone in freezing cold water. His surroundings were now dimly visible in the grey light. The window was white – presumably from the fog, and as he pulled himself upright with much painful stretching, Chris took his first look around the bathroom.

It was bigger than he had thought. Still stupefied with sleep he began to search for a towel, knowing full well that there was unlikely to be one. On the floor there was a threadbare white mat, the centre of which was worn away into a patch of damp rubber. He stepped gingerly onto it, suddenly feeling dizzy. He became aware that in fact the bathroom was partitioned down its centre by a shoulder-high screen of painted wood, at the end of which was a gap whereby one bather – should he so choose – could slip through to visit his neighbour. Just above this little entrance there was a single-bar electric heater fastened to the wall. Tiptoeing across the floor Chris went to turn on the heater in order to dry himself. He tugged the string and gazed up at the fixture, noticing with satisfaction the slow spread of orange across its width as the bar heated up. There was a terrible smell of burning dust, and a deep humming sound, but soon he began to feel warm again. After a while he put on his trousers and pullover, and then wondered whether there was a basin on the other side of the screen in which he could clean his teeth and freshen his face with cold water.

He pushed by the screen and then stopped in his tracks.

Lying in the neighbouring bath, in water which looked black, there was a woman, eyes open and horrifically fixed on his. Too shocked to make a sound Chris stood perfectly still, trying to take in the sight. He had never seen a corpse before.

The woman looked to be in her early thirties. Her face was fleshy, and rounded, her hair a premature grey. She reminded Chris of his mother, with silver-blue eyes, and broad, freckled shoulders. The black water was nearly up to her chin, and her mouth was slightly open. On the floor beside her there was a pile of clothes – a maroon pullover and an old black skirt. On top of these was a brown plastic handbag. In the peculiar luminosity of the morning light it seemed as though the body was laid out in a field of snow. The wallpaper beside the bath had come loose over the years, and people had obviously passed the time in tearing strips of it away, thus revealing areas of plaster. The woman's hands had risen to the surface of the water, and now they floated beside her, white and puckered.

Chris didn't know what to do. He was too afraid to go any closer to the body, and too shocked to move away from it. He stood quite still, trying to make certain in his mind that the woman was dead. Her white body, touched with patches of grey, left him in no doubt.

He rushed back to his side of the bathroom – now quite unable to think of anything save the dead body on the other side. Fumbling with his belongings, he quickly made ready to leave. He had no thought to report the death – in a blur he pictured himself being accused of some murder – and soon he was half-running down the long corridor towards the stairs.

Pausing on the staircase he tried to compose himself. He didn't dare attract any attention. Putting his bag under his arm he tried to look surly and in every sense unremarkable. The night manager made no comment as he put his key on the counter and then walked out into the street.

Once outside he felt sick. The sudden cold, mingled with the heat of the smoke in his lungs as he lit a cigarette, combined to create faintness and nausea. Having run down the street towards King's Cross he then sat down on the curb, his bag beside him in the gutter, and put his head between his knees. He took deep breaths, and retched once or twice, his chest heaving painfully with the exertion. His hands were shaking and he felt hot and cold in swift succession. In his mind he could still picture the woman's eyes, staring at him. He would never know what story lay behind her expressionless gaze, except that it was a tragedy, and had found conclusion in the opening of veins.

★

The fog had cleared, leaving in its place dark skies and damp. Yellow leaves lay flat upon the pavement, and in one of the Bloomsbury squares a tennis net sagged between its posts, weighed down with moisture.

Chris made his way slowly southwards. He wandered through Russell Square, pausing for a cup of coffee at the cafe in its centre, and then he walked through Holborn, his mind a blank. Towards lunchtime people began to crowd the streets, pushing past him and hurrying on errands, some to the banks, others to restaurants, but all with a sense of purpose – or so it seemed.

Finally Chris reached the river, and feeling in need of both solitude and a view he sat down on some steps leading down to the water and began to think.

Firstly, and for reasons which had become habitual as opposed to rational, he thought about Douglas. He blamed Douglas for everything, and wished that he could meet him again, if only to be abusive. But coupled to this hatred was the fact that he missed his former lover. They had, after all, spent nearly three years together, if not in peace then at least in comfort.

And then Chris thought about his own situation, and the approach of winter. This was too horrible to dwell upon. The grey water lapped noisily against the steps, throwing up litter and fallen leaves. A Christmas tree had been fastened to a crane on the building site on the other side of the river. Its red and yellow bulbs stood out against the grey sky.

Just then Chris's thoughts were disturbed by a shout. The voice had a curious accent, and seemed to be beside itself with mirth. 'Hey, you boy!' shouted the voice, and then 'Hey yes you . . .'

Chris turned, wondering who could possibly want to speak with him. His stare was returned by a cheerful wave from a complete stranger, a boy of about his own age, who had started striding towards him.

'What are you doing boy?' said the stranger, slapping Chris on the back.

'Nothing,' said Chris, 'who the fuck are you anyway?'

The stranger sighed, and lit a cigarette and sat down next to Chris. He had fair hair, and a beard, and was wearing old army trousers, big black boots, and a dirty blue coat which was open at the neck. He began to reach into his pocket. Chris got up.

'Want a drink?' said the stranger. Chris sat down again.

'My name is Carrol,' (there was a pause) 'and I am from Amsterdam. I have been in your fucking shit town three months. I am bored though now . . .' Chris nodded, and then asked for a cigarette. Carrol immediately gave him one.

'Thanks . . .'

'And you? What are you?'

Chris paused. 'I'm just here really – I live here . . .'

Carrol nodded, and put on a pair of small dark glasses. 'Good eh?' he said. 'Punk . . .'

'Yeah . . .'

For no particular reason, except for the fact that Carrol

wouldn't go away and he had both whisky and cigarettes, Chris began to talk with him, realising as he did so that he hadn't spoken with anyone properly for weeks. He began with the fact that he didn't have anywhere to live, and then, gathering that Carrol wasn't some kind of do-gooder in disguise, went on to tell him about Douglas, and the corpse in the bath.

Carrol was impressed. Chris embellished the story, introducing police, a chase, a curiously mislaid gun and so forth.

In the end the two boys began talking about all the things they hated most. Carrol seemed to be in hiding from a previous girlfriend, but he wasn't clear about the details. Finally, when Chris suggested they go and buy a hotdog (he had a little money left), Carrol agreed, and the upshot was that the Dutch boy invited Chris back to the house he was squatting in, south of the river, near Vauxhall. The virtues of the squat were extolled in broken English. It was a place with 'no fascist cunts' and 'no shit trouble'.

Towards mid-afternoon the two boys set off for the squat together, Chris thinking that at least a few nights' sleep would give him a chance to think out a new plan. He was to stay at the squat for some months.

★

Whilst Chris and Carrol were eating their hotdogs, Stella Walker-Jones and Miles Harrier were greeting Stella's parents outside Fortnum & Mason. They were going to have tea.

Enough time had now passed since the funerals of late summer to make conversation much easier; indeed, as Mrs Walker-Jones made her way towards the well-dressed couple standing on the pavement, she thought how relaxed Harrier looked, pleasant and dependable in his black overcoat, standing beside Stella with his hands behind his back. Stella, of course, looked delightful.

The object of the tea party was to discuss Stella's forthcoming move to Telford, which was to be almost immediate. On their way to Fortnum & Mason, Stella had expressed some worry to Harrier as to how her parents would regard the situation.

'I'm sure that Mummy will worry,' she had said, 'she'll worry because she'll think that it's too far away . . .'

'I honestly don't see why she should take that line,' replied Harrier, sensing his role as a diplomat. 'I mean it isn't as though you were going to Burma or something, and you are old enough to look after yourself . . .'

Stella nodded, but looked far from persuaded. She was worried that her parents would find some objections to the move, but as usual her fears were without grounds. Mr and Mrs Walker-Jones were only concerned that their daughter should find somewhere nice to live before she began her work.

Shaking hands with Stella's father, and giving Mrs Walker-Jones a vaguely filial kiss on the cheek, Harrier escorted the little party up to the tea room on the fourth floor of the department store. This was a duty at which Harrier excelled, combining, as he did, the correct sense of respect for the older generation with a degree of aristocratic worldliness which raised him high above the slightly intimidated negotiations for tables being made by the more suburban classes.

As soon as they were seated the conversation divided into two, with Stella and her mother discussing the shops whilst Harrier and Mr Walker-Jones exchanged *basso voce* comments about the state of the world in general. Whilst avoiding the rapacious attitude of mere fortune-seekers, the Walker-Jones would in no way have objected to the idea of Harrier becoming their son-in-law.

Telford was raised over sandwiches.

'So – you're off to the cold north . . .' said Mr Walker-Jones, more by way of statement than question. Stella nodded.

'Well, it's certainly a good opportunity – have you given

any thought as to where you might like to live? Are you going to buy a house — I'm sure I can speak before Miles' (and here he laid a hand on Harrier's arm) '— by which I mean we want to be sure that you're started off properly.'

'I've got to go up to the studios next week,' said Stella, 'and I thought I'd perhaps look around whilst I was up there . . .'

'Perhaps I ought to come with you,' said her father (and here her mother nodded), 'that way if we find anything suitable we can at least put a deposit down.'

This piece of generosity was received with an obedient nod.

'Do you know anything about property prices in Telford?' enquired Mr Walker-Jones of the table in general. 'I would have thought that they're considerably lower than those in the south-east . . .' He looked at Harrier, who made an intelligent comment about relocation grants.

'Quite, quite . . .'

'Don't your parents have property in Yorkshire?' enquired Mrs Walker-Jones sweetly.

'Yes — but it's rented to an American research foundation. When my father inherited it he couldn't afford to live there —' (a look of concern took its place on Mrs Walker-Jones's face) '— and nobody particularly wanted to buy it, so we put it out for rent — it just about pays for itself . . .' (Pleasure replaced concern on Mrs Walker-Jones's face.)

'Do you ever visit?'

'I haven't been there for years except to sign papers and things. My father drops in sometimes but mostly it's all done through the lawyers.'

'I see . . .'

'You have a place in town?' (This time it was Stella's father who looked concerned.)

'Yes. Chelsea. It's very convenient . . .'

'James was telling us that it's lovely — but then, James is so lucky over there with his friend etc. etc.'

And so the tea party continued on its course, with invitations exchanged, and best wishes extended, and business mingled subtly within the conversation so as not to ruffle the general air of informality.

After they had contemplated the crumbs of their patisserie for a suitable length of time, Stella and her mother excused themselves on the grounds of shopping and Harrier and Mr Walker-Jones stood up to see them off. Stella would meet Harrier for dinner later and gave him a little kiss as she left.

Once the ladies had gone, Mr Walker-Jones asked for the bill, and then turning to Harrier, said, 'You've known Stella and James for quite a long time now – do you think that this move is the best thing for Stella?'

Harrier immediately upheld the plan, finding all kinds of reasons why it was the best possible thing in the world for Stella to do. Mr Walker-Jones nodded. 'Well, I'm sure you're right. I don't know anything about modelling' (and here they both laughed) 'but it strikes me that one ought to jump at these opportunities whilst they're still there . . . and who knows, she may decide she wants to have children in a few years . . .'

Miles nodded seriously.

'I must be off,' said the older man, 'good to see you again and make sure you keep in touch. I'm sure that Stella will soon have you running up to see her once she's settled . . .'

And so the two men parted, the elder to seek out a first-rate thriller in Hatchards and the younger to stroll through the wet afternoon to his home.

★

Walking through Green Park, Harrier thought about how beautiful Stella had looked at tea. He believed himself to love her desperately, and could not think without jealousy and sadness about how much he would miss seeing her on a daily basis. He tried to believe that nothing would change between them, but then again he felt as though it already had. Was it just his imagination, or did she now seem to resist him slightly when he kissed her? On the other hand what right had he to be constantly seeking her embrace?

He tried to reason the thing out, but he always arrived at the conclusion he least desired, which was that he wanted her more than she wanted him. His anxiety grew.

He turned towards Belgrave Square, deep in thought. Drifts of leaves had piled up on the pavement, and they glistened in the streetlight. He wondered, just slightly, whether Stella found him unattractive. She seemed to dislike any form of casual affection, and even in other ways . . . But then Harrier accused himself of being unreasonable. The idea was silly; after all, one didn't simply fall in love with a person because of their looks, now did one?

Thus pitting speculation against fact, Harrier made his way towards Walton Street, determined when he got in to do nothing save think of further and more effective ways to make Stella love him.

THREE

Death In Telford

Stella bought a Mallard home in Telford.

The ramifications of this purchase were extensive, and they prompted, above all (in the conversation of those who knew her), the observation that such a modern and curious town on the border of Shropshire would be quite a change of scenery. To James, for instance, the contrast between place and personality was resplendent with irony, but there his comments ended, incapable of realising the wider psychological aspects of the move.

For the Honourable Miles Harrier it was a question of 'irony be damned', and to him Telford became privately synonymous with 'the end of earthly happiness'. It was a difficult position for Stella to be in, but she had determined to take up her new job and, having determined, was stubborn.

Whilst the practicalities of the relocation of his girlfriend were getting underway, Harrier gave himself over to extended periods of self-pity. But it was one thing to moodily pace the paths of Green Park, and to speculate (whilst sighing at the gradual approach of winter) on matters of body and heart, and it was another to adjust to the bald reality of the facts. He took down his *Motorists' Guide to Great Britain* and looked up the offending town on the map. Having placed it geographically he felt no better.

If it was Harrier's ambition for his love to be pure, that is, to somehow coerce beauty and truth into an omnipotent moment of harmony which was the essence of a myriad mutual sympathies (like a benign bubble in which only lovers may sit, viewing the world through an iridescence which protects even as it beautifies), then he felt that Telford was most likely to become the acute intrusion into the scheme which would skewer such hopes. Having burst this metaphorical bubble, neither love nor beauty would bother to deny the sorrowing couple the chance to live in the clinging wetness of its remains for as long as they both might live. Thus it was that 'dampness' entered into Harrier's interpretation of the word 'Telford', and joined with the 'end of earthly happiness' as his gloomy readings of that hitherto innocent proper noun.

He wished that he had a friend to discuss the matter with, but the sorry truth was that Harrier had no real friends. He had been content for so long to exist merely within the requirements of his amorous schemes, that what with one thing and another the only people whom he now knew were those integral to the success of these schemes. His friends were waiters, and barbers, taxi-drivers and shop assistants; in short they were the people whom he paid to like him. Other than these there was only James, and Harrier found James's view of the universe too removed from reality to be of much use.

Above all, Harrier dreaded having to walk past the space where Stella sometimes parked her car when she came to visit him. Cynics would argue that, in relation to the other degrees of suffering which can befall a young man, Harrier's lot was by no means drawn from the bottom of the barrel. (There was Douglas Stanshaw for instance, another man trying to adjust to his circumstances, and his retreat into narcotic semi-awareness had created a nasal condition which would draw a long, low whistle from those to whom it was described. Harrier, at least, had his health.)

The real victim of the upheaval was Stella. As she sat in her Mallard home during the first fortnight of living in Telford, or as she learned to be dressed, repackaged and filmed as the totem of the carefree girl, she felt that she was walking a thin line between panic and oblivion.

★

The Mallard homes were brand new (and in some cases unfinished), and they formed a small and exclusive cul-de-sac of 'Architect Original' houses which branched off a residential estate called Greenside, just a few minutes drive down the motorway from the centre of Telford.

The Mallards differed from the Cannings and the Tewkesburys in as much as they were new houses built largely out of old materials. Thus, where a Canning would offer the potential buyer a standard mixture of slate-effect tiles and a single gable of chemically seasoned timber, the Mallard was constructed out of a mixture of salvaged bricks, 'period' front door, Regency-style bow-window, and a turn-of-the-century porch-light. When they bought the house Mr Walker-Jones had stood in the estate representative's bungalow and said, 'There's no point in buying something less attractive when the prices are so competitive.' The young man in the Mallard blazer had agreed, and Stella, whose ravishing appearance in jeans, black polo-neck and leather jacket had won her cause some special favour, could only smile, put her name to the papers, and be handed a set of keys. And then father, daughter and estate representative had made their way down the unfinished road towards Stella's new home. The purchase had taken place during the afternoon of a cold, overcast day.

The row of Mallards terminated in a field. This field was unkempt, and colourless, with wiry grass combed by the wind into clumps of black hawthorn bushes. A simple fence of wooden stakes and netting separated the grow-bag and green water-barrel (now tomb to several sparrows) of the last house in Stella's row from this wilderness.

Whilst her father and the representative were talking in her driveway, slapping walls and stamping on patio, Stella walked down to the fence and looked out over the field. It dipped away steeply after the first few hundred metres, and at the point where the last bush disappeared out of view the resulting prospect seemed gaunt and bleak. In the middle distance there was an artificial lake, flanked by two smaller ponds; these were rectangular in shape and fringed with grey bushes. The surface of the water looked perfectly still, despite the sudden gusts of wind which blew up the hill towards Greenside. Beyond this there was the motorway, overhung with tall white lights and stark blue signposts. There was very little traffic. On the other side of the motorway a dark escarpment rose sharply to a low ridge scattered with silver birch trees. Above this an angry sky hung low upon the horizon, with black, bulbous clouds stretching out towards the glow of the railway station. On that first visit, as Stella surveyed the countryside in which she would be living, a narrow bar of light beneath the clouds seemed to be all that was left of the day. Looking at this strip of brightness Stella shivered, and felt a little bit sad. She wondered what Harrier would think when he realised that this poor environment was all that she had to offer him.

A few days later, accompanied by a small removal van, Stella moved into her new house properly.

Affirming the representative's guarantee that certain fixtures were included in the price of the house, Stella's home was carpeted throughout with a cement-coloured, pristine pile. From the narrow hall, with its convenient downstairs cloakroom and overwhelming smell of paint, one was faced with either the dark staircase directly ahead or the drawing room on the left. The drawing room ran the length of the house, from the bow-window at the front to the patio doors at the back. Painted white, this room was light, and an Adam-style fireplace, complete with ribbed pillars and presentation carriage-clock, stood magnificently in the centre of one wall. Beside this there were some fitted shelves, especially deepened to accommodate a television and video-recorder. As Stella unpacked her new television set, so beautifully encased in its dark grey shell, she began, for the first time, to feel house-proud. From this moment on she started to enjoy home-ownership.

From the drawing room one went into the kitchen, and here there was a varied selection of domestic technology: fitted oven and microwave, fridge-freezer, wall-units, dish-washer and washing machine all sat in colour-coordinated symmetry beside formica worktops and sparkling new sink, the plug of which had been wrapped in blue cellophane. On the ceiling there were track-lighting fixtures, and soon Stella had arranged these to create an appealing – some would say seductive – mood of semi-darkness.

Towards the end of her first week, after a day spent modelling micro-skirts against a backdrop soon to be colour-animated, Stella heard a ring at the doorbell. 'I wonder who that can possibly be?' she thought, and leaving the task of changing the water in her aquarium she went to answer the door. Peering cautiously into the darkness Stella was confronted by a cheerful young woman with a toddler in tow. 'Hello,' smiled the woman, 'I'm Emma Welles – I live next door.'

And so Emma and Timothy (the Welles's youngest) were invited in for a coffee, and soon the two women had begun a quiet conversation about the merits of their respective properties, occasionally giving little bursts of laughter and looking down at the infant between them. Emma and her husband Tony had moved to Telford the previous spring, and after some months of virtual isolation, alone in their Mallard, they were glad that the neighbourhood was beginning to fill up.

Stella took Emma on the guided tour, and Timothy asked questions about the fish.

'They were a present from my boyfriend,' Stella said, by way of a more sober explanation to Emma, who had never felt that tropical fish were practical.

After her guests had gone, Stella settled down in the corner of her Chesterfield sofa and watched the play of the aquarium lights around the room. So much newness! It seemed strange to her that now, surrounded by so much comfort and so many recently bought and created things, she was sitting in a space which six months earlier had been a muddy field, not unlike the one at the end of the row.

Had she been of an analytical turn of mind, or had she delighted (as did her brother) in making romantic conjectures about the meaning of things, she might well have alighted on a semi-Biblical reading of her situation. For here, on the outskirts of Telford, where ancient wilderness and contemporary town-planning sat so close, and so silently, together, there was the potential for a new Eden; a place committed to new beginnings, and the flourishing of health, and happiness. Here was the fresh start, an opportunity which verged upon the prehistoric, and here, should discord be avoided, there was the chance for love to take root, and blossom.

But Stella, quite possibly with justification, thought neither of Eden nor of the burgeoning responsibilities towards the potential of their wilderness which the citizens of Telford had acquired; she thought instead about the various things that she would soon take pleasure in buying in order to stave off the ever-present loneliness which lay outside her door, between the field, and the dark lake, and the curious town just a few minutes drive down the motorway.

★

Telford may one day qualify, in terms of population and the establishment of a cathedral diocese, as a city, but in the time that Stella first came to know it, exploring as much by accident as by inclination the growing grid of roads which encircled the shopping centre upon its levelled, concrete island, the place had the atmosphere of a feudal township.

Leaving for work in the morning, Stella would turn her car first out of the row of Mallards (here and there noticing lines of washing which had been left out to freeze overnight: striped shirts, children's underpants, and denim jeans with rigid legs, solid above the frosty grass), and then drive down the hill away from Greenside. From here a sliproad ran swiftly into the main flow of the motorway traffic, and then, pausing first at the enormous roundabout in the centre of which was the Telford monument (three steeply rising and unadorned concrete parabolas, reminiscent of a Soviet space-achievement memorial), she turned up into the business hinterland of Telford itself. The roads – some of which, like her own, were unfinished – ran in lateral vertebrae from a central spine which curved at the summit of its climb to fold around the northern edge of the shopping centre – thus continuing the moat-like effect of its passage – before descending down the other side, thereby creating a loop effect, not dissimilar to a noose. Where this main road began and ended (above the knot so to speak) there were several acres of carpark, a lower road leading to the railway station, and a bright and impressive-looking building – usefully visible from the motorway – which was the Telford Moat House Motor Motel and Conference Centre. This was an extensive complex of low buildings, serviced with many restaurants and amenities.

But the hub of the town was the shopping centre, and this was the area contained within the middle of the noose. Stella's workplace, a relatively minor development of dark blue offices with a single red roof upon which were satellite dishes – stood close to the motel. As she slowly got used to the routine of her days, Stella's formative impression of the town was coloured by the dark winter sky. One of the effects of this weather was to make the horizon seem low and the gaps between the buildings immense; one never really seemed to reach the centre of the town. One would turn a corner, and there would be a small ornamental lake, neatly filling the shape which had been prepared for it and sitting apathetically before the pagoda-like shelters to one side and the kiddies' adventure park to the other. From the lake there would be a perspex canopy which led to the covered marble precincts of the shopping centre, but just as one was anticipating the transition to which one is accustomed – of entering the 'old town' – nothing happened, and lo, there one was in another carpark.

To Stella's colleagues at the studio, who lived primarily for photographed reality, this other-worldliness was considered rather good. Benjamin for instance, a young assistant on the fledgling show with whom Stella sometimes shared a carton of grape juice, maintained that Telford was the perfect cinematic environment, and referred her to several French films which had made this point. For Stella, a girl who was growing slightly tired of theorists who found her scar 'significant' (even as they instructed the make-up man to 'work with it'), the disorientation was profound. She took to lunching alone in the motel, eating her salad in a pink-curtained dining room where the tables were weighed down with wine glasses of various heights and pink vases of white nylon bluebells. Here, surrounded by grey-suited men whose business personae had grown to overlap the insubstantial outlines of their original selves, and watched by many frustrated and lustful eyes, Stella would sit alone, and here, at the beginning of her second week, she met Linda, a young business studies graduate, herself from London, who was a trainee conference planner.

The two girls enjoyed their first lunch together, both delighted to have found someone with whom to discuss the peculiarities of the town which their careers had forced upon them, and both amazed to realise the similarities of their situation.

Linda lived at Woodside (having first considered a smaller house in Snefeld), and her parents lived in Mitcham, Surrey. She was twenty-three, and had a boyfriend studying engineering at Imperial College, University of London, who had worked for a year in Spain. Telling Linda about her own job, Stella was proud to notice that her new friend was quite definitely impressed by the glamorous conjunction of the words 'model' and 'television'.

'I thought you must do something like that,' Linda had said, 'you wear such lovely clothes . . .' Stella gave a little shrug, as if to say, 'Oh – it's nothing,' and smiled.

Concluding their conversation with the discovery that they would both be shortly returning to their homes for Christmas, the girls exchanged telephone numbers, and agreed to meet again in the New Year.

As she left the motel and walked back to the studios, Stella looked with a happier, more confident eye, upon her surroundings. The shops, trimmed with tinsel and fairy lights, and hung with fibreglass lanterns, no longer seemed the uninviting dens of commerce which they had previously been. It was, Stella reasoned, people who made a place, not buildings.

★

The following weekend the Honourable Miles Harrier arrived in Telford – it was his first visit to the place – to see Stella's new house and then take her home for the Christmas holidays.

He arrived on the Saturday morning, beneath freezing, dark grey skies. On his way to Greenside, driving with Stella's humorously annotated local map on his knees, he had looked up and seen the lights of the shopping centre, fluorescent against the snow-filled clouds. He reached Stella's house just before lunch, in visibility so poor as to make it seem like late afternoon.

Stella had spent the previous day preparing for his arrival. She had dusted and hoovered, laid out fresh towels, cleaned the aquarium, and (so Harrier noticed with an aching in his heart) baked a cake. The cake reminded Harrier of the days of his youth, when he and James had been honour-bound to taste all the biscuits and puddings prepared by Stella and Lucinda in their domestic science classes.

The visit, despite all best intentions on both sides, was not a success. The lovers felt restrained, and on their best behaviour, this feeling being caused by the strangeness of meeting for the first time in a new place. Harrier politely offered his coat to his hostess in order for it to be hung up properly, and Stella formally gave him permission to smoke.

For the first few minutes after his arrival, Harrier and Stella stood holding hands in the drawing room. How beautiful she looked to him! And how sharply, and with what fervour, did he recognise the manner in which her beauty seemed apparent in all the things around her. The white drawing room, with its Chesterfield sofa, the scent of paint mingling with her perfume, the turquoise digital lights on the video-recorder, the flicking of the fish in the dim glow of the aquarium; the whole house, and beyond that the whole concrete townscape between the frosty fields, seemed to echo Stella's beauty. She was wearing a simple black dress, drawn in at the waist and hanging in precise, elegant pleats about her knees. Her features appeared to have adjusted to winter, soft and white in comparison to the sultriness of her summer tan. About her throat she wore a crimson and black scarf, held in place on her shoulder with a silver brooch. As they stood in the semi-darkness, neither speaking, Harrier could imagine no greater bliss than to make love with the girl beside him, slowly revealing her entire body to the warmth and half-light of the brand new room. He slipped his arm about her waist, thrilling to the feel of her hips and the lightness of her dress as he drew her gently towards him. She turned, and kissed him quickly on the nose, laughing slightly as she did so, and then she suggested that they go on the guided tour. Harrier reminded himself sharply of the time of day and the circumstances under which they were meeting. But within a second he was cursing both Stella and himself.

The guided tour did not take long, but Harrier made sure that he found plenty to praise; here a well-placed window, there a space reserved to accommodate some particularly useful or imaginative new purchase. Stella was especially proud of her bathroom, for here, with its long, carefully lit mirror, black and white fittings, and luxuriously verdant houseplant, was where she created herself.

Her bedroom too, was delicately furnished. The bed – Harrier could not determine whether it was a single or a double or some peculiar half-size in between – was covered with a mother-of-pearl-coloured duvet, and the only other furnishing in the room was a white wicker chair, over the back of which was hung a pale blue shawl. The guest bedroom contained only a camp bed and a telephone. The smallest bedroom, which looked out over the rooftops of Greenside as opposed to towards the motorway, Stella had converted into a wardrobe and dressing room. Harrier was given only the briefest of glimpses into this room.

They returned to the drawing room, their plan being to go out before the shops closed to visit Telford itself. Whilst Stella was fetching her coat and gloves, Harrier sat on the sofa and watched the tropical fish. There was one bright blue, and one a primrose yellow, with sleek scarlet markings. Between them swam the neons, little bars of silver which darted like cars through the darkness. Outside the first snow was beginning to fall. It was a heavy fall, a swirling curtain of thick flakes which obscured the whole view from the bow-window to the low hill in the distance. The lights along the motorway had been turned on and beneath their glare one could see the action of the blizzard, buffeting around the traffic. The cars left grey lines on the virgin surface behind them.

'Stella!' called Harrier. 'Look – snow!'

And Stella came running down to look.

The field at the end of the row was already turning white, the snow catching first on the raised clumps of grass, and then beginning to coat the twigs of the bushes. Beyond this the little lakes were just visible, their surfaces looking even blacker as they stood out first against grey and then against white.

'We ought to stay in and just watch,' said Harrier. But at this Stella looked disappointed. 'I wanted to show you the town,' she said, and pouted childishly. When Stella allowed mimicry to break through her reserve Harrier was incapable of arguing with her. He immediately picked up his car keys, and with a slight bow escorted his girlfriend to the door. Deep down he felt sure that she was looking for an excuse not to have to sit with him, and possibly risk his caress.

From this point on the visit became a battle of nerves.

Had Harrier not found himself becoming blind to all save Stella's beauty, and had his dark imaginings that she was withholding herself from him not thereby converted his lover's desire into latent resentment (bordering on hatred), then all might have gone quite well. But as it was he became fixated on Stella's body, and as he could detect no reciprocal desire from her, he began to behave atrociously.

As she showed him the town, making special detours to allow them to visit buildings she thought either impressive or funny, he greeted each new sight with a graceless shrug of the shoulders or a forced smile. Outside the Telford Racquet Centre – the last card in Stella's hand – where she gleefully pointed out to him the slogan 'Where Leisure is Always a Pleasure', he simply glanced and said, 'It's cold,' before turning on his heel to light a cigarette.

He became patronising, and mingled his condescension with snobbery. At each fresh insult Stella faltered slightly, her worst fears coming true. The heart of this sad episode was the fact that Stella, aware of Harrier's desires and terrified of confronting them, began to believe that she deserved such cold and hostile treatment. Had Harrier possessed the self-control to try and negotiate the difficulty of the moment, then maybe the afternoon, and the visit, could still have been saved. But Harrier was floundering in darkness, caught between love and lust, and no power on earth could have stopped him from acting so unpleasantly.

When Stella reached out to take his hand he pretended not to have noticed; and when she put her arm about his shoulder he kept both his hands in his overcoat pockets — although he did brighten up a touch at the gesture.

As they walked into the covered shopping centre, Harrier wished that he had the nobility of mind to simply contemplate the world, as opposed to looking particularly at the female mannequins dressed in gift selections of coarse, erotic lingerie. He resented these figures even as he found them vulgar, for he was excited by them. He looked around enviously at other strolling couples, his eye occasionally lighting upon a pretty girl beside her boyfriend, and then he imagined them enjoying all the sexual theatre which was suggested by the black suspender belts, crude basques of transparent scarlet lace, and minuscule, frilly knickers which hung untidily off the plastic hips of the white dummies. He hated himself for thinking in this manner, and gradually, as he saw Stella's face filled with sadness and bewilderment, he began to calm down. After all, he thought, there were other factors to be considered . . .

But the problem went deeper than that, and had already caught both Harrier and Stella in its spreading, inescapable swell; the lovers were floating upon its surface, welcoming sleep even as they drowned.

★

It was late afternoon when they drove back to Greenside. Their progress was slow, for throughout the afternoon it had been snowing heavily. A thick whiteness covered the roads and the countryside; here made orange by the streetlight, there extending in smooth, luminous sheets, rising to drift against the low fences which ran along the slopes above the motorway. A few fine flakes were still falling, and a grey half-light was reflected off the fields. The landscape was silent, and after they had parked their car near Stella's house their footsteps made a crisp, trudging sound as they walked towards the front door.

'I wouldn't like to be out in this tonight,' said Stella, and Harrier agreed.

'We ought to try and leave quite early tomorrow,' he said, 'we don't want to be caught somewhere on the way home . . .'

The newness of the house closed around them once more, with its smell of perfumed paint and recently unwrapped products. They sat beside the fire in the drawing room, slowly feeling the heat take them in its grasp and warm their minds and bodies. Other than the glow of the fire, the only light in the room came from the aquarium and off the snow outside.

'We must eat your cake later,' said Harrier.

Stella nodded, and looked at her lover; the firelight made his face seem dark, and shadowed, and as he lay back, propping himself up on his elbows, the fabric of his white shirt stretched tightly across his broad shoulders. His collar was unbuttoned and he had rolled back his cuffs. Stella sat to one side of him, with her knees pulled up to her chin; she came and rested her head on his shoulder, and then, sliding to lie in his lap, she drew his face down to hers and kissed him.

The kiss became increasingly passionate, and Stella tried to abandon herself to its power. She tried to let her senses open up with desire, but even as she tried she felt herself go rigid with self-consciousness; her spine seemed to turn to iron, and her limbs, in attempting to become supple and relaxed, became numb and uncomfortable. She lay in Harrier's arms feeling distressed and irritable, but this was only a prelude to the old and only-too-familiar sense of panic which now began to rise up in her. She imagined a sudden intrusion into the scene, like that of the shout of a teacher breaking in on a pupil's daydream – the same shock, the same exposure to embarrassment, ridicule and punishment.

She opened her eyes and saw Harrier smiling at her. He had been pleased by the kiss and now his desire was evident. Stella wanted so much to please him, but deep in her heart, where she knew the currency with which lovers rewarded one another, she felt bitterly resentful of the price she was expected to pay. She lay motionless, her eyes dim with thought. Little scenes from her past formed and dissolved in her mind, the way that her teenage suitors had sometimes reminded her of excited dogs, straining at the lead, and the way that male desire so frequently struck her as similar to the rumbling of a stomach. But then she thought about Harrier, and her resentment and analysis turned into despair. She believed herself to be in love with him – why then would her body not respond to his?

There are many possible answers to this question, but it is by no means certain that had Stella found the 'answer' she would also have found a solution. The grip of the problem, the pliers which seemed to grasp her sleeve and pull her away from desire, was the fact that self-consciousness never left her, and thus her fears became primary, creating a complex and insurmountable circuit of dread. Deep-rooted in such anxiety, Stella's 'problem' could no more be labelled and set to one side than could Harrier's desire be isolated and conveniently withdrawn. Behaviour could be modified on both sides, but it could not be brought to order. Desire could not become domesticated, and tamed, for although a wilderness can be built upon, a jungle always grows back, insidiously flowering amidst those structures which have not already been torn down.

Stella's sexual experience, although slender, had been extensive enough for her to recognise all the symptoms of her distress almost before they had occurred. She had lost her virginity at a party two years earlier, more or less by accident. The experience had coincided with the only occasion upon which she had been truly drunk, and the memory of it – darkness, noise, and illness – was not a thing she cared to dwell upon. She had no feelings at all for the man to whom she had given herself at that time, but now, when she believed herself to be in love with the person who had become in regard to this issue 'the enemy', the situation was far worse.

She lay still for a moment in the darkness, running her fingers nervously across Harrier's shirtfront. Outside it was snowing hard again, with large flakes which batted gently against the window. With sudden determination Stella got up and left the room, gaily saying that she 'wouldn't be a minute'. Harrier turned, and caught her smile in the darkness. He felt confused, and tired, so he lit a cigarette and went to look out of the window. There is a mystery and beauty about a first fall of snow which never fails to excite. He wondered what the precincts, offices and carparks of Telford looked like that evening, and was half-tempted to suggest to Stella that they drive down and witness the sight. But then he heard the drawing room door open, and turning . . .

Stella had changed her clothes. After she had quietly closed the door again, and once Harrier's eyes had grown reaccustomed to the darkness, his senses shuddered with delight at the sight of her. She had taken off her dress, scarf, shoes and stockings, and in their place was wearing nothing more than a black cotton T-shirt (the sleeves pushed up above her elbows), and a pair of black knickers, not cut in the coarse, suggestive style of those on the mannequins, but simple, and minimal, like the briefs of an expensive bikini. And that was all. She walked towards him, smiling, and then lay down on the sofa, gently resting her foot on the floor. She beckoned, he approached her, she took him in her arms, he placed his hands about her waist, she began to undress him . . .

Half an hour later, with convulsions which racked her
whole body, and with frightening, guttural sobs which rose
between breaths into sharp cries of inarticulate despair,
Stella was pressed in rigid anguish against Harrier's chest,
soaking his open shirtfront with her tears. The violence of
her emotion was not the paroxysm of orgasm, but the
shudder of dread, and terror; fear swam about her semi-
clothed body in the darkness, bringing with it a panic
which broke down all defence. No sexual intercourse had
taken place. The bodies of the lovers had barely touched
before Stella's distress became apparent, quickly causing
Harrier to release her. Holding Stella in the darkness, gently
trying to calm her shaking body, and not knowing what
best to do, Harrier felt as though he was sitting with a
stranger, a person suddenly taken ill on a street, or in a shop.
Stella's mouth was trying to shape various words, but her
face was working with tears, and no intelligible sound was
forthcoming. She sat still on the sofa, now with both feet on
the ground and her legs pressed close together. Harrier had
quickly dressed, fumbling for his clothes in the dark. When
he next turned around Stella was sitting with her face in her
hands, still crying. He went over and knelt down in front of
her, hoping that she would look at him. Eventually she did,
with reddened, shining eyes around which her make-up had
smeared. She looked completely unprotected, like a
damaged child. In the stillness she began to shape some
words.

'I'm so sorry,' she murmured, 'I'm so, so sorry . . .' And
then, with a scared, pleading stare, 'Please don't leave me;
oh please, please don't leave me . . .'

Without pausing to think or reflect, Harrier said firmly,
'I love you Stella; I'll never leave you.'

She nodded, and took his hand, and then, without looking
at him, smiled sadly into the darkness.

★

The following day the sky had cleared, and a brilliant sun was shining over the snow-covered countryside. Stella woke first, having gone to bed early, worn out with crying. She woke with a start, feeling as though she had been asleep for weeks. The sunshine was pouring in through her window. The blue sky surprised her, and for a moment she was disoriented, unsure of what day it was, or whether she was about to go to work.

And then the events of the previous night re-formed in her mind, their rawness softened by sleep. She was alone in her bed, and wondered where Harrier was. The house was warm, and silent, echoing the slightest sound – the rustle of her duvet, the clicking of her door handle, the muffled bumping sound as the water-heater switched itself off. From this last sound Stella knew that it was ten o'clock. She went quietly onto the landing, where shadows and sunbeams were crossing outside the bathroom door, filled with minute particles of dust. The door of the guest room was ajar, and inside it was dark. Stella peeped in, and there, on the uncomfortable camp bed which she had never thought of using, Harrier was fast asleep, his black leather hold-all beside him and a blanket pulled up around his bare shoulder. The sight of him so clumsily and thoughtfully in repose stabbed at Stella's heart. She wanted to wake him, and tell him that everything would be all right. But instead she went to wash, and then, having quickly dressed in an old pair of jeans and a white shirt, she crept softly downstairs to make herself a cup of tea.

The sight of her kitchen, sparkling in the morning sun, began to revive her spirits. She pulled back the curtains in the drawing room and opened a window, as if to let out the atmosphere of the previous night and allow fresh, cold air to wash the scene clean. She laid the table prettily for breakfast, and then she began to pack, in preparation for her ten-day Christmas holiday.

When Harrier came down, half an hour later, he was

almost depressed by the normality of the scene which greeted him. The waiting coffee cups and cereal bowls on the white cloth, the empty toast-rack awaiting its load, and the deft, business-like manner in which Stella was organising her packing, all seemed to cheat him slightly of the deep emotion he had felt the previous night, when she had been so helpless and in need of his support. In some ways it seemed almost blasphemous to him that she was capable of such cheerful practicality when they had touched so recently upon a dramatic fissure across the very heart of their love. Having (he thought) controlled his feelings so well in the wake of being more or less denied access to the bliss which he had so fervently desired, and in which he so deeply believed, could it be that now he hoped for Stella to be permanently weak and incapable – wearing her problem visibly as it were, as recompense for his martyrdom?

Set against Stella's earlier agony, this attitude, which combined both selfishness and cruelty, also began to lay the foundations for a fundamental dishonesty. In the brightness of morning, casually clothed and moving with a cheerful countenance, Stella seemed – if such a thing was possible – to be even more beautiful to Harrier, and even more seductive. His desires returned with redoubled force, but coupled to them, adding, as it were, an exquisite eroticism, was a sense of risk, born of frustration, as though fortunes could be won if chances were played correctly. When she affectionately kissed him 'Good morning', the crispness of her shirt-sleeves against his arms disturbed his senses, and when she bent down to fasten a bag he was forced to turn away.

Thus it was that beneath his veneer of self-control and sophistication, Harrier was becoming a voyeur of his own love affair; and thus it was that he began to feel a voyeur's greed and shame towards the gratifications which he sought. It was a subtle obsession, addictive even as it degraded.

Their conversation was friendly and routine, a burlesque of the domestic. For Stella the horror of sex had closed down – temporarily – and she was happy to be on safe ground with her lover once more. But for Harrier lust raged, calculating its next move, even as he joked and passed the butter.

Shortly after breakfast they packed Harrier's car, and then, having left Emma Welles with a front-door key so that she could very kindly feed the fish, they drove off towards the motorway, and the south.

Beneath the blue sky a thaw had set in. The motorway was black, and wet, and across the huge fields on either side the snow-covered earth turned gradually from white to mottled grey, and then to brown.

Fifty miles away from Telford there was no snow at all, and soon the memory of it, like all those of the weekend, seemed unreal, and scarcely credible as fact.

★

Having returned Stella to her parents' house, the Honourable Miles Harrier was obliged to travel to Paris, where he would stay for three days with his parents. This visit gave both the lovers a chance to contemplate their future together, honeying whatever bitterness or anxiety they might have felt by forcing them to be apart and miss one another.

Stella and her mother finished the remains of the cake which had been baked in honour of Harrier's visit to Telford, and whilst they sipped their cups of tea they touched upon the subject of the relationship. Stella, who missed Harrier dreadfully, was full of coy pride about her love for him. Similarly, on the other side of the Channel, Harrier was speaking enthusiastically about his girlfriend.

It is probable that both sets of parents, in their different ways, were beginning to scent an engagement. On neither side had they ever heard their offspring speak so warmly of a partner, and, moreover, both the young people were of an age when marriage has ceased to seem precipitous and has become almost necessary. Thus, in Paris and on the outskirts of Henley-upon-Thames, two families began to feel their way towards a wedding. This was the general tone, and Christmas, with its air of celebration, began to work upon the tone, and conspire to realise it. Apart from this gathering of momentum – which was a question of atmosphere informing action – nothing official had yet been said; indeed, the lovers themselves had not mentioned the subject of marriage to one another, but they had both thought about it – in one way or another.

It had long been a tradition at 'The Leas' for James and Stella to decorate the house on Christmas Eve, this being a seasonal event which both of them had always enjoyed, and, on more than one occasion in the past, they had shared it with Miles Harrier. This particular year, having returned from Paris the previous evening, Harrier filled his car with beautifully-wrapped presents and drove to 'The Leas' in order to follow the yuletide custom.

It was late afternoon when he arrived, and the hedges and trees of Bushy Lane were dripping in a wet mist. The lavender bush beside Stella's front door looked black against the warm glow in the windows. It was unusually mild for the time of year.

Stella greeted Harrier with hugs and kisses. She was trailing a piece of tinsel as she opened the door, and the sight of her face, so flushed with love and excitement, was the dearest thing on earth to Harrier. James followed, looking portly and fraternal. It was a scene of childish friendliness, and Mrs Walker-Jones looked fondly upon it from the hall-way.

A large Christmas tree stood in the drawing room, and Stella, her efforts drawing many humorous comments, was busy covering its branches with decorations. Finally, with a little cry of triumph, she fastened the star to its top, carefully balancing the eternally youthful fairy beneath it. At this point, according to their ritual, all the lights were turned out in the drawing room in order to see for the first time the brilliance of those upon the tree. Too self-conscious in their late twenties to give the little gasp of wonder with which they had greeted the sight in earlier years, the young people contented themselves with saying 'Yes – that's lovely,' before deciding with a laugh to open a bottle of wine.

A little later there was a family dinner – again part of the tradition – and then they all played Monopoly until it was time to go to the Midnight Mass at St Dunstan's. James in particular seemed keen to attend the service, but his enthusiasm was submerged in the general air of festivity which had pervaded the house.

Such was the picturesque routine with which Stella, Harrier and James all willingly complied. The absence of Lucinda, a regular Christmas guest in previous years, was too painful, or too awkward, for anyone to mention.

★

After the Midnight Mass, with its cheerful gathering of the suburban faithful to pray and sing carols amidst the holly and candlelight, Harrier and Stella were tactfully left alone in the drawing room. As they lay in one another's arms, peaceful, relaxed, and chaste, the lovers were filled with a sense of the enormity of their love, and this took the form of deep sentimentality.

Stella was wearing a black blouse, shot with pieces of silver thread, and the delicate lights on the Christmas tree twinkled prettily against the gossamer dress of the precariously suspended fairy, so high up and expressionless above the happy couple. A series of reflections from the Christmas tree ornaments made drifting clusters of light about the room, like the endless passage of small, silver planets through the darkness, and looming down over all of this, to lay itself flat on the carpet, was the enormous shadow of the star.

Harrier stroked Stella's hair, and drank in the beauty of her face, and felt as though he would willingly die for her if asked.

Stella felt warm against him, and safe in the bosom of her childhood home she was quite sure that she could never feel as secure or in love with any other person. Telford seemed distant, and tamed even; a benign satellite to their happiness, viewed with fondness across the distance of its orbit.

In the grip of such contentment the two lovers felt optimistic about their future. They talked in low voices, making holiday plans of the extravagantly romantic kind, and continually sought for one another's fingers and hands in the darkness. From time to time they kissed, deeply, and luxuriously, and then they would be silent again, wrapped in their own thoughts.

In the early hours of the morning they began to feel happy enough, and safe enough, to discuss what they had begun to call the 'physical side of the relationship'. Stella explained her immense 'difficulty' with it, trying to choose her words with extreme care and ending up by sounding vague. Harrier listened closely, never once letting go of her hand, and imagined that something definite was going to be said – some set of guidelines, or some all-revealing anecdote from his girlfriend's past which would set everything into perspective. No such statements were forthcoming. Stella made no attempt to conceal the truth of her feelings from him, that she had never been able to envisage having a happy sexual relationship, but also that she had never loved anyone the way she loved him, and that she would try . . .

Harrier, in depths of love which permit credence only to those words which speak in favour of love, was filled with a need to do simply that which would make Stella happy. This magnanimity caused him to believe that he had risen above mere desire, and shortly before three o'clock on Christmas morning he asked Stella to marry him. Her eyes filled with tears of joy – provoking the same response in his

– and then they clasped one another in the darkness, repeating 'I love you, I love you' until their voices intertwined and became one.

Just as their lips were meeting for a sealing kiss, their happiness was disturbed by a sudden rustle, followed by the sound of something falling off the Christmas tree. Harrier turned just in time to see the fairy, somehow worked free from her uppermost position, plunging head first through the branches and the lights, her arms apathetically by her sides, and her little gauze dress catching on twigs. In a second the doll lay broken on the floor, her porcelain face quite smashed by the fall.

★

With the exception of attending Midnight Mass, Christmas was a largely secular occasion at 'The Leas', pursuing the usual course of food, presents, television and contented hearthside torpor.

Now dropped into this mixture was the excitement of Harrier and Stella's engagement. Harrier, following the proper course, formally asked Mr Walker-Jones for Stella's hand in marriage shortly before lunch. Mr Walker-Jones said 'Of course, of course,' thought it unsuitable to ask a junior member of the aristocracy for precise details about his income and prospects, and cordially re-welcomed Harrier to 'The Leas' 'as a real member of the family'.

From this point on the day revolved around the lovers. Toasts were drunk, James was asked to be the best man (a role which he cordially accepted), and the debate about banns and dates became the foremost topic of conversation. Amidst all the excitement some time was found to mourn for the broken Christmas Fairy, and her bits were put in a box.

Harrier telephoned his parents with the news, was congratulated, and then Mr Walker-Jones spoke with Harrier's father. The wedding would be a small one – and here both the lovers nodded sensibly – and could, as Stella preferred it, take place locally, at St Dunstan's. To do the Walker-Jones credit they did not dwell too fancifully upon the social triumph of the engagement.

Indeed, the engagement was to be as short as possible; Stella and Harrier, after tender consultation between themselves in which they combined many kisses and thanks for their good fortune with an excessive degree of mutual respect for one another's 'careers', had decided that Stella would work her contract through in Telford whilst Harrier remained in Walton Street. In short, they would begin their married life by living apart and commuting, an arrangement which Mr and Mrs Walker-Jones found both sensible and modern.

The wedding would therefore take place in February, a grey month, but frequently quite mild.

★

The white winter sky closed over the outskirts of Henley-upon-Thames, and over the lovers, and over their decision to get married; neither dark, nor light, nor grey, it stretched in interminable blankness; neither celebrating, nor condemning.

Beneath the white sky were the towns, and the roads, housing passion, hatred, acts of kindness and hours of boredom. The streets turned into ringroads and the ringroads, eventually, became motorways, connecting city to city, and life to life, speeding beneath tall lights – the markers of civilisation – to cut a passage across the dark countryside which spread out on either side.

Within this landscape was all emotion, and all morality, a vast diversity of life whose very size is too overwhelming for the mind to accommodate it. And yet even as one turns to appreciate the breadth of this landscape, and to think of some profundity, or philosophy, which at least will serve to label even as it fails to describe, one's eye is drawn to the details – arbitrary, and anonymous, yet somehow evocative of something further, and something splendid, or terrible, which radiates out from the glinting minutiae to roll across the wilderness and fill it with a sense, or a resolution.

But resolution is difficult, for it requires faith, and the business of life does not appear to be faith but rather the ordering and response of a million impulses, complex, and hormonal. The triumph of physical beauty is a triumph of the senses, and may appear to be a total victory, but a victory over what, and reaching what kind of apotheosis?

There can be no true apotheosis without faith, and for Miles Harrier it was simply the shape of Stella's body which had declared the code of love, and this was the code he had determined to live by. As codes go it was not an uncommon one, but it was delicate, and vulnerable, and thus it took its place beneath the blank Christmas sky, alongside all the other codes, and all the details which had informed them.

FOUR

'Please tell me at what time
I must be carried on board . . .'
[Rimbaud]

There was a belief – if a rather half-hearted opinion can be called a belief – among the middle-ranks of the pop music world, that Douglas Stanshaw (a man whose career had been largely a question of unfulfilled optimism) would one day do something remarkable within the business he had served so loyally and for so long. He had had his successes in the past, but they were minor successes; enough to keep him in full employment, but lacking the triumph out of which legends are made.

Douglas believed fervently in pop music, and what he liked most about his life was being a part of pop music's machinery. He believed in its slang: 'the biz', and 'the kids', and he took its controversies seriously. To Douglas, pop music was something of a religion, a calling whose credo should be obeyed to the letter, but it was this devotion which he had for the industry which had so far kept him back. He lacked the irreverence to be original, and thus he plodded along, doing 'good work' with an archaic enthusiasm which earned him a degree of ridicule even as his expertise was respected. The world to which he aspired was one of stadium concerts, limousines, celebrity medleys and backstage parties. In short, he believed in 'rock 'n' roll', and enough of the world believed in it with him to sustain his faith.

Two things happened to Douglas Stanshaw which caused him to jolt out of his cherished system. Firstly, he parted company with Chris Patterson, and thereby met Erik, a successful young publicist in the pop music world. Erik and Douglas became lovers (in a brisk, rather businesslike manner), lived together, and realised that they could help one another's careers. They became a team, and 'the biz' loved teams, and Erik (who was fashionable) did much to update and revitalise both the appearance and the beliefs of Douglas. After three years of Chris, who had exploited Douglas even as he grew to despise him, Erik was a welcome change, and although Douglas did not find Erik beautiful, or feel particularly involved with him, it was a good relationship, and they were genuinely fond of each other.

The first thing that Erik did for Douglas was to make him start wearing sober, black suits, of classic Italian design. And then he gave him a businessman's briefcase, and made him throw away the awful plastic and metallic things which he had previously used. Finally, it was his glasses, and in place of the semi-reflective, drop-framed monstrosities through which Douglas had previously squinted, Erik bought him a smart new pair, with tortoise-shell frames and dull, green lenses. With the suits Douglas had to wear a collar and tie – the era of 'tour' T-shirts was over. Baseball boots were also forbidden, and sensible black brogues replaced them.

The result of this transformation was dramatic. People started to take Douglas seriously; young musicians asked for his advice (indeed some of his minor successes of the previous decade were now beginning to find a new audience), and record companies, confronted with such a professional-looking person, began to talk to him more quickly. Erik, who was tall, and thin, who dressed in black and seldom smiled, was pleased with the result.

The second factor which altered Douglas Stanshaw's perceptions was related to the first. He was given 'The Statements' to produce, and 'The Statements' – as can sometimes happen with these things – suddenly became hugely fashionable, before they had even released a record. For the first time in his life, Douglas Stanshaw was at the centre of a 'cult', and the particularly curious thing about his position was that his surprise came across as highly professional reserve.

The people who had sometimes thought that Douglas Stanshaw would one day 'make it' congratulated themselves on their foresight. Douglas, in the meantime, began to work on 'The Statements' debut records, and this he did rather well, guided in part by Erik, who 'knew a good mix when he heard one'.

'The Statements' were a version of a long-established model, four personable young men who combined a certain degree of boisterous humour with a talent for good tunes. They also had a sex symbol in their lead singer, Chico Hardwick, and this (as Erik had stressed) would contribute enormously to their success in the teen and pre-teen markets. Douglas nodded, and continued to work on 'the sound'.

'The Statements' liked Douglas, and he, in his turn, liked them. They discussed the possibility of him becoming their manager, and at this he nearly cried. Advised by Erik, Douglas told 'The Statements' to wait and see how their first record fared before tying themselves up in anything too legally binding. 'The Statements' thought that such an attitude was both trustworthy and sensible. After all, it was still early days.

★

Amidst a great deal of activity (both in public and behind closed doors), 'The Statements' prepared for the release of their first single. This was called 'Oh look! It's me', and had been written by Chico Hardwick. The refrain of this song: 'I reach out to touch you and you move' figured heavily in the advertising campaign which surrounded the release of the record. It became a curious kind of slogan, and was printed in various colours across the sleeve of 'The Statements' forthcoming long-player: 'Oh look! It's us'.

The single was due to be released at the end of January, and meanwhile, surprised at having a 'hot property', the record company to whom 'The Statements' were signed decided to make a video to coincide with the release.

This was all done in a great hurry, with Chico and his colleagues swiftly involved in a series of 'image' meetings. They asked Douglas to accompany them through this process, and flattered, he did.

★

Although he did not know her name, Chico Hardwick had long been attracted to the image of Stella Walker-Jones. At an early production meeting he timidly asked (having first proferred a cherished collection of magazine cuttings) whether the 'girl with the curious eyes and beautiful body' could feature in the video. Telephone calls were made, story-boards were hastily prepared, and 'The Statements', with Douglas Stanshaw, headed off to Telford in early January to make their film with Stella. It was generally agreed that Telford would make the perfect urban backdrop.

For Stella, life was suddenly full of excitement. Already filled with nervous joy about her approaching marriage, the chance to feature in a pop video added to her well-being, and so she telephoned Harrier to tell him all about it.

Harrier, of course, was thrilled for her, and he looked forward to coming up to visit her for the weekend directly after the filming. Secretly he was afraid that he would not be able to compete with the glamour of the four young pop stars.

The filming of 'Oh look! It's me' took place in and around the streets of Telford. There were even two policemen on hand to make sure that no reckless member of the public tried to disturb the work.

Stella's role was largely incidental. Her main duty was to

look surly and unobtainable, staring darkly through shop windows, or disappearing mysteriously up concrete stair-cases, pouting moodily as she did so, whilst Chico mimed the famous refrain.

One surprising outcome of the episode was that Stella became friendly with Douglas Stanshaw. She was attracted by his nervousness (which was due to his fear of women), and found in his shy reticence a certain degree of empathy with her own personality. Eventually, when her involvement with the video was over, Stella invited Douglas to dinner with Harrier and herself the following evening. He accepted. As an afterthought she invited Linda as well, 'to make up the numbers'. The dinner would take place at the Telford Moat House Motor Motel, in The Four Seasons dining room, on Friday evening, shortly after Harrier arrived.

★

One of Douglas Stanshaw's more recent ambitions was to achieve 'respectability', and by this he meant to develop a certain social tone, part domestic, part bourgeois. This was to some extent a reaction against the wildness which Chris Patterson had preferred to affect, but more fundamentally it was the result of growing older. There were certain aspects of behaviour (his use of cocaine for example) which Douglas couldn't alter, but he determined to cease making these habits social, or visible. As a consequence Stella's dinner party was the kind of entertainment he had come to enjoy. It was restrained, quiet, and 'respectable', and it was a fair replacement for the drunken Charlotte Street lunches of the previous five years.

Linda, who had been told that Harrier was an Honour-able, was curious to meet him. She decided to take what she perceived to be the exoticism of aristocracy in her stride, and had prepared herself to be stoutly unimpressed. In the meantime she was keen to report her impressions back to her boyfriend at Imperial College. (The boyfriend, sad to say, was stoutly indifferent when she later described the evening to him. His aims were more practical, and Linda loved the gruff severity of his reactions even as she pretended to play the socialite in front of him.)

Harrier, indifferent to everything save Stella, made himself charming, and tried to be witty. He asked a continual series of questions of each guest, whilst nodding, and saying 'very good' to each of their replies.

'And you are . . .?' he said to Douglas, inclining slightly to catch the reply. He completely failed to recognise Douglas from the scene in the Spanish bar, and this was due mostly to the elderly record producer's drastic change of image. Douglas thought that there was something familiar about Harrier's face, but he couldn't place it, and after a few minutes gave up trying. Instead he extended a confident hand, and said 'Douglas Stanshaw – pleased to meet you.'

'Very good; and you . . .?'

'Oh, I work with the band that Stella's been . . .'

'And they are . . .?'

'"The Statements". . .'

'Oh yes – Stella mentioned them . . .' etc., etc.

The dinner party was of the sort which favours discussion between the diners because their knowledge of one another is too slim to permit conversation. Harrier and Stella, viewing their guests from the tenuous bubble of lovers' security which they had so recently created, were pleased with the event; it seemed to affirm them, and to suggest a good omen for their ability to bring together an interesting social mix. They were seeking occasions for self-congratulation in this manner, for despite their engagement they still lacked the confidence to face one another intimately. When Harrier and Stella were alone together, their confidence failed even as their love increased; there was an impasse between them, which they both knew the nature of, and in order to ignore it they were beginning to devise all manner of social distractions.

Added to this was the aura of the lonely streets of Telford, which was informing their evening. This created the effect of dining in orbit. The Four Seasons dining room, nearly half an acre in size, was decorated entirely in shades of brown, and this muted spectrum seemed to absorb all sound, sucking in voice and gesture, and deadening the sense of being alive. Through the long picture-windows one could see first the motel carpark, bathed in forecourt lights, and then some strange pyramidal shapes, silhouetted in the middle distance. The cold January evening was still and silent, its darkness scattered with the distant red and yellow lights of residual Christmas decorations. Beyond these the fields began, and mile upon mile of Shropshire countryside. One could almost hear the emptiness.

A discussion about new towns began, and everyone spoke in favour of them out of loyalty to the two girls and deference to the pleasant evening they were all having. Linda (whom Harrier thought very pretty, with her short black hair, smart suit and sensible blouse) said that her boyfriend was seriously thinking of working for a big company in Telford when he graduated.

'That would be ideal,' said Harrier, and Stella and Douglas nodded.

Douglas asked whether there were any local concert venues. The girls thought that the nearest were in Birmingham. Everyone laughed at Birmingham.

Despite the amusing or critical things which were being said about her adopted town, Stella, in her heart, did not dislike the place. She liked her house, and her neighbours, and the ease with which one could get from one place to another. There was no need to look for short cuts in Telford. In realising this Stella had recognised a certain truth, and she rather resented the manner in which the simplicity of the system was being humorously belittled.

She said nothing however, and watched the waitress wheeling the sweets trolley toward them.

Later, over their coffee and the presentation mints, the party decided in a moment of well-being to go to Fountains, the local Telford nightclub.

★

The entrance to Fountains took the form of a fairy-lit lean-to on one side of the small piazza near the shopping centre. On the piazza itself there were raised strips of ice, like black weals, and between these were flattened patches of grey, granular snow. A freezing wind cut between the buildings from time to time, buffeting the public Christmas tree. Outside the club there was an oblong, shallow pool, lit from underneath and fed by three fountains. The water made a loud splattering sound, like someone strewing pebbles on a bare wooden floor. Beside the illuminated fountains there were some statues, of ordinary citizens. These statues were cast out of grey metal, and were now rimed with ice. They depicted, in life size, a man with his hands in his pockets, contemplating the water, and a young mother, dressed in skirt and anorak, holding a baby on her hip and grasping a small child by the hand. At first Douglas thought that these people were real, and was about to make a shocked comment regarding the smallness of the children and the lateness of the hour. Everyone laughed when he told them about his mistake. The frozen family was caught in the pink glow of Fountains' neon sign. The rest of the piazza was deserted.

Once inside the club the little group was directed to a small booth where they all had to fill out membership forms. Having borrowed pens, made jokes about their addresses, and returned the slips of paper to the girl inside the booth, they were free to enjoy themselves.

A quiet corridor, with black, portholed doors, ran in

semi-darkness to two much larger doors at its further end. On the walls of this corridor there were framed collages of photographs and newspaper cuttings which recorded various events which had taken place at Fountains. The group paused to scrutinise these. There were the usual theme parties – 'bad taste', '1950s' and so on, and then there were also snapshots of more adult occasions, a wet T-shirt competition, and a presentation cabaret by a leading firm of sex-aid suppliers. These latter events had been photographed inhouse as it were, and consequently had the look of cheap pornography. Bathed in white flashlight which blackened all surrounding detail, professional models and selected members of the public were documented in various stages of undress, their performance surveyed by crowds of young people, red-faced, tousled, shouting, grinning and entwined around one another. They looked completely unselfconscious, captured for all time in the midst of their enjoyment. There was a crude eroticism about these photographs, and a sense of licentious freedom, but it was neither shock nor prudery which made Harrier turn away from them quickly. He was filled with an ill-placed and overwhelming sadness by the little exhibition, and his sadness was heightened with envy and lust. The photographs reminded him of his own mind, for the sensitive conditions which surrounded his desires had made him prey to the slightest erotic detail. Within his love for Stella there still worked a dynamo of frustration, and the shiftiness of the voyeur. His sexual psychology had lost all perspective, and created false illusions, not the least of which was deep jealousy. He was filled with a need to know whether Stella had sexual fantasies, and if so, the nature of them. On this subject Stella gave no indication of her predilections, and Harrier, his self-confidence diminishing even as his desires increased, resented her for her silence and hated himself for the coarseness of his curiosity.

Linda and Stella laughed at a photograph of a male

stripper, and Harrier felt his insides curdle. Within lust he was at war with sex, and by extension he went into conflict with himself, and with Stella. Most of the time he could control these hostilities, and was disturbed only by considering whatever similar anxieties might be upsetting his fiancée. But Fountains left him defenceless, and thus his determination to marry increased, ever seeking a future when love might speak for itself more harmoniously, in the language of requited passions. In the meantime he watched Stella's every move, learning to recognise every passage of expression which moved across the features he found so dear. At times the slightest of these (the way she touched her scarred eye with the tip of her finger, or the manner in which she would close a car door) would set off a terrible chain of mental pictures in Harrier's mind, always culminating in her giving herself to him, joyously, determined, and obscene.

But what of Stella? Stella too had her fantasies, but they demanded no testing against reality. Years of guilt and worry, resulting in depressions too acute to bear, had driven her to know that certain avenues of thought should not be followed. When she did feel desire for Harrier, which she did, the realisation of the desire presented itself as impossible to achieve; the time seemed wrong, or the surrounding circumstances not propitious. Any joy or abandon that her mind allowed her body was usually explored when alone; as regards her marriage Stella hoped at least to be able to make physical movements which would fulfil a duty. She suffered terribly as a consequence of these hopes, for as ever, behind her love, was the terror of being found out.

★

There were very few people inside the nightclub. The little party from the motel stood in a self-conscious group on the edge of the dance-floor for a little while, and then they

went to sit in a quilted booth. From time to time they
shouted various comments to one another about the antics
of the dancers, but their words were drowned by the music.
Lacking the confidence to dance they all became rather
bored. Stella put her arm around Harrier, Linda smiled, and
Douglas disappeared for a little while, to attend to his nose.

After two drinks they left, all saying 'Well!' and 'We
must be getting old!'

As they were saying their goodbyes, Harrier and Stella
invited Douglas and Linda to their wedding. Addresses
were exchanged, handshakes and kisses followed, and then
the evening was over.

Stella and Harrier returned to the Mallard home on the
hillside. Stella had decided that she must make Harrier
happy, and so during the night she attended to him, in
much the same way that Douglas had attended to his nose –
fuelling an addiction by lessening an immediate need.

★

Upon his return to London, Douglas Stanshaw was told by
Erik that 'The Statements' had been offered a special concert
at a large club in Shaftesbury Avenue. A television company
were going to film the event, journalists from a wide
variety of periodicals and newspapers had requested compli-
mentary tickets, and public interest had been such that the
show was now completely sold out. The concert would
take place at ten o'clock in the evening on the last Friday in
January.

Two of the public tickets for this concert had been sold to
Chris Patterson and his new friend, the Dutch boy, Carrol.

In Carrol, Chris had found if not a lover then a soul-
mate. Carrol was full of stories about wild and violent
incidents in which he had been involved at home – club
fights, football riots, bar murders and so forth. The two
boys spurred one another on in the telling of more and

more outrageous incidents, and between them they had covered nearly every form of unpleasantness. They were careful never to make themselves the hero of whatever deed was being recalled, as if to transfer the real glory to another character would heighten the legendary status to which they both aspired. Also, in describing the activities of someone whom it was unlikely either would ever meet, there was more room for exaggeration. Thus Carrol came to hear about 'Big Neil', 'Savage Harry' and the Millwall F-Troop, whilst Chris was regaled with the thirst for blood displayed by 'Seppo', 'Tulmann' and various gangs of Amsterdam brigands who patrolled the canalsides in search of policemen to kill. Conversing in this manner, Chris and Carrol became quite fond of one another. Carrol had girlfriends, and urged Chris to join him in the enjoyment thereof, but Chris was not interested, and sneering he would say 'Tarts', in a manner which Carrol could never resist. Carrol found his friend's misogyny puzzling, and was amused by it. He called him 'fucking queer' in the nicest possible way, and agreed wholeheartedly that Douglas (whom he had never met) was a 'cunt man'.

The house in which the boys squatted was visible to the stares of commuters passing through Vauxhall towards Waterloo Station. It had once been an end-of-terrace mansion, but the rest of the terrace had been demolished, and so now it stood alone, shored up on one side by yellow beams of raw timber, and derelict on the other, looking out across a hole filled with muddy water and a broken fence of corrugated iron.

It was unlikely that the property would remain unclaimed and decrepit for much longer, but it served as a transit camp for a variety of people, none of whom the two boys ever came to know. The empty days of January were cold and bright, with sunny mornings of blue skies, and the undersides of the clouds tinged with gold. Chris and Carrol meandered through their days, keeping warm, drinking, and, in a meagre sense of the word, living.

★

Chris Patterson had a talent for making his prejudices infectious. Over a matter of weeks he had thus drawn Carrol into his obsessive tirades against Douglas Stanshaw. Despite the fact that Chris himself was unclear as to why he was so involved with this largely academic war, he managed to make it seem like something of a crusade, meaningless in itself yet standing for a variety of forms of struggle against oppression. He lectured Carrol on the subject, citing examples and nodding wisely over the subject of his cause. Despite having never met Douglas, Carrol began to regard him as the enemy, standing for 'being cold', or 'not having any money', or 'the reason why life is bad'. The documented success of 'The Statements' was therefore regarded by the two boys as a form of provocation, like the crowning of enemy propaganda, and thus they determined to go to the big concert, partly to watch and partly to look for trouble.

By the time the day of the concert had arrived, Chris and Carrol were tense with excitement, and so they set off for the West End in the late afternoon. It was bitterly cold, and of course they arrived hours too early.

Carrol was wearing a T-shirt with 'The strength of the country lies in its youth' printed across it. Chris wore a long black coat which he had found in one of the rooms at the squat. Upon arriving outside the club, they looked at the locked doors for a few minutes and then went off in search of drink.

The fighting mood would not sustain itself. The boys wandered aimlessly into Fitzrovia, their hands in their pockets and their faces turned down against the biting wind. Their spirits rose temporarily when they went into the off-licence, to buy a bottle of vodka. Then they went to a pub, and feeling bored sat down in the corner with their drinks. The pub was virtually empty, and the two boys sat close to the fire, eating crisps and sipping their drinks in silence. There were three hours to pass until the doors of the concert hall would open, and they had very little money to drink with. A depression overcame them, and once or twice they began to argue about the cost of the evening in proportion to the entertainment that they were likely to get out of it. Chris defended their need to be there – but it was a slender defence, based only on his hopes of seeing Douglas – and Carrol was eventually too bored to argue with him. The time passed slowly, and as it did the pub began to fill, and people crowded into the boys' space. The boys had finished their drinks a long time ago.

At about seven o'clock they decided to go and buy some food. There was a little kebab shop on the Tottenham Court Road which was open to the street, and there they bought paper cones of chips. They sat to eat these on a bench beneath an office building, beginning the vodka as they did so. The vodka made them feel a little better, but by now they were simply cold and bored, so they set off for the concert again, not to prove a point but to get into the warm and see something to distract them.

The scene at the venue was completely transformed. A large crowd of young people were standing on the steps, drinking cans of lager or waiting patiently for friends. Those who were waiting alone looked slightly nervous, and others, not wishing to be associated with the crowd, stood with plastic bags propped against their feet, and read news-papers, or stared dully at the traffic. In the alley beside the venue there were three large vans, none of which had any markings on them, but one of which was trailing long black cables which were fed through a small window into the heart of the club. Such a display of power acted as a stimulant on those who saw it, and the sense that the long-awaited event was shortly going to happen began to pervade the waiting audience.

A camera crew were also installing themselves, and people looked curiously at the busy young men who were rushing about with boxes and headphones. One of these was Erik, wrapped in an expensive cashmere coat, and barely noticing the waiting crowds as he pushed through the foyer to find Douglas, who had been with the band all afternoon.

Erik walked swiftly through the maze of corridors which led to the dressing room. He looked cold, and business-like — an executive amongst troubadours. He swept up to Douglas and took him to one side, murmuring various little details about who ought to be met and who ought to be invited to the party after the concert. Douglas nodded, and was grateful to have such a practical and attentive lover. He left the all-important social side of the event to Erik, who was only too happy to organise it.

Chico and his colleagues looked very young, lost, and nervous. They had another hour to wait until they were due on stage. Outside in the hall there was a deafening clamour of voices over the taped music which was playing.

A supporting group played with the energy of underdogs, and were largely ignored. The noise rose up into the high black ceiling; people stared, or drank, or talked to their friends. Up in the balcony a boy was leaning over the rail, his chin resting upon his folded hands and his mouth open. His bored stare was illuminated for all to see by a trick of the spotlights.

All the time more and more people pressed into the hall. The film crew were now practising their shots, with cameras in the balcony, halfway up the hall, and on the stage itself. Many people were absorbed in watching them, and as they did so congratulated themselves on being at such an important event.

It was a query from one of the cameramen which led to Douglas Stanshaw's downfall.

Shortly before 'The Statements' were due to begin their concert Douglas was asked to go and see one of the film crew. He made his way up the side of the audience, pushing a way through the dense pack of people. His route took him past one of the bars – and here the crowd was packed even tighter – and then to the foot of a staircase. It was here that he caught a glimpse of Chris. Surprised, and not quite sure whether he had seen correctly, he paused for a second and then began to walk towards the two boys. It was difficult to see in the darkness, and just as he was leaning forward to speak there was a tremendous roar of applause from the audience as the taped music was turned down and the lights began to dim around the hall. Douglas turned back again to see the arrival of his protégés, picking up their instruments and striking experimental chords. Chico walked over to the central microphone and said 'You reach out to touch me –' his statement prompting an even louder burst of applause. And then Douglas felt a tugging at his sleeve. He turned around in time to see Carrol – who was staring drunkenly at him – and for a second he didn't understand what was happening. There was a confused blur, and some inaudible shouts, and then he saw Chris again, raising his arm. At first Douglas thought that for some reason Chris was making a gesture of salute for the magnificent concert, and then he saw something glint in the lights. It was a broken glass. Douglas swerved, fell, and then felt a searing pain across his cheek where Chris had tried to crush the glass into his face. And then the two boys fled.

For a moment or two after the assault Douglas knelt down and clasped his face in his hands, not daring to move. He was bleeding heavily, and could feel the warmth of the blood against his collar and neck. He shouted for help, but his voice was lower than he thought and nobody could hear him. 'The Statements' were roaring through their songs, and so Douglas, feeling sick and faint, found himself being jostled by the crowd. After what seemed like a very long time – in reality it was only a minute – a couple beside him began to stare at his face, and then confer between themselves, looking at him anxiously. Douglas lowered his hand for a moment and saw that it was covered in blood, and then he collapsed.

He was taken backstage by one of the security guards, and then, with his head leaning against the side of the car window, he was driven by Erik to hospital. He was cut from the right cheekbone down almost to his chin, and he required fifteen stitches. The wound was not deep, but it was complicated by traces of powdered glass. Erik asked for many details – who had attacked him? Why? But Douglas was unclear.

'I was just going to see Graham about one of the cameras . . . then I saw Chris . . .'

'Oh Jesus,' said Erik, turning away, 'I should have guessed . . .'

'But I'm not sure – there was this other guy – I don't know who he was . . . I think it was him. The band had just come on, it was all very quick – Oh dear . . .'

And then Douglas began to sob again, worn out with shock.

After a few moments Erik spoke again. 'I thought that little animal had gone away. Why don't you get the police onto him? It's obvious it was him . . .'

Douglas groaned. 'I don't know,' he kept saying, 'I don't know . . .'

Erik took this reticence as some form of defence which was being put up for his lover's former boyfriend. He became tight-lipped, and practical. 'Well you'd better get yourself cleaned up and go back to the flat. Will you be all right? I must get back to the concert – there's a lot of people I ought to see . . .'

Douglas nodded wearily. He felt tired, and nauseous; he wondered how he was going to sleep covered in bandages. He also felt sad. He had been looking forward so much to the evening.

★

Chris and Carrol, having stopped running, found themselves in Trafalgar Square. Panting for breath they looked at one another for a few minutes, and then Chris suddenly walked away from his friend, and leant against the wall, staring up at the sky.

He didn't move, but kept opening and shutting his mouth, like a fish. He made no noise.

Carrol walked over, and looked at him with respect. 'You got him . . .' he said.

'Oh Christ,' said Chris, and began to walk away.

Half a mile away, in Whitehall Court Mansions, James Walker-Jones was thinking about theology.

★

It is worth mentioning – if only parenthetically – James Walker-Jones's interest in God. Possibly, with a forthcoming wedding to signify The Church, and loneliness to stand for Contemplation, it was inevitable that sooner or later James's aesthetic conjecture would touch upon the institution of Christianity.

However, it is also possible that for James the seeds of religion lay in a crude form of pantheism. As a little boy he had been immensely susceptible to changes in the family garden; he noticed pruning for instance, and mourned for every shortened branch, and the felling of certain trees. Thus he equated the weeping pear tree (it looked like a willow) with the death of the giant sycamore it had replaced, and he saw in these instances of horticultural strife the movements of a greater and invisible power, indurate to sentiment and higher than nature. In the manner of children James ascribed a human personality to the inanimate, and after a little while he evolved his own idea of God as a benign judge to whom the problems of both these speechless colleagues and his own soul could be addressed. With school the literal aspects of this scenario lessened, but the basis for prayer had by that time been established – part fantasy, part superstition, and largely confused.

Orthodox Christianity followed a public school course – Chapel, R E, Confirmation, indifference, and finally, with the discovery of debating societies, intellectual precosity. Then it disappeared altogether, and the more exotic concerns of Platonism and art took its place.

As he grew older James became conscious of sin – not great sins, but the usual ones, furtive and rather dirty – and with this came a desire for cleanliness. The standard decadent texts had already touched him, with their concentration upon the soul, and its corruption, but as James was not interested in the glamour of romanticism so much as the formal pleasures of symmetry, he looked on askance as other young men began the usual attempt to confuse Life and Art, regarding sex and inebriation as the former and books about sex and inebriation as the latter. For James the way was even thornier, because it lacked companions. He regarded the soul quite simply as an opaque, elliptical shape, about the size of a soup plate, whirling unguided through the darkness. All around it were other soup plates, and above them was God, to whom they sometimes ascended, and below them was Hell, to which some of them fell. Our actions upon earth determined the eventual destination of this cosmic crockery, and a good deal of insurance against damnation could be gained through regular and devout church attendance. The Higher Choir, and He before whom we cast our crowns, remained the remote words of scripture for James, and when asked at school about the forgiveness for all men which Christ's death upon the cross had signified to Christians, he replied that he supposed Christ was under a great deal of pressure at the time. But still James felt the desire for salvation, and for the salvation of others, for he was not, by nature, a grasping sort of person.

The great dead languages and the history of art proved far easier to manage whilst at Oxford than the problems of Faith. James could hold his ground on Ruskin, and was pretty safe on altar screens, but there remained, bubbling away in the background, the sense that the daily experience of artists had guided their works towards God – or directly away from Him, which could amount to much the same thing – and that this was a conscious part of creativity which he ought to understand. Faith eluded him, and so he became more and more embedded in theory.

He began to think about whether the love of Beauty as Truth was the same as the Love of God; that if we worshipped human or physical beauty, we were in fact by extension worshipping the image of Our Lord; but this somehow smacked of the carnal, and the sensual end of Pan-Hellenism. Moreover, as James was unlucky with girls, it became impossible to separate the worship of beauty from sexual frustration, and that was no good at all.

In the end the whole thing disintegrated into a muddle of contradictions, but the soup plates continued to whirl in the darkness, regardless of art, or theories.

When Kelly O'Kelly and Lucinda Fortune died, this muddle was set against the reality of death. James had read, shortly before the tragedy, that it was 'not catastrophes, murders, deaths or diseases that age and kill us; it's the way people look and laugh, and run up the steps of omnibuses'; at the time he had been inclined to give a nod of approval, finding in the subtle flippancy of the statement a certain degree of satisfying truth. But when he came across death unprepared, and saw the faces of those who watched the black coffin lowered into the ground, he had felt a powerful desire to believe in Heaven, or Salvation. A soup plate had lost its balance, and he fervently prayed for it to ascend.

He discussed his prayer with nobody, and continued on his intellectual course, concentrating more and more upon the Church. He began to see suffering everywhere, and felt keenly the 'evil of men'. He gave money to beggars and condemned violence; he tried to be a humanist but rejected politics as being largely insincere. He attended church.

Nothing happened. He felt conspicuous when he tried to pray and self-conscious when he sang. He prayed for Kelly and Lucinda, and for the suffering to be comforted. He asked for forgiveness for his sins, and his brow furrowed with concentration as he intoned the Lord's Prayer, his voice joining in with the low murmur which filled the church.

On the night when Chris Patterson attacked Douglas Stanshaw, James Walker-Jones had been thinking about forgiveness again. More precisely he had been wondering whether Lucinda Fortune would have forgiven Miles Harrier for marrying Stella. Was it even a matter for forgiveness? James was not sure, but he felt that there was something – he could not put his finger on it – that was wrong about the forthcoming marriage. Bitterly he accused himself of knowing nothing about women, or relationships, and as he stared despondently into the fire he muttered 'Deep Water' to himself, and began once more to try and reconcile Art, Theology and Life.

There had been something spectacular about Lucinda's death, but to think of spectacle in relation to the killing of a childhood friend was blasphemous. Harrier, who had been so intimate with both the girls, never spoke about the incident, but this seemed mostly to prove that he possessed a remarkable facility to overcome grief.

If one could come to terms with the thing it was all for the best thought James, but somehow he dreaded the bridal procession at St Dunstan's, which would pass so close to the recent grave. It was right that Love should triumph, but this love seemed to sit so uncomfortably close to death.

After a few hours of thinking in this manner, James came to the conclusion – or rather, he determined to conclude – that the wedding was right, and that to question it was wrong.

But despite this resolution he asked Harrier about it a few days later. He had decided that this was perfectly suitable within his role as the best man. Harrier seemed cheerful, and deeply in love. His main preoccupation was with his family, who throughout the engagement had remained as shadowy and remote as ever.

Over glasses of wine the two young men discussed arrangements, and then, in the tone of an afterthought, James asked his friend whether he had any misgivings about the event. After a few amused suggestions as to what these doubts might be, Harrier came to the point.

'Do you mean about Lucinda and everything?'

James nodded, and made a non-committal gesture with his hands.

'Well – yes . . .'

'It's understandable that you should ask, but I wouldn't be marrying Stella unless I felt sure about it . . .'

'Oh, of course . . .'

'It was terrible when – they – died in the summer; for a little while I think I went a little queer in the head, but then it seemed quite clear – Oh, I don't know it was like a light coming on or something –'

(James registered the word 'light'; this, at least, seemed to make sense. He leant forward a little more in his chair, hoping for further clarification.)

'. . . And then,' continued Harrier, 'when I met Stella, or rather, started seeing Stella, I knew I had to marry her. There was no one to forgive, no one to say 'sorry' to – the events just followed one another. It would have happened anyway – does that sound awful?'

James shook his head, and smiled. 'I'm sorry to have raised it,' he said, and so the conversation lightened.

★

The Honourable Miles Harrier and Miss Stella Walker-Jones were due to be married at one p.m. on Saturday 14th February. All the machinery which would unite the two young people was running smoothly. Invitations had been posted, presents were beginning to arrive, and Mrs Walker-Jones was planning the reception, which would take place at 'The Leas'. Harrier and Stella treated all the fuss with becoming levity, Stella preparing for her nuptials in Telford and Harrier keeping a weather eye on proceedings from his drawing room in Walton Street.

There was no doubting that the young couple were deeply in love, ready to step into the niche which society was preparing for them, but beneath their assurance lay a deep and fundamental fear, wholly related to the physical.

They had discussed the problem so many times that it had become a formula. They always ended by pledging their love to one another, and this bound the wreckage together, but at best it was a compromise. Whatever sensitivity and respect they might show for one another's position was always polluted by resentment, but the thought of breaking off the engagement was much more than either could bear.

Instead they developed a system – perhaps many others have developed similar arrangements – whereby each was caused least pain. This involved leaving much unspoken and taking much for granted; there was a silence between their souls, and whilst it would be untrue to say that the union was loveless, it would also be untrue to say that the love was pure. Beauty was theirs, and companionship, but as for love – love was adequate.

Stella continued to make herself pretty and available for Harrier, and Harrier, driven by this, continued to make Stella's well-being his main concern. But in this darkness – for darkness it was – they looked at one another with primeval envy, and touched upon animal jealousy and resentment. A life was being built, but as James had dimly perceived, there was something unstable about it.

A week before the wedding it was Stella who finally said the braver things about their love. This happened quite suddenly, as they were walking up Sydney Street with bags of heavy shopping.

'I'm almost sure it will work,' she had said, suddenly serious after a light-hearted comment from Harrier about their future domestic duties, 'but how can one really be sure? I mean really? Everyone seems to say "I love you" so often, and to think that they're in love so many times – right from the schoolgirl crush; but if only we could go back and hear ourselves, saying all those things – sending all those cards, and little presents, what on earth would we think . . .?'

Harrier was about to say something conciliatory, about 'growing up', but Stella continued. 'I mean, when we went to all those parties, or drooled over people we hardly knew, were we just lying? Or did we mean it? More than we do now? Perhaps it was just the easiest way at the time to get what we thought we wanted – or to keep what we thought we had – saying "It'll work". I mean – I don't know . . .'

Harrier was silenced by this unusual outburst, and sought yet again for some phrase which Stella would only be able to answer by telling him that she loved him. In the end he simply said, 'Well, I love you . . .' and was comforted to hear her say, 'Yes darling, and I love you too – so much . . .'

And so silence was resumed, but Harrier thought deeply about what had been said. It was an uncomfortable process. When had he really believed in all the things that he'd said, all the pledges and confessions, sentimental oaths and 'for-evers'? His love affairs began to seem like 'cases', either legal or medical, with diagnoses and solutions, but to prove or to cure what? Depressed, he sought for conviction, but perhaps he could no more be certain of his love than James could find an absolute way to test the prayers he wanted to call faith. In the end the problem defeated him, and he stopped looking outside of the formula that he had built with Stella. He saw her smile at him, her face bathed in sunlight, and he was happy that she was so beautiful.

★

The Home Counties, however, particularly when they are absorbed in the planning of a wedding, have little thought for doubts and envy and, indeed, why should they? These are not the conditions for which churches are decorated and marquees erected, and as the seasons pass in ordered procession – each bringing its different crises and beauty – so too are weddings anticipated to produce their indigenous range of emotions. Such systems are not invented, but evolved, and despite being challenged by circumstances which step outside their jurisdiction they continue to hold sway, believing in the best and fearing the arbitrary.

It is perhaps ironic that the social system out of which Douglas Stanshaw had been trying to climb was the one in which the arbitrary and the unexpected are most highly valued. His fresh scar was evidence of this volatility, and it determined him anew to make his way into those circles where violence and disorientation are considered alien. For two weeks after the assault he remained indoors, getting on Erik's nerves, and losing interest in even the rising fortune of 'The Statements'.

After a great deal of thought he announced to Erik that he would be going abroad at the end of February, possibly for a long time.

'What on earth are you going to do?' said Erik, not really taking the issue seriously. He was going through some papers, and had barely looked up when Douglas made his big announcement.

'Travel,' said Douglas.

'Where?' (and now Erik was slightly more attentive). 'You must be mad. This 'Statements' thing is going to be really big, I mean massive, and you ought to be here . . .'

'Why? We've finished the L P; there's nothing more for me to do . . .'

'There's a management offer to begin with, and the European tour . . .'

And then Erik began to look concerned. 'Douglas, you can't just go – what about us?' Douglas looked at the floor, gently patting his hands together and smiling. 'You don't need me Erik – not really. I mean, like,' (and here the Americanisms began) 'it's been great, and I'm really grateful to you . . . but . . .'

'But what?'

'I don't know – I just feel like I'm getting too old for all this . . .'

'Oh you poor thing!' (Erik threw his biro onto the table.)

'No, I'm serious – I've got a bit of money, and this flat, but . . .'

Erik could sense an emotional scene being brewed. He hated tears, and confessions, and so he lost his temper. 'So you're just going to "like travel man"? Well you're stupid and I must say that I'm hurt. I wasn't expecting to get dropped like some rent-boy the moment you got moody . . .'

Douglas Stanshaw's eyes flickered. He said nothing for a moment, whilst Erik lit a cigarette, and made gestures of incredulity, puffing out his cheeks and looking from side to side. There was silence for a while. 'Well I've made my mind up anyway,' said Douglas, with just a hint of defiance in his voice. 'I'm sorry if I've treated you badly but I've seen all this before. Nothing really changes. You can either do relationships or you can't – it's like sport. I've always been – oh shit, what's the point anyway . . .'

'Well you can just fuck off then,' said Erik, and a few minutes later went out, slamming the door behind him.

Left to his own devices once more, Douglas began to pack a bag.

★

Chris and Carrol were also arguing. This had begun with silences, and then awkwardness, and then a stream of bitter teasing in which Carrol tried his utmost to make Chris lose his temper.

Ever since the night when he had attacked Douglas, Chris had been silent and preoccupied. He went for long walks, leaving Carrol to lie about in the draughty house, bored and hostile, aware that an era was over.

'What's the matter with you?' Carrol would say. 'What's your fucking problem? You're boring ...' And then he would repeat the word, over and over, chanting it, 'Boring, boring, boring ...'

'Oh leave me alone,' Chris would sigh, and this would prompt yet further attack. Carrol would shake his arm, or kick his foot, or flick his cigarette out of his hand, and then begin questioning: 'What's your problem? Queer boy – what's your problem. Talk to me ...'

'I don't want to fucking talk to you. Leave me alone – or give me some money ...'

'I haven't got fucking money. We need money. Let's steal a car ...'

'Oh grow up ... just fuck off. Leave me alone ...'

For Chris had done something real; turned an emotion into an action, and now he was filled with horror. The incident would not leave him. He saw Douglas Stanshaw's face in his mind, and then saw himself ripping the turned cheek. The dark concert hall closed around him again, and then there was Trafalgar Square, and Big Ben chiming the half-hour. At Waterloo his mind had snapped, and then he felt as though he had suddenly woken up for a second, before falling into an even deeper sleep. He wanted to see Douglas again, and he dwelt endlessly upon the time that they had spent together, neither glamorising nor damning. He simply saw their times, and the city in which they had lived.

Above all, he wanted to apologise.

*

Finally, Stella and Linda had dinner together in Telford, just a few days before the wedding.

The reason for their meal was the fact that Linda would not be able to come down to 'The Leas' for the wedding. They went to Christine's, a little bistro with chequered tablecloths and menus written out by hand. Despite the fact that the girls had been acquainted for only a short time, they seemed to feel relaxed with one another.

'You must be very excited,' said Linda.

'Yes,' replied Stella, smiling.

They waited for their starters, and Linda showed Stella a picture of her boyfriend. 'Oh – he looks nice,' said Stella.

'He's all right,' said Linda, laughing. 'It's strange, we've been going out together ever since we were at school. Childhood sweethearts!'

Stella smiled.

'Have you had many other boyfriends?' asked Linda.

Stella shook her head. 'Not really –'

'Too busy fighting them off I should think!'

'Oh no – not me . . .'

Linda bought dinner. Stella sent Linda a bunch of flowers to thank her. Linda sent Stella a little card because her flowers were so lovely.

★

The days had begun to get longer, and slowly, with the end of winter, Telford was released from the iron clamp of cold which had been Stella's only experience of it.

Her work at the studio enabled her to take a month off to get married, and she began her month in the first week of February, not planning to return until the middle of March.

On the first day of her holiday there was a premature sense of spring. She awoke to sunshine, and the air was fresh and soft, running gentle fingers across the fields and the motorway. Although she knew that it was simply a mild day, unseasonal in its clemency, Stella began to feel as though it was May, and that it would stay light until early evening, promising summer.

She rang Harrier, who said that it was cold and raining in London.

And then she went for a walk on her own – a distinction which is made simply because she had rarely walked alone for pleasure in recent months.

She walked along the quiet roads of Greenside, and then climbed over the low fence which separated the house from the sloping field which led down to the lakes. The grass was long and springy beneath her feet, like a mattress, and although her shoes were soon soaked the morning sun was quickly drying the land. Her footsteps became quicker as she walked down the hill, and soon she found that she was running. Looking up at the blue sky, she spread her arms out to balance, running faster and faster. The landscape spread around her, with low fields and distant fences. The motorway was quiet in the sun, and high in the air a tiny silver line denoted an airliner. Stella thought about Italy, where she would soon be going on her honeymoon.

She reached the first of the lakes, and began to walk around the slender concrete rim which surrounded it. The water was dark, and hardly moving. It was impossible to tell how deep it was. She began to play a game, simple in its rules, to walk along all the different rims of the lakes without retracing her steps. Soon she was absorbed, fearlessly pacing into the middle area where there was only water on either side.

Passing motorists who saw her might have wondered at the sight – a well-dressed young woman, in the middle of a weekday, walking with curious purpose down a thin concrete path between two sheets of deep black water.

FIVE

'Love Divine, All Loves Excelling'

Whether marriage is a full stop or the beginning of a new paragraph is an unanswerable question, but it was one to which James Walker-Jones had given a great deal of thought. The conceit of grammar, and of syntax, was the mainstay of his best man's speech, and he was getting into a frightful muddle. At times the speech rose to paragraphs of such ontological complexity that he was forced to abandon them, unable to work out quite whether or not he had said something offensive or, indeed, said anything at all.

He had attempted different styles, beginning with the traditional references to risqué incidents in his friend's past, but then, unable to think of any, he had passed onto something in a higher tone, and here he got bogged down with metaphysics.

At one point he opted for the safety of offering a simple toast, but then he decided that that was too slender.

The speech became nightmarish; one minute it lay placid beneath his pen, redolent of both meaning and wit; the next it spread out, and became amorphous and unwieldy, neither amusing nor wise, but dense with platitudes and complex lines of thought which found their conclusion as truisms. Placed firmly within inverted commas it would have been a work of genius.

But inverted commas are not the things between which weddings are decently placed, and James was not, moreover, a man of irony.

Sitting in the drawing room at Whitehall Court Mansions, or eating his lunchtime sandwich in Bloomsbury, James wrestled with this most difficult question of how best to articulate his good wishes. He favoured, finally, an epi-thalamium, but he only had a day left to write it in. After one or two promising starts this too was abandoned, and so he returned to his original ideas, making short notes on catalogue index cards, and hoping for the best. On the evening before the wedding he went down to 'The Leas', and there he met Stella, who was surrounded by white cardboard boxes and lengths of ivory-coloured tulle.

The premature spring weather had continued, surprising everyone with its mildness. The evening air was soft and damp, and here and there in the twilight yellow and purple crocuses stood out beneath the trees. This potent hint of spring, following so quickly on the heels of a bland and colourless winter, seemed to suddenly advance the year three months, and make one think of summer. The sun took longer to set, stretching long shadows across the fields, and although this weather was unusual, and vulnerable to sudden change, it made all those who were enjoying it feel optimistic, and carefree.

Shortly before James arrived, Stella was sitting in her bedroom, surrounded by outfits and packing. She was thinking, unintentionally, about her life. A hairbrush lay on the bed beside her, and on the little dressing table there stood a bunch of white carnations and roses which Harrier had just sent. The window was open, and Stella could hear a dog barking, somewhere just down the lane.

Surrounded by so many familiar things, she fell into a pensive mood. Her thoughts came at random, welcoming the freedom not to concentrate on the following day, or check through mental lists of jobs that had to be done, and points that had to be remembered. With the thoughts came memories, and with the memories came reflection.

Whilst her engagement – or rather her readiness to be engaged – had taken Stella by surprise, the thought of marriage did not disturb her. It simply seemed to follow on. She had weighed the good and the bad aspects of the situation in her mind, found the former to far outweigh the latter, and now there was added the sense of novelty, and excitement, and these qualities she joined to her love of Harrier – to make him complete as it were.

Despite her calm, and her happiness, Stella soon discovered that she was recalling a whole succession of incidents from her past which made her wince with embarrassment. There seemed to be no stopping them. Once or twice she got up and then sat down again, saying 'Oh really!' as some particularly acute scene returned to her. She remembered the times she had sulked, or been punished, or made things up. She ran over the occasions when she had done something wrong in public which had drawn attention to herself. And then she remembered various boys, Richard, who had been sweet, and Stewart, who had not. She remembered a time when one of her early conquests, inflamed with passion, had tried first to undress her, and then, having failed, to undress himself. It didn't make her smile.

She remembered the hateful mornings of school, and, most hateful of all, the nausea of Sunday evenings, with her hockey clothes, freshly washed, waiting in a plastic bag in the hall. Then there was the hell of French pronunciation classes, where the mistress had made the girls hold French conversations with one another in pairs, standing before the whole class. The sadistic mistress, knowing Stella's shyness, had always shouted at her to 'speak up', and then made a joke, mimicking the girl's voice, and setting the whole class off into roars of laughter. Stella had sometimes wept for whole evenings before French pronunciation, her supper uneaten, her other homework books untouched, and her parents, alternately soothing and annoyed, refusing to realise quite what pain the following day would bring.

Lucinda had used to help, with her jokes and cheerfulness, but Stella jumped quickly over the thought of Lucinda, who had always said that she would be her bridesmaid. Despite the jump Lucinda too came rushing back, but curiously unclear. It was always her face from a photograph which Stella recalled, taken in the garden after they had been hosing the flower beds one hot afternoon. Lucinda would have been about fifteen at the time, when she wore her hair very short, and she had been wearing an orange dress. But now Lucinda had been dead for seven months, and so much had changed.

Other impressions came sweeping back to Stella, random and disjointed, but none of them would flatter her, or sit peacefully in their place. The sentences, or paragraphs, as James too had discovered, refused to come right.

★

Harrier stayed at Walton Street on the eve of his wedding. He too was in a pensive mood, but whereas Stella found that her thoughts and memories came flooding back uncalled for, Harrier found himself searching in drawers for souvenirs of his past. He did this, primarily, because he was nervous, and wanted to pass the time.

His main excavations took place beside a cupboard in the hall, where he kept his old school trunk. This was a large wooden box, oblong in shape, and bound with brass and leather. Upon its lid there were the initials of both his father and himself. At first he had opened this trunk simply to locate an old fountain pen, made of ivory and silver, but then, as one by one he descended through the layers of material which had been thrown in over the years, he became absorbed.

Much of what he found was banal, but the chronology was interesting. At the top, so heavily compressed as to be quite flattened, there were various papers from work, and presentation pamphlets from property companies which he had never read. Amongst these was the brochure from Telford, and with that some old magazines in which Stella had featured.

Harrier burrowed further, into things he had forgotten. There were postcards from galleries and museums, some with little notes upon them ('Enjoyed our day so much – more foolish things!'), and then there were photographs, and Christmas cards, endless invitations to balls and dances, printed on stiff white card, and, of course, letters.

There were also ties, an old pair of sunglasses, the pen that he was looking for, and several old desk diaries. Beneath these there were scrapbooks, and holiday projects, and old school essays. There was also an old notebook, with 'Black Hand Gang' written upon it, and 'Secret'. Inside, carefully written – Harrier remembered the time when it was done, in the summer-house, with the four children grouped earnestly around – was the following:

The Black Hand Gang: CODE: One wave = Someone's coming.

Two waves = All clear.
One whistle: Danger.
Two whistles: Follow me.

And so on.

Beneath these signals there was 'The Black Hand Code'. This was a list of good intentions and vows to act honourably, whatever danger might present itself. The resolutions stood out upon the page, clearly written in careful handwriting. Beneath them were the signatures of the four children – Harrier remembered them passing round the pen. The last of these simply read: L. Fortune. And then there was the date, August 7th.

Harrier tried to remember what year it must have been – 1971, or 1970? They would all have been quite young.

He carefully put the Black Hand Code back into the trunk, and then began to pile all the other papers and cards on top of it. Then he closed the lid of the trunk and locked it, returning his past and the list of good intentions back to their storage space in the cupboard.

★

On the morning of the wedding Chris Patterson got up as soon as it was light, drank a cup of tepid and bitter coffee (there was no milk or sugar), and then packed his few belongings into the British Airways bag. He took a last look at the squat: dank and stale-smelling behind the old curtains nailed over the windows, and then let himself out. He would not be coming back.

Outside the sun was shining, and all the streets and parked cars were silver with frost, here melting in the warmth and there kept intact according to the shape of the shadows.

He walked to the end of the road, and then he caught a bus to Earl's Court. He was going to find Douglas. The bus rumbled through the quiet streets, and then went over the river. It was a beautiful day. Chris watched a motor launch bouncing across the water, with two plumes of white spray behind it. The sun glinted off the cabin windows, and then it disappeared out of sight. He felt calm, and determined.

Shortly after nine o'clock Chris arrived at the end of Douglas Stanshaw's road. He thought that maybe it was too early to call, but on the other hand he didn't want to risk Douglas being out. The flat was in a small, modern apartment building, set slightly back from the road, with a carpark in front of it. Chris slipped lightly between the crowded cars, and then rang on the entry-phone. Nothing happened. He waited for a moment, and then heard someone coming down the stairs. A well-dressed young couple let themselves out of the building, and before the door could close again Chris ran inside.

He made his way up the familiar staircase to the third floor, where Douglas lived. The air smelt of cleaning polish, and brought back many memories, but before Chris had time to dwell upon these recollections he noticed that the door to Douglas Stanshaw's flat was open. Treading very quietly he made his way towards it, and then, not hearing any noise, gently pushed it open with his fingertips.

'Hello?' he called, and stood with one foot in the doorway, not knowing what to do.

'What is it?' snapped a voice, and then Erik came out of the drawing room, clutching a bundle of clothes. He looked pale, and distracted, like someone who was not interested in talking to anyone. 'Oh it's you,' he said, 'you've got a fucking nerve showing up here; you ought to be in jail, but –' (and here he poked Chris in the shoulder with a long and bony finger) 'you don't frighten me . . .'

Chris pushed away the finger. 'Where's Douglas?' he asked.

'I neither know nor care . . .'

'What are you doing then?'

'Packing – in short my sweet I've had enough. You can both go to hell . . .' And Erik started throwing items of clothing and toiletries into a large black suitcase. After a few seconds he paused, and then turned around again. 'Are you still here?' he said. 'I'd ask you to wait but really . . .'

'Where's he gone?'

'God knows.'

'Didn't he say? He usually does . . .'

Erik took a cigarette from a packet on the table and lit it, exhaling long streams of smoke through his hooked nose. Chris also took one, and leaned against the door, determined not to be put off.

'Now listen,' said Erik, 'I've got a band to run now that the Mystery Man's buggered off, and I'm not really very interested in wasting time talking to you –' He looked at his watch. 'We've got to be in Manchester tonight –'

Chris interrupted him, 'So you don't know . . .'

'For what it's worth he's gone to a wedding . . .'

'A wedding?'

'Yes, and . . .' (Erik took a card off the mantelpiece) 'you'll find all the details right here – now do piss off; just please me by going away . . .'

Chris took the card, and a ten-pound note which was ill-concealed beneath a bunch of keys. He wagged the card at

Erik, smiled, and then left. 'Bye,' he said. Erik slammed the door.

Within an hour Chris was at Paddington Station. On the back of the card there were road and rail directions as to how to get to the wedding. A taxi from Maidenhead was suggested . . .

Chris boarded the appropriate train; he would work out the rest when he got there. Huge pools of sunlight were falling through the glass roof above the tracks, and the train slid out from the dim green light of the platforms like a fish nosing between weeds.

As the train gathered speed Chris tried to think of a plan. He looked at the card: 'And afterwards at 'The Leas', Bushy Lane . . .' Maybe he ought to go there. There seemed little point in arriving at the church . . .

The city faded away and the suburbs began, these giving way in their turn to fields, and business parks, and leafless clumps of woodland. Every detail of the passing countryside stood out in the sunshine, looking fresh, and damp. In one field there was a huge bonfire smouldering, and its cloud of grey smoke drifted high into the azure, scarcely moving. The train rattled across a level-crossing, and Chris just had time to see four young children on bicycles, waving.

The train stopped once or twice at small, busy stations, and then the conductor made his way between the seats, asking for tickets. Chris stood up and started putting his bag on the rack, as though he had just got on. The conductor was fooled, and only charged him the fare from the previous station.

Sitting down again, and playing with the ticket between his fingers, Chris wondered what he would say to Douglas. It was simple, he merely wanted to say 'I'm sorry'. And then he wondered how much damage the glass would have done to his former friend's face.

★

At Maidenhead Chris made his way across the sunny station forecourt and then went up to a taxi. 'How much would it cost to get to here?' he said, pushing the card towards the driver. 'Depends on the traffic – it's about six miles down the road there . . .' Chris got into the cab. 'Tell me when the meter's up to five quid,' he said. The driver shrugged, let off the handbrake, and turned slowly out of the station.

Soon they were on the main road. On either side there were tall trees, and muddy fields, separated by low hedges. It was warm in the back of the taxi. Chris tried to start a cheerful conversation, in the hope that the driver might take him all the way, but this didn't happen.

'Five quid,' said the driver, pulling in to the side of the road. Chris got out. 'Do you know which way I go?' he asked. The driver pointed to a spire, visible across the fields. 'It's about a mile or so that way,' he said, pointing. And then he drove off, shaking his head in irritation.

Chris set off across the fields. He reckoned that it couldn't be that far. He walked in a straight line towards the spire, his feet growing steadily heavier as the thick mud caked his shoes. He took off his coat, and carried it with his bag.

Having got across one field, he then went down the side of another, partly in the shadow of some trees, and here the ground was still hard with frost. It was just half-past eleven.

At the corner of the field, beyond a hedge of evil thorns, there was a small road which seemed to lead into the village where the church was. Chris gashed his arm on a length of barbed wire as he pushed himself through, throwing his bag before him. He wetted his palm with saliva and rubbed the blood off the wound. It left a dirty red smear. And then he began to walk down the lane towards a low bridge; it couldn't be that far . . .

★

'Mrs Beetons', a local catering service, were busily installing themselves at 'The Leas'. Mrs Walker-Jones had
immediately found out the Christian names of the four
local girls, now dressed in neat black uniforms, who
would be responsible for the serving. She was soon ordering
them about. 'You do dry sherry dear, and Sharon . . .' etc.,
etc.

'I think it will be dry enough to stand in the garden,' said
Mr Walker-Jones, opening the french windows.

Stella was upstairs with her bridesmaid, dressing.

There were already about fifteen guests at the house,
mostly relations, and these were sitting in the drawing
room, talking in quiet voices, suddenly remembering things
they needed from their cars, and all behaving like a polite
theatre audience, waiting for the curtain to go up. Amongst
these were Lucinda Fortune's parents, for whom the day
was proving very difficult to endure. Mr Walker-Jones
went over to them, and soon they were talking in hushed
voices. A little later they left, Richard Fortune shaking Mr
Walker-Jones's hand, and Mrs Fortune trying to smile through
her tears as she leant forward for an understanding
embrace.

A few minutes later there was a ring on the doorbell. Mr
Walker-Jones went to answer it, brushing the lapel of his
smart morning coat as he walked across the hall. Chris
Patterson was standing in the porch, his bag at his feet and
his old overcoat draped over his arm. His shoes were covered
in mud, and his face was red and dirty from where he had
wiped it with the back of his arm. His pullover had torn,
and his trousers had brown rust stains upon them. He was
smoking a cigarette.

Mr Walker-Jones frowned. 'Yes?' he said.

'Is Douglas Stanshaw here please – I'm a friend –' The
words fell into silence. At that moment James hurried
past, on his way to meet Harrier in the village. He was
looking for his top hat. 'Oh James,' said Mr Walker-Jones,

completely ignoring Chris, 'do you think that you could deal with this – I must go back to our guests . . .' James walked over to the front door, wondering at the dishevelled boy outside. He was in a hurry to meet Harrier, and had so many things on his mind that this latest event did not surprise him as much as it might have done.

'Yes?' he said.

'Is Mr Stanshaw here – I just want to have a word . . .'

'I'm sorry – I think you must have the wrong address –'

Chris produced the card. 'I've just got to see him quickly,' he said.

'Wait a moment –'

James went up to Stella's room, and gently knocked at the door.

'Stella?' he called.

'I'm not decent!'

'Do you know a Douglas Stanshaw?'

'Who?'

'Douglas Stanshaw – there's someone outs—'

'Oh.' (The voice sounded preoccupied. There was obviously a matter of greater importance being discussed to do with the veil.) 'Oh – Douglas – he's not coming, he rang last night . . .'

'Ah.'

James went back downstairs. Several people were giving Chris curious looks as he stood in the porch, the sun directly behind his head. 'I'm frightfully sorry,' said James, 'I'm afraid that Douglas isn't here – apparently he called last night to say that he couldn't come – can I help?' (This last question was offered quickly; James did not really want to get involved with the strange-looking boy in front of him.)

'No – it's all right –' There was a pause, and it looked for a moment as though Chris was going to ask for something, but then he simply smiled and said, 'Thanks anyway – bye . . .'

James shut the door again. A moment later he remembered his buttonhole, and went through to the kitchen to look for a pin.

Chris walked slowly down Bushy Lane. The big houses, locked and barred between lawns and trees, seemed to be sleeping in the sun. A car drove by, carrying two women wearing large hats, and then there was silence again. The boy began to walk back up the road, aiming to return to the dual-carriageway. He would hitch to Plymouth – it wouldn't be that difficult . . .

The sun beat down on the back of his head, but the breeze was sharpening and a white haze was beginning to settle over the countryside. Chris stopped to put on his coat. 'Well, at least I tried,' he thought. And then the church bells began to ring out behind him, filling the misty air with their echoing chime.

Chris began walking again with powerful strides, his mind clear.

*

Fifteen minutes later, self-conscious in their morning suits, James and Harrier were drinking little glasses of brandy in the 'Coat & Coachman'. Here and there various wedding guests were also waiting. When they saw the two young men they nodded, and mimed drinking gestures, the ladies wrinkling their noses as they gave little waves above bright smiles.

Presently the wedding guests began to make their way up the damp path to the church. Once again the green of the graveyard was vivid against powder-blue, lemon-yellow, and lavender-coloured dresses. Wide-brimmed hats bobbed beneath the trees, and standing in the porch, the vicar, in his white robes, murmured little greetings to each new arrival.

Harrier's father arrived in a great hurry, and as he passed by people leant their heads together, and tried not to point.

Kuzumi arrived, small and exquisite in a grey suit. Again the heads turned. 'Japanese,' said someone, nodding.

Soon the church was nearly full, and there were just five minutes to wait until Stella was expected. A low hum of voices rose from the pews, whilst here and there people were leaning backwards or reaching forward to greet old friends and relatives. Two large displays of yellow and white flowers stood to either side of the altar rail, and upon the bronze lectern the Bible was open at a passage from Corinthians which one of Harrier's schoolfriends was going to read. Harrier and James sat stiffly in the front pew, with their hands on their knees. And then an unpleasantness happened.

The area in which the Walker-Jones lived had long prided itself upon connections with rural life. There were several farms in the neighbourhood, over whose fields the local families went for walks on Sundays, and to speak of 'Old Tom', or cutting through 'Cherry Bottom' was an affectation to the simple life which many of the suburban residents loved to employ. There was also a poultry farm, and a man who kept pigs.

It was unfortunate that one of the farmers had been forced to halt his little truck at the foot of the path which led to St Dunstan's in order to allow a large car to park. In the back of the truck there was a mulch of manure, and some rotting turnip heads, and on top of these lay one of the farmer's dogs. The dog was a large mongrel, part Alsatian, and part, it seemed, Airedale. It was chewing on something it had found amongst the turnips.

It was impossible for anyone to tell quite what happened. The farmer, getting out of his truck to see if he had enough room to pass by the large car, heard a strangled whine, and then, with a speed which denied close observation, and clutching something in its mouth, the dog bolted towards the church.

A terrific commotion ensued, with little screams, and bursts of laughter, and people suddenly getting up. The dog, turning in circles beside the font, seemed to be choking on something. James got up, and ran down the aisle. Harrier followed. In the distance Stella's car was approaching, decked with white ribbons. People passing by could see the beautiful blonde bride inside, pale and lovely against the ivory silk of her dress.

'My dog! My dog!' shouted the farmer.

The dog ran into the churchyard pursued by James and the farmer. Its eyes stared with panic and there was foam about its mouth. It seemed to be eating a piece of rope, or gagging on a turnip root. As Stella's car glided to a halt outside the church, the dog stopped, and then coaxed by the farmer, offered itself for inspection. James turned away. It had seemed to be a grass snake, or a slow-worm perhaps. The farmer ripped it out, and pacified, but still nervous, the dog allowed itself to be returned to the truck. Uncoiling slowly, the snake slid back into the grass.

A moment after this, Stella, her father, and the brides-maids made their stately procession down the aisle, seeming to float in a mist of white flowers. The chords from the organ rose in crescendo, the congregation pulled itself to-gether, and the vicar, who for some minutes had been afraid for the safety of his church, opened his prayer book. His deep voice began: 'Dearly beloved, we are gathered together here in the sight of God . . .'

A NOTE ON THE TYPE

The text of this book was set in a digitized version of Bembo, a
well-known Monotype face. Named for Pietro Bembo, the
celebrated Renaissance writer and humanist scholar who was made
a cardinal and served as secretary to Pope Leo X, the original
cutting of Bembo was made by Francesco Griffo of Bologna only a
few years after Columbus discovered America.
Sturdy, well-balanced, and finely proportioned, Bembo is a face of
rare beauty, extremely legible in all of its sizes.

Composed in Great Britain
Printed and bound by The Haddon Craftsmen, Inc.,
Scranton, Pennsylvania